One Last
MURDER

One Last MURDER

FRANCES ZANE

PARTRIDGE

Library of Congress Control Number: 2015955006
ISBN: Softcover 978-1-4828-5398-8
eBook 978-1-4828-5397-1

Print information available on the last page.

To order additional copies of this book, contact
Toll Free 800 101 2657 (Singapore)
Toll Free 1 800 81 7340 (Malaysia)
orders.singapore@partridgepublishing.com

www.partridgepublishing.com/singapore

THE SCENE WAS LANANG DISTRICT; the year was 1918. This story retells the experience and trauma of the people in Lanang. This is Peninsula Malaya. This is where it begins!

PREFACE

"THERE ARE SO MANY MURDERS . . . . .
This is alarming! And the police can't find a clue. Do you call this redemption, Detective John Hayes?"

Dr Janet Walker's look was ashen and cold.

"Cool down, Dr Walker. I know you are a doctor and a surgeon. We are closing down on these mysteries. We will get them. I don't believe in failing my duties as a cop.

They left us the skeletal remains for the police museum. They want to play a game. The police department will trace them.

"In a trailblazing cat-and-mouse game, there is more murder. Too many murders rest on a thread of cotton. One last count, we have the seventh murder.

CHAPTER 1

THE MORNING RAYS CAME DOWN with a cold breath of air. The rays pierced through the tiny holes on the wooden wall of the old house, shining lines of light across the living room. The house had been standing there for three decades in the face of strong criticism.

A Chinese teenager named Lee Ai Ling planted joss sticks at the prayer altar at the sundry shop's front door. On the altar was the porcelain figurine of a beautiful woman in long white satin robes. The small idol was the Chinese goddess of mercy, Quan Yin.

Lanang District's people were usually quite agile, but a small segment of the people took to their daily activities with the pace of a camel walking through a desert.

Ai Ling's mother called to her daughter. "Ai Ling, have you prepared breakfast and fed the goslings? See that they get enough green cabbage; slice it thin and small. I do not want those poor fellows to choke in the morning."

"OK, Mum," was the quick reply.

Twelve footsteps away lived a Malay family with three daughters: the plump and quack Lily, a characteristic that reflected her voice; her pretty sister Iris, who was more voluptuous than her siblings; and the youngest, Nur Salmi, beautiful with a slim pug nose and the sweetest smile, captivating and refined.

Ai Ling rode her red Penny-Farthing bicycle (named for two British coins, the large penny and the small farthing) with its one big wheel in front and a smaller wheel trailing behind. She circled a few times with the big wheel. It was an amazing invention, testing both balance and skill. She had fun riding but tired quickly and stepped down. She held the handlebars and walked towards Salmi's house.

The normal daily attire of a young Chinese girl was a pair of cotton pants that went down to the upper part of the calves. Ai Ling looked gorgeous. She was receiving her education at the convent school, just like Salmi. She had a small black mole on her cheek. She was pretty with short hair that ended along her silky, narrow shoulder line. Her light brown hair was intertwined with light orange and gold. She was around five feet six, had beautiful hazel eyes, and had an oval-shaped face. Her lips were crimson, and the rest of her face was pallid but mesmerising. Her smile was sweet, with very tender contour lines running down her jawline. Her neckline attire was usually round or U-shaped, slightly revealing her creamy white bosom. Her wide cleavage gave her the look of an athlete from marathon races.

Salmi was dressed in similar pants. They were like twins and were classmates in secondary school. Salmi was eighteen years of age, like Ai Ling. She spoke English but stammered most of the time when finding the right word. During conversations, she would interject with a Malay word. Her eyes were beautiful. A beguiling, thin smile added beauty with her very well-formed cleft and dimples. Her chest was wafer-thin with two small, slender breasts close to each other. She stood at five feet six with fine, thin hair resting on the nape of her neck. Her hair was tied at the middle with a hair band, making her long ponytail flow backwards like a pale flag.

Salmi called to Ai Ling. "I'll be out in a minute." She pushed her blue Raleigh bicycle out of the house. They cycled to the lake and caught butterflies with a net near the water. The girls went to convent school and liked to sing hymns and other spiritual songs. The lake was a desolate place.

A pair of great hornbills flew low above the surface of the lake, gliding for a while and then raising their altitude to find a tree trunk to end their flight. The two girls stared fervently at the beautiful scene, and Ai Ling sighed. "It's so magnificent."

Salmi nodded and said, "They must be a happy couple."

There was a strong wind blowing intermittently, and it grew stronger each time. Dried leaves shifted positions in a whirlwind. Small and light leaves and other objects rose higher, resembling a vortex in a whirlpool. Trees swayed, yielding to the continuous assault. The two girls felt a sudden spasm of fear. They thought they heard horses running along the pathway, a short prancing that came to an abrupt end. The frightened girls ran to their bicycles and cycled as fast as they could. Neither of them had the nerve to look back.

When they reached home, their panting and sweating lasted many minutes. With blushing cheeks, Ai Ling said, "What was that the sound of running horses?"

Salmi was still heaving slightly. "I think they are ghosts playing with horses."

Ai Ling exclaimed, "My hunch is that they could be ghosts from the past who drowned in the lake!"

"Are we standing on troubled ground? We are standing on the lake's concourse," murmured Ai Ling.

"Do you think we ought to consult the elders regarding this?" Ai Ling said, quivering with fright.

"I'd rather find out what's holding this place," Salmi replied. "It could be invisible hands at work, or perhaps our anxiety and fear have given us the glimpses of the dark side." She pulled her sleeves higher and wiped the sweat from her forehead with her fingers.

With chattering teeth and quivering lips, the girls held each other's hand and hugged. They were quite scared. "We have lost two colourful butterflies; we could have caught them," said Salmi.

Ai Ling assured her. "We'll have better luck next time." They went home quietly.

There was a community celebration at the district's hall. Timang Sani headed the district council. He was a man who was not bothered about his attire. He was articulate but had a speech pattern similar to Sir Winston Churchill. The ceremony began at 4:00 PM, and the turnout was overwhelming. The hall could seat almost two hundred people. The scene was quiet but lively, with the people of the Lanang District quenching their past problems with representatives from the district council.

There was a poor old Indian man by the name of Reindran who had lost two adult cows to thieves. The cows were never found. "I still want the thieves to be caught! God blessed the souls of my two cows, Run and Rim. They are both eleven years old. They are so obedient and intelligent," he told the district officer in a slow, wailing voice.

"Salmi, are you ready for the evening?" Ai Ling asked.

Salmi laughed. "Let me see your hidden magic."

Ai Ling was wearing a sweet corsage-adorned pink cardigan over a V-neck top, exposing her small, cream-white bosom. She was gorgeous in her knee-length, thigh-revealing skirt. Salmi had on a greyish-white camisole that bared part of her chest and skin over the shoulder with a light-blue cardigan. Ai Ling paired this combination with a bright beige satin blouse. Salmi wore maroon flat-rope sandals, and Ai Ling put on pink low-wedge, round-toed platforms with classic straps.

After the community celebration, Salmi and Ai Ling went home, took the butterfly net, and cycled to the lake without informing their parents.

When the girls did not turn up at home after 6:30 PM, Ai Ling's mother, Su Ning, and elder brother, Lee Chan Chan, were very worried. So were Salmi's mum and dad, Liyan and Remang. The orange sunset was slowly dimmer as each minute passed.

Lily and Iris took their bicycles and headed for the lake, a distance of almost two miles from the Lanang District dwellings. It had long, narrow roads with bushes on both sides, making it look like an aisle with thick undergrowth and thorny four-foot trees. Most of the tracks were undulating and rough. When they reached the lake, they alighted from their black Raleigh bicycles. The women had a small torchlight with them. Lily carried a four-and-a-half-inch lance made of bronze in the shape of a dagger with uneven waves. It was a headpin to hold her hair, combed into a bun. The lance was at her waist for critical situations.

Lily and Iris started a frantic search for their youngest sister and Ai Ling. They searched at the lake and the surrounding bushes. Their faces and sorrowful, pinched expressions turned blanched as beads of sweat rolled down with desperation.

Lily was grim and shouted, "Just show up. We're dead worried. Please show up!"

Lily yelled to her sister and Ai Ling, "Where are you both? Answer now!" Tears welled in her eyes.

Only echoes from their voices came across the lake and the surroundings. Moments later, there was only silence. Lily and Iris were never to be found again.

Salmi and Ai Ling used the other route downwind to reach home. There was chaos in the district; commotion and unrest were everywhere. People spoke of the girls' disappearance. When Su Ning saw her daughter, she was delighted. So were Liyan and Remang parents. "Oh! Dear, you're back safe. Where have you been? The townsfolk are also worried," lamented Salmi's parents.

Ai Ling's mother almost cried. "Hou choi, nei mou sie. Ngo chan nhai tam sam. Tai wan ngo em chun nei chut uk kam chee," she spoke in Cantonese. "Seongtheen yau ngan. The gods and the / heavens have eyes," she wailed further.

"I am an old widow, and my white and black hairs are receding. Don't make me worry," the old woman said as she looked up to the small lamp on the dinner table.

Meanwhile, Liyan and Remang noticed something was wrong. The other two daughters, Lily and Iris, were missing and were not in the house. The muez'zin azan, the Muslim call to prayers, rang across the district. The men had completed their *maghrib* night prayers. Remang, Salmi's father, informed the residents that Salmi had reached home safely – but the other two ladies were nowhere to be seen.

Old Reindran came over to Remang's house. He walked slowly with a red meranti walking stick, and it took some minutes until he reach the doorsteps. He said in a soft slow tone that he noticed Lily and Iris had cycled past him in a hurry. "I asked them where they are going. They replied they were heading for the lake to look for Salmi and Ai Ling."

Remang and Liyan, with the help of Chan Chan, informed the village folks regarding Lily and Iris. There was an avalanche of confusion. The men started running with torches and gathered at the community hall. Timang Sani took to the rostrum. "Listen now, people of Lanang District. This is a sad moment. We have two missing women, Lily and Iris. We will mount a search operation immediately. Ten men with their leader will search each point. There are thirty groups. We will split from here and start searching till we reach the lake. Each leader will carry a whistle."

Ahmad Naning joined the search party with three police constables and John Simon. The reverend from the Charismatic Church, Reverend Peter Palmer Eldrich, and John Simon followed the other groups.

"Good heavens, can't you hurry, Simon?" remarked the reverend.

"I'm getting ready with the torch and sabre, just in case we encounter wild boars in the dark," replied John Simon.

"OK, then get on with it," said Reverend Peter.

When the search came to a standstill at the lake, it was a desperate attempt to find any evidence. Ahmad Naning, Simon, and the mayor shone their torches one more time. but nothing surfaced.

The two young women never came back. There was no trace of them in the wilderness and around the lake. Their disappearance remained a mystery. The victims were lost with no trace whatsoever, not even a shred of evidence to confirm their presence near the lake. The search parties scoured every inch up to the far end but could not find any trace of the missing women. After three hours of searching, they finally quit. The police party went home disillusioned and numbed. So were the people of Lanang, who came in full force to help find Lily and Iris. A new search team would start in the morning. It went on for two days, but nothing significant surfaced.

The ordeal was exhausting and became part of the town's history.

When the anxiety about the disappearances subsided, a group of boys who scavenged the lake surroundings for catfish and *ikan haruan* at the shoreline chanced upon something very scary. They saw two skeletal remains at the shorelines. In the shallow, one-foot-deep lakeshore, two unidentified skeletal remains floated face downwards.

At the crime scene, the police and District Commissioner Stephen Lark cordoned the area. The other onlookers were not authorised to go near the crime scene.

A police photographer named Mark Stone came to the scene and photographed their positions.

The two Jane Does were hauled up, laid on stretches, and placed on the ground. Shots taken from different angles were for forensic analysis. The skeletons were placed in two coffins are to preserve any residual evidence as much as possible. The skeletal remains were women based on the width of the pelvic bones.

"Yes, they were women."

"Looks like they were skinned and cleaned to the bones," cried the commissioner.

"It's done by experts – no blade marks on the bones, sir," a constable in a khaki uniform said. "No flesh left for identification."

"But we have a gunshot wound near the chin that pierced through the trachea," Stephen replied.

"This is not the work of art done by cannibals."

"They want to be artistic," the commissioner told the young constable. "We are dealing with psychopathic personality."

"Were they raped, tortured, and killed before the skinning began?"

"All we know is that the victims were skinned to the bones. Fish in the lake later consumed the flesh remains. That is why the bones look very clean on the surface.

"Constables, scan this area within a two-hundred-feet radius," Stephen said. "Look for new burnt spots, Sergeant."

"Yes, sir!"

The constable said, “Sir, why do they leave the skeletal remains in perfect condition?”

“Our guy here is an artist and a satirist, young man. “He wants us to collect bone specimens for the police museum. This man wants to squeeze police protocol. He wants us to play his game. Sooner or later, we will identify the killer’s prints.”

CHAPTER 2

THE NEXT MORNING THE BODIES became the talk of the town. A day later, local dailies – *The Straits Times*, a daily in the English language, and the thrice weekly *Utusan Melayu* – reached the people. The headlines read, "Murdered victims found. Scary. Skeletal remains."

A small Malay boy in a cocked hat raised his mellow voice again, standing on the cobblestone pathway with a stack of newspapers. His eyes looked dole, and his obese body gave him the confidence of a great orator. His cheeks were a fine mild scarlet that raised the flesh into a half-blown balloon that sunk his eyes into a shallow ravine. He began to move, and his steps were a swaggering humble walk, wavering gently and stretching his shoulder blades.

He raised his jawline, looking up at anyone passing by. He spoke louder this time in the Malay language. "Quick, quick, buy newspaper. Don't miss the news. Buy now, sirs and madams!"

Sophisms became a reality and turning point for kids, adults, old folks, and the underprivileged. You can call it redemption or life after death. I wandered the hopes of everyone in my visions.

Hope can sometimes be a deception and fantasy, always floating out of reach.

Life is not a spectator in a game; it is just a sojourn, and you are part of the game.

The folks in the town were shocked and disillusioned. They were not singing lamentations. The newspaper boy raised the levitations in a sad chorus of hymns. "Whose daughter died? Oh God! Our daughters, are they safe? Who did this murder?" he yelled.

The papers sold within an hour. Everyone wanted to catch the story. Timang Sani was holding a cigar, and he intermittently puffed the nicotine into his lungs. He told Chan Chan to pass the message and paste the notice at all entrances to shops and at tree trunks at shoulder height. "There will be an emergency meeting tomorrow at 5.00 PM. Attendance is compulsory."

Chan Chan was one of the most trusted young men. He had done social work with the townsfolk to rebuild collapsed houses on stilts. Old folks whose children had forsaken them owned the staggeringly old houses. Chan Chan was also a master in Chinese gung fu, the secret art of arm and leg manoeuvres.

"Was there any evidence found at the scene of the crime?" asked Timang. "Check with me regarding the agenda. Inform the police department."

Chan Chan replied with a slight bow. "OK, I'll get it done immediately, sir."

The two young friends cycled downhill along the lagoon area, fascinated after capturing three butterflies. They lost control, and the brakes failed to hold them from falling. Salmi's bicycle hit Ai

Ling's wheel, and they found themselves landing in the water. The huge splash sent ripples of water upwards like a tiny meteor hitting a lake. They managed to pull their bicycles up the banks. They were not worried at the sight of the lake. The lagoon at the lake was near the shorelines; this was the place where the skeletal remains were left.

"Ai Ling, are you hurt?" murmured Salmi. They had no bruises. "It's a miracle, after such a fall," she noted.

"I remembered Tom Sawyer, and Huck Finn! Their lives are full of adventures," replied Ai Ling.

"We were lucky this time." The butterfly net fell on the foliage of a two-foot flowering plant, the red bunga raya, the flowering plant chosen as the national flower of Malaysia in 1957 for Independence Day.

"Dear Salmi, the butts are still alive. I think there's no one around this area. I think I want to find a place with tall bushes to rinse these wet clothes."

"That way, by the time we reach home, our clothes will be almost dry from the wind and sunlight," Salmi said, grinning with a flirtatious wink. "Look, that side is just what we've been looking for. Are you sure there are no peeping Toms?"

"Looks like we have good reasons to do this. I hope no one is watching us. We are going into indecent exposure."

"Get ready, Ai Ling. We will flaunt our nakedness in these bushes."

Both girls went into the bushes and hedges, which looked like a wall and were conspicuous to anyone looking at them. The girls began to undress. They rinsed the wet clothes and hung them on the branches. Two pink-coloured Triumph bras landed on the small branch, and they had a sudden bout of shyness as they looked at each other.

Unknowingly, their partially naked, beautiful bodies became the pleasure of strangers. The girl's instincts failed to notice the hidden eyes in the bushes. "Good heavens! Look at those young and subtle *pink strawberries.* They sure taste delicious and are finger-licking good," heaved Jacki Lanun.

Then they reeled down their panties. The light blue and pink panties hung on the row of sunflowers. The sunflowers turned into two bright scarecrows standing tall with their new attire.

Tuck Heng's and Chandran's lust were drowned with wild imagination. The men exclaimed, "Look at those fleshy and lonely valleys. I want to taste them."

"Salmi, be careful with the thin tree near you. That's Rhus Radicans, I think. In English, it's called poison ivy. You'll be scratching your body after you touch it. The foliage looks attractive, but it's pretty messy and causes severe skin problem."

"Thank God that you know the names of foliages and trees in the forest."

Billy Smallboy whispered and reprimanded the people watching the girls. "OK, boys! Haven't you hungry wolves seen enough? Let's get to work, you sex-deprived, lonely angels. Don't call me Messiah. I'm no angel or prophet either. Let's deal with the real situation. The Big Boss wants to know the whereabouts of the red meranti, black cenggal, and jati (teak) growing region. Once we identify the exact point, an application for timber clearing will be filed by the company clerk with the land office," Billy reiterated. "We are paid by the boss to do scouting for new frontiers, not indulging in passionate peeping. Do I need to paint a picture? Why can't you people understand? All right, let's get moving, you hungry old cats."

The girls arrived at the town. Both had revulsion and second thoughts when they undressed earlier near the lake. Had anyone seen them?

That evening at 5.00 PM there was a musical show by a fun fair group. They would remain for three months in a town or district before ending their sojourn. They had a colourful show of skits, dances, and songs that often poked fun at personages and fashions. The satire always overstepped protocol. There was no law to control their limitations, even when it involved revered personalities. The revue usually last for thirty minutes for each sketch or session. Some of the sketches were rhetorical.

The satirical parody in every show could be entertaining, but some were plain insult that drove people's nerves up the wall. Most pantomimes were short, and they changed the acts every week. Some were old-fashioned and put people to sleep. One could watch and hear it, or one could simply walk away. This revue group had twenty-seven people. Even the owner was part of the performing team.

The revue of *Romeo and Juliet* was a favourite with the folks here. However, the revue on *Pygmalion* was a hit with the younger people and schoolteachers. The girls also enjoyed the opening act of *Macbeth*, where three old witches spoke to each other, and then there was the curse ...!

John Simon was having a cup of tea with Ahmad Naning at 8.00 AM. It was cold with the clouds of morning fog capturing the landscape of hills and mountains. The white fog was so thick that it was impossible to move ahead clearly. It looked like a promenade in a Garden of Eden.

John said, “One can thank his lucky stars if he doesn’t encounter wild boars on a stampede.”

“I’ll have my bullets ready for the assault,” giggled Ahmad. “I’m sure their meat ain’t kosher for dinner.”

“I’d rather use my Winchester rifle for flying ducks,” laughed John.

Meanwhile, the breeze of thick coffee captured everyone’s mind. Then a group of drifters walked past; they looked haggard with tattered clothes. Two men had cigars, and the other three were lean and tall. One of them had a distinctive character: he looked quite old-fashioned and commanded astute leadership. A benign macaw stood on his left shoulder. He had a small Italian percussion conversion pistol marked “C. Nicoli” strapped to his waist with a brown leather holster. The macaw looked disciplined and tame. The other man had a slight limp.

Two of them spoke Italian, and the other three French. The speech was alien to the inhabitants here, but not to John. John was a linguist and had studied European history. The other Frenchman was around six foot three inches tall. He was a lean tough-looking man with very fine, thin hair and a moustache. He had a French An XIII percussion pistol in a red leather holster hung below his waist belt, and it was fit snug to his thigh by a thigh strap. It could be ornamental without any bullets. He had a beautiful face and good looks. An artistically done tattoo of a blue green dragonfly sat proudly on his left arm's thick biceps.

The other two Frenchmen were twins, standing around six foot one with captivating smiles. They were quite lupine in character.

Leman's granddaughter from his late son's marriage had a chicken pox infection. Old Reindran paid him a visit. Reindran came in and said, his parched complexion was so pallid and dry from old age.

"Don't worry, old friend. It takes time to heal with the Neem tree leaves."

"The Neem leaves can cure fever, inflammation, and infections. It's also useful for dental pain and skin diseases," wailed Reindran. "I have used it on my children and grandchildren, but they have deserted me. God blessed them. God is great."

The sharp morning sunshine had vultures flying high above. They circled at a small hill about fifty feet above the ground. A group of small kids came running down the hill with pale faces. Lena, the eldest boy, was panting for air like an asthmatic having an acute exacerbation of bronchial asthma. His hand was leaning on Eugene's thin shoulders. Lena and Eugene cried. "We saw a ... a ... a woman. A dead woman, lying on the hills tall grass! She's not breathing anymore."

The tense news gathered everyone near the community hall. Chan Chan ran to inform Mayor Timang Sani. The others shouted that another dead body had been found. Ahmad Naning, the constable, and John Simon rushed up the hill on foot.

"Oh God! Someone must have suffocated her. There is no strangulation marks on her neck and no stab wounds," exclaimed Ahmad.

Simon replied, "Looks like she was not molested or raped."

"She could have been dead for ten hours, since midnight," Ahmad said. By then the townsfolk had gathered at the scene.

Timang Sani held his pipe, which was not lit, and he scratched his head in disgust. "Get the corpse to the district hospital for a post-mortem. OK, folks, just get back home."

Dr Janet Walker was having a short lunch. She was blonde with hair that curled at her temple. A beautiful, small black mole sat on her lower cheek area near her chin. She was tall at five foot nine and was slim at her waist. She had a studded necklace containing with a red round stone called a delima, along with three oval white stones slightly larger than the tip of a teaspoon.

The white stones were the legendary batu keduduk putih, considered by the Malays as the favourite heritage of Soloman. The creation was from the flow of fluid from the atmosphere during the cold night that formed the dew. It then landed on a tree in the paranormal realm called keduduk putih and ran in the trunk's middle lines as a fluid. When one dislodged the roots from the ground, the fluid turned into stone.

The white stones were identical to the pair of white stones worn by Salmi. They could have been derived from a different period.

The dead woman's body was sent to the casualty department on a trolley. They identified her as Dandy, a forty-something Malay widow with no children who lived by the stream, weaving baskets to store vegetables for the market.

Dr Janet came out after the post-mortem. "It was quite a struggle before she died. Her lungs collapsed; they must have used a thick blanket to stop the flow of oxygen into her lungs. It could be a few perpetrators. There were marked provocations in the upper and lower lungs. It could have taken six to seven minutes before she passed."

Dr Janet filled up the form on the medical report. "I had a hectic day doing surgery for accident victims," she said to herself. "Two kids had deep wounds from barbed wire near the river. They must have slipped and fallen near the riverbed.

John Simon appeared and asked Dr Janet, "How was the finding?"

"The coroner's report is with the district police. The post-mortem can't help much," she said. "We have a difficult situation. In addition, no one seems to know the answers. We live in a small society, and they walk among us. They are like people wearing masks. You won't know their identities until you pull the thread with various colours and find the other end."

John gave a nervous laugh. "Looks like we can't solve this mystery. Even the first murder case involving the two young women is still pending police investigations. It's intriguing how it happened, and yet there's hardly any evidence to probe the missing link."

The sad episode soon reached the Colonial Office, High Commissioner at Kuala Lumpur Headquarters. That night British

High Commissioner David March, who was working at Kuala Lumpur, wrote a letter. It was addressed to the New Scotland Yard, Metropolitan Police Headquarters, England.

David March narrated while his secretary named Mary Flint wrote as instructed. He said, "Mary, do you think we need further assistance from England? It has been quite a while since the two unsolved murders."

"Sir, I'm sure the case will unfold when the police trace the suspects," said Mary.

"Nay!" David quipped. It's not so easy. But I have a hunch our boys back home in the Yard will be able to crack this mystery. I will seek help from Scotland Yard, asking for two experienced officers. Such elusive crimes worry me, and the presence of Marxist followers in the peninsula scares me to death. The second piece of fear is the mushrooming of Marxism. The emergence of Chinese triads is still a small storm over a cup of coffee. But the emergence of Malay nationalistic inclinations is still far from being a threat to British colonial rule. Still, this *'ism'* can grow bigger one day." He sighed and lifted his pipe.

It took a month and a week for this episode to take its stand. High Commissioner David March reached the railway station at Port Swettenham. The arrival of the two men from Scotland Yard at the railway station was expected.

The morning breeze was cold. David March was waiting with Mayor Timang Sani from Lanang District. These two men each used a wooden stick to support their arthritic bones. Both men were dressed in light brown suits with a bow tie. David March was wearing a round hat. Ivory pipes sat between their dry lips. Chan Chan was standing near Timang Sani. He was the mayor's old bodyguard and was very loyal to his work.

The sound of the train's horn rang from a short distance, signalling its arrival at the station. The train itself was loud and deafening. When it came to a standstill, the engines and wheels reversed its gears to get the balance to a complete stop. The door opened, and passengers alighted from the steps.

Two very tall and big men stepped down from the train. They were dressed in mackintosh coats and hats, and they carried luggage. The first detective was a Caucasian with green eyes, and the other had blue eyes.

David March and the mayor introduced themselves. "So you have finally arrived. Welcome to Peninsula Malaya, gentlemen. Welcome to the land of legends and folklores." The commissioner smiled broadly at the two big men.

"I am Chief Inspector Detective John Hayes, and this is my partner, Sergeant Blue Deighton. You can call us Big John and Sergeant Blue."

"OK, Detectives, we will stop at a saloon for refreshments and food, in case you need anything before we proceed back home to Lanang District. Here is the peninsula map. We will pass through Taiping railway station, and further down we will see the Tapah, Perak police headquarters. Along the journey we will cross over the southern part of Pahang and down to the border with Perak and Johor. That's where Lanang District is gentlemen, in the golden triangle. It's a long journey back home, gentlemen. We hope you enjoy your experience here. You'll be fascinated by the beauty of the peninsula. Now, I want you to meet the Mayor Timang Sani and his assistant, Chan Chan."

"It's nice to meet you, Mayor and Mr Chan."

"They will be working hand in hand with you detectives, doing surveillance work and more, I think. The mayor and Chan Chan will use one four-seat carriage, and I will travel with both of you in another carriage. "I hope you'll enjoy the journey back home while I brief you men about the gruesome murders."

When they started their trek back to town, David March said, "Gentlemen, this train will pass by Lanang District. The reason why we came up here north to Port Swettenham's railway station is nothing personal. We want you to see the landscapes in the peninsula on the way back home with the stagecoach. You will see the beauty of Malaya."

The two Scotland Yard men were taken to Lanang District in disguise. Their duty was to mingle with the townsfolk and drifters in order to find the murderers. John Hayes was six feet, five inches tall. He was very big, broad, and muscular, with a forty-two-inch waist. Blue Deighton had a height of six feet, three inches. He had a moustache and a soft beard. Big John had olive green eyes and was Irish. Blue Deighton retained the traditional, strong Scots blue eyes.

David March said, "Gentlemen, your presence here is to solve the gruesome crimes and conduct surveillance on the emergence of

Marxism in the peninsula. The British High Commission in Malaya is answerable to our London consulate."

A stranger came in the evening. He was old around sixty but still commanded a strong physique. He walked with a rattan, and the cradle had roots in a herringbone pattern. He had a coolie hat that covered his face.

He walked into the coffee shop and sat down.

"Sir, what would you like to have?" the waiter asked.

"Give me a cup of coffee."

The man was thin and tall, an athletic type, and he had a very fine, short, raven beard and a clear baritone voice.

The waiter held the tray with coffee with an indulgent smile.

The man said, "Thank you, this is a privileged moment." He looked at his cup of coffee and cradled it with his fingers, smelling the aroma. He was out of breath from a long walk, wheezing like a tired man. His eyes looked lifeless, and his sulky face was ashen."

After the evening's coffee, he excused himself and went on with his sojourn. No one knew who he was or where he was heading.

Across the moorland and bordering the paddy fields, kids were playing with mud and dipping in the paddy pools. The rainy season was over and the days were getting drier.

Buffaloes, with their horns and nostrils strapped with the jut rope and tied to the ground, were feeding on the daun pegaga (centella asiatica). They seemed attracted by the ulam consumed by the Malays, Chinese, Indians, and the entire South-east Asian. The plant had greenish, small, rounded leaves. The people on the Asia continent were very fond of shrubs for therapeutic value.

From afar, a platoon of little red herons serenaded the meadows. They sat on a fallen tree trunk that rested its stump on a tilted, willowing coconut tree trunk that almost touched the ground. It looked like no one was oblivious to this premature situation. They looked bereft from the tapestry of solitary freedom.

It was a life without human bondage, like the merbuk tekukur (spotted dove) and their distant cousins, the talkative but charming magpies. The fronds of weeds in water swayed from the gale of winds like lilies flowing down from the Hanging Gardens at Babylon. The rare beauty captured the little red heron's attention. Their cold sanity turned to stone.

They were subdued by audiences attentive to the ancient Greek play *The Iliad* by Homer, staged at the Colosseum.

CHAPTER 3

THE HEADLINE FROM PREVIOUS DAYS was still lodged in the minds of the townsfolk. People had fears, and everyone's encounter was different. A police station with just twenty-one men was meant to monitor the entire district of Lanang, and it was exhaustive work.

At Lanang District, John Hayes and Blue Deighton were trying to fit into many new hats. John and Blue Deighton disguised themselves as odd-job workers and carpenters who could fix any household issues.

When John Hayes retired at his quarters, Blue Deighton, who was seen planting lady's fingers at a small plot of land, followed him.

John removed his shirt and sat next to a table, facing the window. On the table was an old *Strand Magazine* dated February 1892. The front cover read, "The Adventures of Sherlock Holmes" followed by a subtitle: "The Adventure of the Speckled Band."

John yawned and soon fell asleep.

Blue was still erecting bamboo stilts for the vegetables. He called out, "Big John, are we going to the lake this evening?"

There was no reply.

"Big John?"

The long echo from Blue's voice woke John. He stood up and walked towards Blue.

Blue "Come on in and have a cup of coffee that I prepared earlier. It's still hot. We will survey that area at 5.00 PM, as planned."

Soon, two rickshaws appeared to take them to the designated place. One was pulled by a mustang, and the other one was a breed from Mongolia. They looked strong enough to carry Big John and Blue.

"Where to, sir?" asked the riders.

"Take us to the lake," ordered John.

"The fare is three cents each way," said one rider with a Chinese coolie hat used in tin mining. The other rider was Malay and had a headdress of the Bajau from Borneo.

"It's a deal," replied Blue.

"OK! Move, my boy!" The horses started running.

They passed by the sundry shop where Ai Ling and Salmi were playing and skipping. John did not bother to look around. He had one intention: to find evidence and the missing link for the murders.

Salmi tossed the skip around and told Ai Ling, "Isn't he the primary one school teacher from England with his friend?"

"They're pretty big guys and would make good husbands," chuckled Ai Ling.

"What do you have in mind, my sweet sister?" Salmi said after tapping her on the shoulder.

There was a mysterious sighting of the flying storks at the lake landing sites. There was a huge swarm of the milky stork, known to the Malays as burung upeh; the exotic blue pelican; the fabulous grey herons; and the painted storks. The birds took to the lake's perimeter and shallow waters. Joining the colourful party were the meticulous egrets and the notorious ospreys.

The egrets were friendly neighbours but could turn ferocious when scavenging and haggling for tiny fish. John and Blue reached the famous landmark of Peninsula Malaya. The famous Lembah Laut surface sparkled from the sunrays and was magnificent.

"This must be the exodus period of the year. The flying storks have landed. There are so many different species," John noted. In the hue of the moment, he also noticed a piece of wood painted with the word "Danger" and a skeleton sign.

"This is where the poor ladies Lily and Iris were found dead." Blue said. He sighed after the bouncing journey uphill from the long ride with rickshaws.

The two rickshaw riders found a place to sit and smoke their rolled cigarettes. This cigarette was made by rolling tobacco in a square-cut tobacco leaf. Sometimes they used very thin white paper rolled with tobacco. They seemed oblivious about the tragedies.

Big John and Blue were busy looking for any small evidence that may link the killings. John ordered the riders to join in their search. "Can you guys help us?"

"Sure, we will be obliged to help as long as the murderers are tracked down," replied Ming and Pitung.

The four men looked all around for clues. In the search, Pitung noticed an object that was buried almost to the rim. A sharp, protruding object caught his eye. He called out, "Sir, come and take a look at this."

Blue, John, and Ming rushed to Pitung. Pitung pierced the soil with his hands and unveiled a bronze dagger. It was small, but quite surprisingly it was stained with dark patches.

"A good find, Pitung," exclaimed Big John. "This may be the tip of the iceberg."

The frantic and tiring search proved fruitful, and the men soon returned backed home.

That evening was breezy and cold. Remang and Liyan were weaving the traditional Malay carpet made of *mengkuang leaves.* They were experts in this old tradition.

Remang's voice was a sign of retribution from the loss of his two daughters. He was almost over the edge, and it took him some time to simmer down from that tragic grief. Liyan was speechless when Remang cried.

"We lost our two daughters. Is destiny so dark and cruel? Do we deserve these tragedies?" He was sad with tears. He was contemplating a future without hope, with only one daughter to survive them. "Salmi must survive no matter what happens in Lanang."

"To be a saint is a journey of a lifetime," Liyan said as she held her husband's hand. "You have to stop feeling guilty, and remorse isn't going to help you. There is nothing much you could do to bring them back to life. Say your prayers and let justice take its path. Those responsible will be caught."

Bereavement, wrath, hatred, and fear appeared in his eyes. He reeled away from the dark moments and whimpering oaths. Finally the old man simmered down. “I have to live with it,” he cried with tears streaming down his old skin.

Chan Chan was talking to Mayor Timang Sani. Dr Janet Walker walked across the street and smiled at them. She took long strides to meet Ahmad Naning and John Simon, who were discussing something in a low voice.

“Good evening, Dr Janet,” John and Ahmad said together.

“Good evening,” was the reply from Dr Janet’s sweet voice. “You guys look great.” The evening breeze was dry, and the musical renditions of crickets filled the air. “Can I join this evening party?”

“By my guest, Dr Janet.” They smiled grimly.

“Thank you, gentlemen. I have had a busy day at the hospital. There were three surgeries from accidents. And one boy was stung by bees, but he is recovering.”

“That’s a very noble profession,” John Simon said. He lifted his hand and put a cigarette between his lips.

Ahmad stole a limpid stare at Dr Janet, unbeknownst to her.

“Can we have coffee for this evening?” she asked.

They went to the nearby cafe and sat at a round table with wooden stools. Dr Janet gave them a rundown of possible links to the post-mortem. She believed the crimes were bold and cruel.

The cafe was an old and very archaic Chinese facade coffee shop. They had round marble tables with three-legged wooden stools. One of the stools had a loose leg. While sitting down, Dr Janet wobbled, and her hat fell off. She stood up and held the hat. Her auburn hair flipped over her eyes, and her hair from the sides and the back of her nape rested on her creamy white chest. She blushed, and her face looked sullen. "I'm sorry, guys," she murmured. "I think I lost my balance."

Ahmad's eyes were sly at all times, but he was able to recover each time Dr Janet stared at him.

Dr Janet took a sip from the cup, and her voice was wet and sharp. "So is there any good news today, Inspector?" She took a thin breath and said, "Any links yet with the killers of the two Malay girls?"

"No, nothing at the moment, but we are working on that."

At one corner of the cafe sat a tall, lonely man with a coolie hat. He could be someone from the tin mine nearby. He was quiet but attentive to conversations. He wore a maroon raincoat made of leather that was quite worn out at the edges, with torn corners of the chest pocket. He was smoking a pipe, and the mouthpiece made of ivory. The tobacco smelled like the famed Indonesian tobacco roasted with clove, bunga cengkeh. He had an object wrapped in a black cloth; it was laid on the table across from his coffee cup. He had a fixation on his object; he was like a pathetic, wheelchair-bound patient with a saintly look, but he couldn't lift his gaze from the wrapped object while staring at Dr Janet with dreamy eyes.

Dr Janet spoke without any intimidation, but suddenly her eyes shifted on the guy sitting at the corner. She stole a stare at the guy and avoided confrontation to hide her observations on any strange characters.

"Those killings were not done at the spur of the moment. I believe they had motives dictating a cold, calculated murder."

"Sounds like a twisted rhyme that hits a blank wall. We do not know where it came from and where it ends," murmured Ahmad.

"I'm still working with my colleagues, and I can't disclose them."

Simon sniffed the heavy coffee scent and grinned at them. "I'll keep an eye on everything that's strange and questionable. Meanwhile, Dr Janet, you're a doctor, pathologist, and brilliant biologist and scientist. Please keep us informed."

Dr Janet excused herself and bade farewell to the two men. She had to assume duties at the hospital at 6.00 PM.

At the hospital, she pushed her hair back and tied a blue ribbon to hold it into a bun. She looked into a mirror and said, "Well, time to work again, Doctor. You're lonely, and you need a good man." She giggled and flung her stethoscope over her thin shoulders.

As soon as she sat down at her chair to write a note for Detective John, two nurses operating the reception entrance called her name. "Doctor, we have one new case."

"Bring the patient in, Nurse."

A woman with a baby held in her arms walked towards Dr Janet. She had a child who was three year's old tucked in to her blue silk Chinese pants. The small child looked pale and yellowish.

"Doctor Janet, help my baby. She sick, got fever, crying no stopping, but I no money to see doctor," sobbed the poor woman. "I no talkie good English."

Dr Janet stood up immediately and placed the baby on a table covered with a scarf she had worn that evening. She checked the pulse rate and tapped the chest and stomach. "This baby is very sick with jaundice and tonsillitis. Come with me to the hospital."

A beige-coloured carriage driven by two white horses came by, and they boarded. Dr Janet calmed down the worried woman. "Don't worry, I'll get her warded, and you can stay next to her bed.

Just say your prayers, Mrs Chin," assured Dr Janet, trying to calm her with fake confidence.

At the emergency and casualty department, the hospital attendants rushed out with a trolley as soon as they saw Dr Janet holding a baby. The mum trailed behind, her reddish face flushed with anxiety and small drops of tears. "Oh! My poor baby, don't cry, Mummy is here. Doctor will cure you."

Dr Janet did her usual routine. Within minutes, the baby was placed on a trolley. "Get me the drip needles." She did it within minutes without the small baby crying. "I hope this saline drip will reverse her dehydrated, frail body. Give an IV with glucose hourly. Get her warded at children ward nine. Keep me informed if the fever and blood pressure goes up. Right now, the pressure is at 150/95. It's very critical for a small baby. The baby's mouth is almost completely ulcerated. I am afraid it is Steven Johnson syndrome," Dr Janet told the staff nurse and the two student nurses. "Put this baby on the drip with cortisone six hourly. She will recover in a few days, I believe. Let me know if there are any complications, I'll be at the doctor's quarters."

Dr Janet sat beside the poor mum and told her to remain with her baby in the ward. She gave the woman a blanket for the night. A lazy chair was carried by two nurses from the store room. She needed the chair to lie down and sleep while watching over her baby.

Meanwhile, Old Reindran and Imam Banjar joined Timang Sani, who was with Chan Chan. They had a brief discussion on something confidential.

Old Reindran's incessant shrill cough and panting was quite alarming, "Don't worry about me – I'm old but not a dotage. My younger days as a clerk with the colonial office are just a faint memory. My job was typing and translating the Tamil language for the estate workers. It's just liaison work. Now I breed cows and goats, and they are my good companions." Reindran gave a long, shrill chuckle. "My eyes are still as good as an old eagle. Do not underestimate an old man. I'll pretend and look for details and information."

The mayor told Mazian and the rest to be extremely careful. "Don't cause any ripples to be seen by the perpetrators. Chan Chan will remain with me; there are so many clues we need to write down. Good luck, everyone. May God bless us."

"The police superintendant has given us the order to call possible suspects for questioning. We have screened the drifter's group, Billy Smallboy, the giant with his timber boys, and of course the revue people. So far there is no lead," Ahmad said. He gave his half-smile and readjusted his pistol holster belt.

Timang Sani ordered them to disperse one or two at a time in different directions to avoid suspicion. Soon they left the community hall at their own paces.

The two young women, Salmi and Ai Ling, were doing their yoga exercises at the porch. Salmi's wooden house was quite spacious. It was made of a hard wood derived from the laksa tree. A mat made of mengkuang leaves laid on the ground.

The pants up to calf worn that they wore made them look like the soulful white Panama dove orchid in a nesting stance.

"Can we do the breathing position together?" Salmi asked.

"Sure," Ai Ling said, smiling.

The two girls went on with their orchestrated stances until they were tired. They rested with a glass of orange juice.

Ai Ling stated, "The State Wildlife Department put up a banner to inform residents on illegal poaching by ruthless people. They are after the Sumatran rhinoceros and the poor Malayan tiger for aphrodisiac elements."

"Ai Ling, they believe in such twisted tales," muttered Salmi.

"People with strong sex drives use it as stimulant. It's like a metaphor. Just empty hopes to keep their hungry souls alive," remarked Ai Ling.

Old Reindran passed by the two girls on his bullock cart. A big brown cow pulled the old man to his destination. "Good evening, ladies. Old Reindran is heading back home. Have you had your evening tea?"

"Yes, we have replaced it with orange juice. Uncle Rein, we saw you at the post office yesterday with a few police constables."

"Sort of looming around as the years go by, ladies. See ya again."

Billy Smallboy was pretty happy about the findings at the designated sites of Meranti and Cenggal. "We are in the middle of the golden triangle in Peninsula Malaya. The Belum-Temenggor Forest, Tasik Bera, Tasik Chini, Langkawi Island, Gunung Tahan, Gunung Ledang, and the famed Malaccan historic archaeological treasure trove. Then we can go across the peninsula to the tip of Isthmus of Kra in Southern Thailand and the massively dense tropical forest that stretches for thousands of miles. We're right here in Lanang District, the star gate to everything that opens up the green Pandora's box."

"Remember the Koh-I-Noor diamond in India, and how was it discovered?" Billy went further. "The Koh-I-Noor is one of the biggest diamonds discovered, after the Moonstone. Not even the diamonds mined in Johannesburg, South Africa, could come close to it. A peasant in the muddy land for cultivation in India found it. There it stood buried in the mud, and the sparkle caught the attention of the peasant. It must have been thrown out from the earth's crust during a volcanic eruption in the early period." Billy laughed.

"Peninsula Malaya and the Borneo Islands are older than the Amazon. It is a basin of riches," interrupted Jacki Lanun.

"You're right, Jacki. We could strike gold if we are lucky, and this land is full of folklore legends, which is true. You may not know what's ahead and hidden behind the curtains."

Back at the other edge of the lonesome retreat, Ahmad Naning heaved in silence. His imagination was running wild with despair. He had this sense of remorse, and his soul needed salvation. Ahmad lit a 555 cigarette and puffed on it. He whimpered to himself, "I was in earnest when I proposed to her. She is sexy and beautiful. I can't live with dejection. Why did I destroy the nest? I could have cherished it with her." He laid down his pistol after emptying the bullets; that was standard police procedure. "We have a sinking ship now, and everyone will try to avoid it. I think it's double indemnity from now on. It's just a matter of time before the police will unravel the murders."

This man knew how to play his cards and pretend he was oblivious to everything. His face was always sullen. He had the sly face of a man filled with hate. He had failing eyes that twitched in every direction.

He murmured to himself, "No one knows what's going on."

CHAPTER 4

IT WAS VERY DARK WITH little refuge from the dim moonlight. The quietness drowned the romantic dreams of Dr Janet Walker. She was in her light blue nightgown with a half-laced bra hanging precariously from her long and voluptuous neck. The cleft was devastating to any man who would be drowned by lust. She longed for the masculine arms of a man, for hands that would caress her emptiness, a void filled with earnestness that would run along the bare skin of her body.

She looked kinky but a little dry from the long hours of tiresome work as a doctor and surgeon at the emergency and casualty unit in the hospital. She was at the balcony overlooking the terrain across the meadows.

Dr Janet whimpered to herself, "I'll look forward to having all the answers to this mystery. We're the only town in the region with more than ten thousand people. People know everyone; you just cannot walk around Lanang District without anyone noticing. There must be an answer to these cold, calculating murders." She strode through the pink satin curtain and passed through the arched entrance to her bedroom.

She peeled down her maroon colour panties and threw them on the edge of the bed. Soon her fingers unbuttoned the hooks of her bra, sliding it down her arms and she threw her lingerie into the air. It spread like the flight of a swan sensing danger while on still waters, and it glided to find a target hung on the wooden wall, a genuine reindeer's branching antler. It was a beautiful species from the Alps Mountains. The antlers were a family treasure left by her late father, Dr Walker Reinmarck. The bra landed on the fine twin edge of the antler.

"Wow! I'm delighted," she exclaimed. "I hit the jackpot again."

Her balanced frame engulfed in the nightgown showed her delightful contours simmering in the dim lit bedroom. Her body was like a beautiful mannequin, and men would go to war to win her prized status. Her Anglo-Saxon, Germanic descent added beauty to her features.

Dr Janet lanced her hands upwards and every direction, dancing in a circle. She started a slow dance like a marionette, a puppet with constrained movements. Her movements looked natural; she was alluringly amazing.

Then she slipped into bed under the thick cover of her cotton-sandwiched blanket. She put her face on her pillow and fell asleep immediately.

The birds were chirping; it was the magpies. Birds were twittering on the ground below. Tiny sparrows were in abundance, dark and light brown feathers with white and yellow breasts. They were the friendliest tiny birds, not bothered at all by the presence of people. The birds scratched the ground and shook the dust. The morning dew had watered the surface, which made it easier for the tiny birds to dig and extract small worms and tiny insects.

Two magpies were skirting at the balcony pillar, hopping two and fro with its small light body. The long and thin baritone voice of the tiny bird was loud enough to wake Dr Janet from her sleep. The swift manoeuvres of the magpies cast a painted image of black-and-white pictures moving incessantly against the morning sky.

She opened her eyes and brushed her eyelids with her thin cotton blanket. "Wow, its morning already?" She sat up in her bed, yawned, and covered her mouth with her soft palm. "Time to get up and get to work." Her bleary eyes were still half-closed.

She leaned forward and did three basic yoga stances. She looked into the mirror and took a deep look at her aging face. "I think I'm getting older each year. I need a man to lean on. I hope to meet someone who understands my work schedule in the hospital."

She took her big towel and headed for the bathroom. After a good shower, all that she needed was her beauty and charm.

She had a fine morning, with breakfast of fried egg omelette, white bread, and a hot cup of tea. While she was reading a journal from the British Medical Association, a Malay police constable came knocking at her door.

Nancy Kwan summoned Dr Janet to her house because there was an emergency case. Nancy's husband had just collapsed from seizures. When Dr Janet arrived at the scene, Nancy was with her husband, Timothy Wong. She was sobbing, and tears fell down her pale white cheeks. Her grimace indicated she felt lost in her mind.

Dr Janet rushed in to see the patient and held his wrist to get the pulse. "I'm afraid he's gone, Nancy. I'm sorry. His heart stopped after I made the first twenty counts. I will write the time of death at 9.15 AM, 15 May 1918, for the death certificate. The hospital will have him taken to the morgue for further medical procedures. You can follow, if you wish."

At the hospital, Dr Janet went in with her assistants to conduct a preliminary medical diagnosis. She had a hunch there was something mysterious. Timothy Wong's medical records showed he'd had heart problems; however, he was on medication. There was no marked provocation to show he encountered any contraindications prior to his death.

She left the deceased in the morgue for the time being and called on Detective John Hayes to get a coroner's inquiry to ascertain the cause of death. This would give her the jurisdiction to conduct a full medical investigation and to find the cause of death.

Detective John went back to Nancy's house to scan the area. Nancy was told that the police wanted an inquest; a post-mortem would be conducted by the hospital.

"I assume that Timothy's death could be due to other reasons far more remote in the right sense of the word," said Detective John. "Could you come to the police station for a recorded statement on your husband's death?"

"Much obliged," remarked Nancy. "I have no objections."

At the end of the moorland was a large farm with cows and goats. The animals were barricaded with wooden gates to keep them indoors. The cows numbered eighty, and there were a hundred goats for meat. Some of the stock for meat consumption was from the other districts near Lanang.

A shepherd named Kimby Singh owned a big piece of land at the outskirts. The exhausted shepherd was leaning on a sliding slope, watching over his flocks. He was thirty-something and was six feet two with big shoulders and a long beard that shrouded his old scars on his cheeks from a spear wound when he was robbed some years ago.

Kimby Singh wore a pair of spectacles with round rims because he was short-sighted. Kimby wanted to save enough money to read law in England. That was his ambition, and with his intelligence and command of the English language, it looked like he'd make it.

On the evening of Nancy Kwan's murder, Kimby was walking across the street and facing Nancy's house. It was dark from the rain, and his eyesight failed him. However, he did see a character from afar with a long mackintosh raincoat standing at the doorstep. That character was tall and thin. The figure vanished as soon as it turned towards Kimby, like a sort of premonition by someone who could sense being noticed. That thing, whatever it was, was faceless. Kimby could hear the sound of dragging footsteps from a distance. Sepulchral or not, it was real.

A long, continuous, shrill mewing and cry from a pack of stray cats entertaining their mates was audible. An old stray dog raised its neck, giving out a sad long growl and fearing the scenario that lied before it.

Kimby had a shock. He felt his heartbeat skip from the fear of the strange character. He was numb to his own senses and could hardly move.

As an orphan without family obligations, Kimby decided to feign his presence near the scene. He went to the side of a shop nearby and lit his cigar with a matchstick. Five minutes later, he heard the sound of hooves with a moving caravan. He peered at the doorstep but only noticed the back of the caravan's wheel whisking past the victim's house, about thirty yards from the doorstep. There was no one standing at the doorstep.

This was all he could recall.

"If I had remained standing facing the doorstep, at least I could have seen the intruder," murmured Kimby with a sense of remorse.

After dawn, a stranger travelled on a twin-horse carriage, heading towards Lanang District. As the morning fog grew thinner, he reached his destination but almost hit a pack of wild foxes running past the carriage. The last frightened fox was almost run over by the wheel but escaped. It ran with howling cries and vanished in the bushes.

Another stranger walked to an inn near the Heong Fook Inn, the Fan Yat Man Lodge. He wore a dark coolie hat worn by the Chinese tin miners in Malaya. His face was hardly visible because the brim almost touched his lower cheeks. He was around five feet eleven inches with broad shoulders. His Spartan physique revealed his defined, well-built chest.

He pressed the bell on the reception counter and spoke in *Cantonese*. "Chow San, yau mou yan cheong looikun."

There was no reply.

"Hello?" he said in English.

Eventually, out came running a young woman, almost falling forward as her fox trot in a shuffling half walk. She managed to hold her balance by placing her palms on the table. "Sorry, sir. Good morning. I'm April Hwang."

"I ... I was practicing the fox trot dance. I was clumsy doing it the first time."

The man lifted his coolie hat and held it in his arms near his chest. "Not at all, and good morning," replied the tall stranger. "I need a room for the time being. I'm Brandon Kwan. You are the proprietor? May I have a room for tonight?"

"Sure, Mr Brandon. The price is two cents for per day," said April Hwang to the handsome guy standing before her. "Breakfast is toasted bread or noodles, and supper is noodles again. This is a free courtesy of this inn." Her lips quivered. "We are having competition with the other inns, and it is quite monotonous these days.

"You don't look like any of those men who came here," April Hwang prompted the conversation further. "You're very positive and confident. And I suppose you don't put your head in the clouds, do you, sir? Just a wild guess – don't get alarmed, Mr Brandon." She chuckled with beaming eyes.

"You're indeed very beautiful, Miss April. You have two very subtle dimples on your cheeks and a pretty cleft on your chin. I presume your mum and dad must be good-looking too. I have that hunch." Brandon Kwan gave a shy half smile.

"Here are your keys to room number five. I'll carry one of your bags, if you don't mind."

"Much obliged, Miss April. Very kind of you."

They walked towards room five, and April said she'd get the noodles and bread ready. "Do you want coffee or tea?" She ignored his intent smile.

Brandon looked into her eyes and said, "Yes, my dear, I'd prefer both if you don't mind. "Coffee hits the mind, but Chinese tea cleanses the throat and body." He smiled, anticipating a further response from April Hwang.

Brandon checked in the room as usual. However, no one knew he was the younger brother of Nancy Kwan, who was deliberately murdered. Several thoughts came to his mind. "I'm here to find out how she died. Revenge is not my purpose for being here," Brandon said to himself in an angry tone. He stood hunched over with a cold, hidden face that could burst into flames of anger. "I have no clues, and this place is new to me. I have to know the people here. Miss April is my only chance because she is quite warm." He sat and then lay down on the bed with stretched hands to revive his energy after his long journey.

There was a knock at the door: April calling Brandon that his food was ready at the guest dining hall. Brandon stood up and combed his short hair, which stood up like cat's fur when wet. "I'm coming, just hold on." He came out in a white pagoda T-shirt and refined light beige tailored pants. Beaming with amusement, he praised her natural beauty again. "Do you realise you have such beauty?"

"No, Mr Brandon, I know my limitations. I am not the kind who thinks she has the cat's whiskers." Her heart beat hard. "In Lanang District only two young ladies are looked upon as the most beautiful. Salmi and Ai Ling won the beauty pageant contest two years in a row. Last year Salmi won first place and Ai Ling was runner-up. This year Ai Ling won the beauty pageant, and Salmi came a close second." April looked sad with defeat, given the colour of her cheeks. "I wasn't even given a place in the top three."

Brandon was quick to neutralise her sadness. "Let's continue with the breakfast, dear."

"OK! Do you want me to join you?"

"I am looking forward to that," Brandon said with a laugh.

Another guest at the inn sat at the sofa and faced the reception in the guest hall. He was smoking a Rough Rider cigarette. This quiet gentleman flicked ash into the ashtray on a small, rounded marble table as he haphazardly skimmed through the *Straits Times* newspapers published a week ago. He was brushing stray flecks from his texture moss-coloured trousers made of wool. It looked like he was all alone in his inspiration. A few minutes later, he stood up and walked out from the inn. He was quite a tough person at five feet ten, and he packed in almost 230 pounds. He went by the name Sujak Ramli, and he claimed to be a poet and writer with the Malay newspapers *Utusan Melayu*, which was published thrice weekly in Singapore. The publisher was none other than William E. Makepeace.

While at the breakfast table, Brandon Kwan was having a whale of a time with April Hwang. April looked so timid with her new acquaintance, but the minutes of icebreaking went smoothly. "Brandon, did you complete your education here in Malaya, or somewhere south in Singapore?" April asked.

"I was raised in the church by the reverends; they were English. I was orphaned when I was five, and that's the reason why I have the accent of an Englishman. The church sent me to England. I went to Oxford and graduated with a degree in history. I came back six months ago and got a job in Kuala Lumpur as a teacher at St. John's Institution."

"What brings you to Lanang District, bordering the states of Perak and Pahang?" asked April with surprise.

"I'll let you know later, April. I just can't at the moment," remarked Brandon quickly. "I have obligations to someone. You can't see my sorrows over a cup of coffee." Brandon sniffed the coffee scent with very thin enthusiasm. His jawline almost touched the cup's edge. "I have my trauma and flashbacks." Her eyes had that look of a million hungry and sparkling moons. Her eyes could sink a thousand ships. "Your eyes are very contemplating, April. At least, I think so."

"Am I a pretty girl?"

"Your passion could mean a million quests in your mind," said Brandon as he smiled at the young and kinky woman.

"Then are you a mind reader or a womaniser?" rebuffed April. "Have you fallen in love with anyone, Brandon?"

"Not in a thousand years. I was never popular with women. In Oxford University and the whole of England, there are many beautiful women, but I prefer to stay indoors. I'm half Caucasian and half Chinese. And besides, I think I'll just stick to my history books." His voice grew thinner.

The room was big and cosy while the young people played host and toastmaster of the evening. Two lonely people together in the evening tea, with Chinese cakes, muffins, biscuits, and Chinese tea. The ceiling fan was an old type from England. The circulation had a creaking, humming sound that sent shivers down the spine. It sounded like a platoon of crickets and cicadas doing their symphony. The blades could spin and fall on one's head at any moment. They could hear the horrifying sound of a horse-carriage that galloped on uneven terrain.

Brandon thought April was a turn-on. Any men could fall in love with her. "April, can I ask you something?"

"What do you want to hear about?" She smiled at him, and it was wide and lasted a minute.

"I was curious about Nancy's death and her husband's. Do you know any stories about them?"

"Well, in Lanang everyone knows she was not happy with him. Their quarrels could even be noticed when they were at the bazaar. He's very rich with plantations and property. As far as I know, the folks said he was a heart patient. But he was a heavy smoker, and he was on opium once in a while. She was a miserable wife, but she looked happy in public. There was nothing much from the coroner's report. The dailies just mentioned her husband's death as somewhere around 15 May 1918."

"Were their marital problems sexual?" Brandon knew his further intrusion could reveal his identity that he was Nancy's younger brother."

"No, I haven't heard about that in all these years, Brandon."

"Could it be he was having an impotency problem? Was Nancy having an illicit affair or love relationship with another man?"

"I don't know, Brandon, but you could check with Dr Janet. She's the doctor and pathologist who does all the post-mortem in Lanang District. She may know the cause of death. Anyway, two days after his death, Nancy was found hanged in her house. I think no one knows what happened." She licked her lips from the lukewarm coffee. "Why do you ask, Brandon? Now you look sad."

"Nothing, I'm just tired. I want to rest in my room."

"I had a wonderful evening with you."

"And there's so much to talk about days from now, April." He took his last sip and put the coffee cup on the plate. "Thanks, April Hwang, and good night."

"I'll see you in the morning for breakfast, Brandon. Have a good rest."

The new stranger in town took long, curious strides towards the post office. He passed by many hawkers' stalls that were busy entertaining their customers. These stalls, or gerai makan in Malay and siew fan tong in Cantonese, were thriving, especially during the breakfast and lunch hours.

Sujak Ramli lit a cigarette again. He took a liking to a Chinese stall selling coffee and ordered one with toasted bread. An old Chinese man greeted him in Cantonese with "Cheng chor, hapkun," failing to notice that Sujak was a Malay man. The cataracts on both his eyes had reached the full-fledged sunset stage, causing extreme blurred vision.

"Bagi saya secawan kopi dan roti bakar sapu kaya, taukeh," Sujak said to him. ("Give me a cup of coffee with toasted bread spread with kaya.")

"OK! Incik, gua in…gat cik o-lang Cina, wa tak tau lu o-lang Ma-la-yau." The old man grinned, revealing thin, fractured, coloured, parched lines on his cheeks. (OK! Mister, I thought you were a Chinese man. I didn't realise you were Malay.")

CHAPTER 5

THERE WAS A COMMOTION AT the mayor's office, and the crowd there grew bigger. A small kid with a ruffled shirt was held captive with his hands tied. He was crying out loud in pain. He was a small boy who of eight years and was skinny but looked intelligent. The poor kid was manhandled quite badly.

Sergeant Blue was on his way to the precinct when he noticed the crowd. He alighted from his single horse buggy and stepped down. "What is going on that I should know about, folks?"

"This boy was caught stealing bread. He's an orphan and sleeps in the streets. His parents died when he was six. No one takes him in for adoption," a big, fat man replied.

"This poor, small boy was popped with fear. Who beat him up so badly and slapped him until his lips bled? This is not the way to treat a kid," Blue growled at the crowd. "We are not at liberty to say and judge what he had done." There was silence, and the haunted look on his face started fading away.

The boy looked at Blue and grinned; he saw someone he could call friend. His fear subsided, and he was smiling with tears.

Blue said, "I think I like you, kid. I'll take you to the police precinct. Now, people, the game is over. Let this kid go. He was caught stealing bread because he was hungry. There was no crime involved for one small piece of bread. Be compassionate for the poor. We're not living in heaven, for God's sake." Blue was firm this time. He took out a handkerchief from his pocket and wiped the almost dried blood from the boy's lips. "Come on, boy, I'll give you a ride. What is your name?"

"Tom, sir! Tom Horn. That's what I can remember my mum and dad calling me. They died when I was six – fever. I think it was malaria, sir." The boy licked his lips from dryness and still looked worried.

They headed for the precinct. Blue took the boy in and sat him on a chair.

Big John was dealing with his papers and held his forehead with both hands, his fingers rubbing his temples. "I was thinking about this police reports, Blue. Maybe I need to start all over again to find the missing links."

"John, I found this boy outside the mayor's office. He was pretty roughed up by the crowd for stealing a piece of bread."

"Kid, you want coffee? Here, take your time." The kid held the cup with his nimble fingers. He was visibly trembling. He took a sip and put the cup back on the plate.

"You have been around for some time, boy. Tell me how old you are."

"Eight, sir!"

"And your name?" John said in a friendly tone.

"Tom Horn, sir! You can call me Tom. I'll be big and tall like you ten years from now."

"Yes, you will be, kid," John said with a smile. "But if you're rude to me, I'll kick your butt out."

"Well, don't ever mess around with me, because I'm a street fighter. Walk away from this slayer, if you want to live long," Tom replied.

"I'm frightened, street-slayer. Spare my life. Please, *please* don't hurt me," John said, trying to boost the boy's pride. "Tell me, where did you learn boxing?"

Tom clenched his tiny fist, showing his stuff and looking very serious. "Look at me when I'm talking. Look at my fist! I hold it like this. Learn from me big man."

"OK, I am listening."

"So I punch like this. One punch left, one punch right, and one uppercut. See, and you move with your legs like a butterfly. I will punch and move around like a rocking ship in a stormy sea." Tom moved around as he spoke. He almost wobbled and fell but got back to his feet. "This will surprise my attackers. They'll be sorry they messed around with me. They will remember my name, the street fighter, until they get grandchildren."

"Wow! That is very amazing, street fighter. How much is the fee for training?" John asked.

"It's easy, man. Just breakfast with a lot of cupcakes and muffins, and a jug of milk. Then I will teach you my kickboxing style, Detective. But you look like a nice guy, so I will waive the fee and charge one muffin only."

"Hmm, I think I can learn from you. Can you be my trainer?"

"How much can you pay me?" The boy looked into his eyes with a wide smile.

"We'll discuss that later, boy."

"I accept the offer."

John grinned at him. "Let's shake hands. Tom Horn, you have a job now as a boxing trainer. By the way, who are your parents? Where are they now?" John smiled and held his chin. "Can you tell me, son? You are a Caucasian. You parents are from Britain. Who are your mum and dad, kid?" John said as he looked into the boy's confused face.

"My mum is a Scots, and my dad is Welsh. Are you a Scotsman? If you aren't, I'll put a dead flower on your head."

"No, kid, I'm Irish, so you will put a dead flower on my head."

"You can bet on that. I can kick your butt, so you'd better be good to me if you want to live, Big Man."

"Here, Big Boss, eat these biscuits and muffins. The vanilla flavour tastes good."

"Thanks. You are a good man." Tom said, his freckled face grinning. "I think I am right this time."

There was a long list of names and sketch pictures on the notice board near John's table. Most of these were men drawn from lists of suspects and descriptions given by victims and eyewitnesses.

"Where do you sleep every night, kid?" John asked.

Tom was gulping the muffin and taking a sip of the tea in his cup. His fingers trembled from the newly acquired tea. His eyes blinked each time he felt the tasty muffin that went down his skinny throat. His clothes needed washing, and he needed to be groomed. John was thinking of sending him to the orphans' home, but first he must be sent to the hospital to get treated for the wounds on his lips.

John asked again. "Where do you sleep at night?"

The boy looked at him and wondered why. "Oh, I sleep at the bazaar's back lane, sir! I have a blanket given to me by kind folks. Sometimes they give me leftover meals. It tastes good."

Then the boy looked at the notice board. He put his hands on his eyelids; he must be tired. He stood up and said, "I think I have seen these people before the skeletal remains were at the lake. Detective John, I have seen them earlier. I was catching spiders with my friend, Harun the Malay boy. He is an orphan too, around ten years old. Since then, I have not seen him around. We sleep at the bazaar and scavenge for food together." The boy looked disillusioned at his friend's disappearance. "Can the police look for him, please? I'm dead worried. He is my only friend."

"All right, kid, we will search for him."

The boy was happy at John's promise to look for his missing friend. The hope to see his friend again showed on his freckled cheeks.

"And then they walked past us. I heard them speak foreign, kind of like Italian or Spanish or French. It was not English. It was midday. I remember now. In the evening there was one more group of men. One was a giant and bearded; he was a white man. The others were Chinese, Malays, and Indians. This is the picture of him – the giant." The kid pointed at the sketches. "We were a couple of miles from the lake." He rubbed his eyes again.

"Never mind, kid. You can speak later, after you get treated at the hospital. Now, be a good boy and follow Sergeant Blue to the hospital."

"Thank you so much, Big Man," Tom cried, and he hugged Detective John tightly.

John said, "Blue, get Dr Janet's medical report, and get Nurse Joanne to put Tom in the orphans' home first. I kind of like this boy; he reminds me of someone when I was a kid back home in Sligo, Ireland.

"During the Depression it was bad – really bad. Coalminers all over Ireland had to migrate. Some migrated to America. We moved on to Dublin for better days. Dublin was just as gloomy and mired with unemployment. I worked as a kid, pushing hay and groceries on wheels." John's eyes slid across the precinct.

John rubbed the boy's hair several times and smiled at him. "Now go on, boy."

Blue took his coat and left with Tom. The boy was given immediate treatment at the accident and emergency department. Dr Janet nursed his wounds and wrote a medical report to support his admission to the orphan's home. Finally, the kid got a place in the home. He was very skinny and under-nourished.

At the orphans' home, when the sun came up the next day, Tom was having coffee and breakfast with the inmates. The kid was bleary-eyed and was sad, with tears in his eyes. This was the first time he'd had breakfast with coffee, and bread sandwiched with cheese. He was gazing at the walls in the dining hall with cold eyes. He knew this would be his place until he was a grown up. His face was white, but the lines on his face grew thinner. He was amazed by the prophetic paintings hung on the wall. It was a tribute of the great Vincent Willem Van Gogh.

At the precinct John was going through his papers again, looking at the long list of suspects and what the kid told him the day before.

"Blue, could you fetch the kid here? I think he is in a better position to let us know what he may have seen."

Soon Tom was walking joyously through the office with Blue. John grinned. "Thanks, Blue, for taking him here." He looked at Tom. "So we meet again, kid. Want some candy?" John opened a small jar. "Do you remember what you told me two days ago? Can you think back what you saw? I just want to know, because this is important police work. We have to know what happened. Now tell me, was there anything you saw about those men?"

"Yeah! Those men on the sketches ... will they harm me?" Tom was afraid and looked pale. "I heard them quarrelling, as they walked down the slope. They said, 'What is done, is done. No one will know what happened.'

"The other shaggy-looking man scolded, 'Shut up idiots – don't put us in danger.' That's all I can remember. Sorry, Detective. I may have forgotten some words.

"And the other group – the giant man, I heard him scold his men." The boy scratched his forehead with his tiny finger. "The giant said 'You sex crazy', and 'peeping Toms'. What is sex, sir?" The boy asked with a set look on his face.

"Well, kid, that is a word for a man when he is older. I think it's time Sergeant Blue takes you back to the orphans' home."

"All right. Can I have some more sweets? Thanks. Mighty kind of you, sir. Bye." He waved a few times in a gesture of appreciation.

It was raining, but the drizzle faded late in the evening. Ai Ling glanced through the window with a big smile on her oval face. She was leaning on the Singer sewing machine, and the wood was made of brown teak. Her elbows rested on the machine with her palm cradling her chin. Soon the faded drizzle turned rainy again. She was wearing pyjamas, and her loose shirt revealed her white chest. She had a thin jade necklace round her slim neck.

She looked at her brother doing martial arts manoeuvres in the kitchen. It was fascinating. Chan Chan was a real expert.

Chan Chan did his usual breathing exercise. He was also practising the crane stance with punching manoeuvres. Ai Ling laughed and tickled her brother's neck while he was still standing on one foot.

"Let's see if you can stand this tickling, my big brother!" Ai Ling said with a broad smile. "You can't even smile, can't you, Chan? I'd like to see April Hwang longing for your presence." Ai Ling leaned her head over Chan's shoulders. "Do you want me to pass a message to her?" She was walking with a mannish stride, teasing him further and flitting around like a butterfly. "'April, I'm in love with you.' Ha!" She giggled and ran out, leaving him alone.

At the hospital, Dr Janet and John Smith were waiting for the arrival of the Yard men. The day was bleak with several patients and casualties.

Big John alighted from the twin carriage on the left flank, followed by Blue. "Good evening, Dr Janet, and pleased to meet you too, John Smith," remarked Big John with a smile. "John Smith, you have to excuse us for a moment. This is strictly police matters."

"OK, I understand, Detective John. I'll go to the café at the back of the pharmacy."

"Dr Janet, can we find a quiet place to talk regarding the post-mortem you did on Nancy Kwan's husband? He died from cardiac failure and cerebral oedema. I need further details, if you don't mind." Big John was cold this time with a hoarse voice, but it returned sombre again after a few choking coughs. "Don't throw the red hat into the air in public yet. We haven't identified the entire suspect trail." Big John grinned at Dr Janet and Blue.

The doctor said, "I think she inserted painkillers or aspirin into his tea or coffee as a first attempt, but that failed to do the job fast. When laryngeal oedema failed to kill the victim, she went into the second stage with strychnine. "The second wave of intoxication did the job, and he was laid to rest."

"I have this fear that keeps coming back. Early revelations may drown the murderers' curiosity and confidence." John walked around with his pipe lit. "They may leave Lanang, or they may remain in a cocoon state and pretend to be innocent..

As I was browsing the cabinets in the deceased's room, I found a couple of brownish, round pastels. A small pastel is enough to cause seizures and brain damage. The seizure can lead to heart failure. The pastel is called strychnine by its chemical name. Dr Janet, I think I have found the murderer for Nancy's husband: it's none other than his wife." Big John puffed air out of his mouth.

Dr Janet looked surprised. "Where do you suppose she got the substance?" she asked.

"In Kuala Lumpur. There is a hamlet near the meeting point of two rivers, the Gombak and Klang. This busy trading hub has shops and small outlets retailing all kinds of foodstuff, household items, artefacts, attire, incense, and hardware materials derived from China, the Middle East, the Dutch East India Company, and India. She may have bought it on one of her trips there."

Blue said, "Let's presume this silent substance is as deadly as cyanide. We have a time bomb here. Criminals may use it to paralyse their victims, to rob and even to kill. That poor woman wasn't able to enjoy the wealth left by her dead husband. In the next episode, she was found hung by rope in her own house.

John said, "Some neighbours, when interviewed, told me that Nancy suffered through eight years of marriage. Her rich husband was a sadist and a wife beater. Her domestic violence was too much for her to bear. They could hear her crying voice, pleading for mercy when they quarrelled. He was heavy on alcohol, wines, brandy like Brandy Jack, and also the detrimental Chinese white wine, which is popular with Chinese men. It looks as though there was no other option for her, except ..." He shrugged. "I may be wrong, and it could be someone else. In any crime scene, everyone is a suspect."

Blue said, "Dr Janet, we have to be decisive. Police work is not just on circumstantial evidence. We deal a lot with real evidence."

Dr Janet told Detective John about a detail kept secret. "When I did the post-mortem on Lily and Iris, the bullet wound at her throat was inclined. I presume it was deliberate, to silence her." She held a stethoscope and a pen in her hand. "One of the perpetrators may have known the victim."

John and Blue thanked Dr Janet and John Smith, and then they resumed their daily work.

Back at the teacher's quarters, Big John lit his pipe with roasted English tobacco. The clock on the wall toned at 10.00 PM. It was getting late, but he was not alone; Blue was still browsing through the police report.

Blue sighed and tapped the table with his fingers, playing the tune "Jingle Bells". It was a faint sign of desperation. His gaze was getting thinner, and with a conspiratorial wink, he released a cold smile.

"Could this be the last murder case? I just hope so." He stood up. "Do you want a cup of coffee, John?" he asked as he put the cup on the table next to his.

"Thanks, Blue, but I feel the killers know we're getting a step closer."

Two of the glass windows were open, letting a strong wind carry in the chill from the drizzle. The paper calendar swayed on the wall, and there was a glimmer of moving shadows criss-crossing frantically as the kerosene lit lamp swayed to the left and right. It grew darker when it hit the right direction because of the blue curtain canvassing the edge.

Suddenly a shot rang out and hit the copper lattice used to support the glass window frame. The bullet whizzed past the curved contour and broke the glass into splinters. It went through the top of the hat that Blue wore.

"Don't run!" shouted Blue at the figure standing outside the glass windows. He raced to the door and rushed out, but the man in a raincoat with a round hat was gone. Sergeant Blue gave chase, but there were no indications of anyone around the dark alleys. "I'll get you next time, night stalker, and I will put these handcuffs on you." Blue gave a lopsided grin and turned around, walking back towards the quarters.

Back indoors, Blue tried to pacify Detective John, who was in quite a shock. “That shot was meant to kill you, John,” reaffirmed Blue to his colleague. “It was aimed either at your head or your heart.”

“Let’s presume there is a connection between the stalkers with some of the murders,” said Big John while unbuttoning his upper button to breathe better. “Deliberate and intentional to silence me, yes, and then you, Blue. I presume he knows we’re on his trail.”

“The clock is ticking, and we need more evidence to tie each murder to the perpetrators,” Blue said. “We need to find the murder weapon that was used on those two Malay girls. Then the man or woman who cuffed Nancy Kwan’s nose with *laudanum* to put her to sleep. After that. tying a hangman’s rope round her neck and throwing the other end of the rope on the wooden trusses below the roof. She must have very strong arms. I suppose if it is a woman we’re looking for, we’re hitting rough waters.”

Big John looked at Blue with a commanding eye. “The forty-nine-year-old Malay woman was a widow. She was deliberately killed to decoy us further,” he said. “She was killed somewhere else, wrapped in a gunny sack, and taken to the hill by at least two or three persons. I’m tired, Blue. I have to teach tomorrow morning at 7.45 AM. Until this episode is over, I’m still a school teacher in disguise.” Big John yawned due to his empty stomach; he hadn’t eaten since noon. “I just told everyone I am just doing liaison and typist work in the police precinct. That’s my reason why I get into the police precinct every day. And you’re doing carpentry and a coffee boy in the department.” He yawned. “Good heavens. After the class ends at 12.45 PM, I intend to see Dr Janet again. In the evening we'll get her to visit the crime scene at Nancy Kwan's house."

"Cheer up, Sherlock Holmes. We are just beginning to scratch the surface. I believe it's going to be a long journey. We'll do further investigation. We may have left some small evidence to close Nancy's murder."

At the hospital, a ten-year-old Malay boy was being treated for dementia. He was found hiding in an empty wooden shack that was evacuated by a poor couple ten years ago. Ai Ling and Salmi found him and took him to a nearby post-office. They saw his moving shadows behind the partly dilapidated wooden structure. When the two girls went in the shack, he was almost motionless and shivering from cold and fever. Then he fainted on the wooden bed.

He had a splint to support his elbow; the long piece of flat wood was self-made. He bandaged himself to support his elbow. His arm could have been fractured due to a fall. He had a cut on his face almost an inch long, from something sharp.

His face was frozen like a flat piece of crystallized ice sunk in dry sands. His nose and eyes went dry from dehydration over a number of weeks. This Malay boy looked haggard and malnourished. He should be in the orphans' home, convalescing for a long period. His shirt was old and was covered with a blanket of black and grey fungal growth spread over the chest and neck area; this was the result of continuous sweat soaked on his body. Loose threads were at every sewn edge of his clothes, and his short pants were torn and worn out after years of wearing them.

Dr Rama attended to him after his admission to the ward. He could die from starvation. He was dehydrated, pale, and weak.

At his bed he looked at the nurses attending to him. The saline drip with cortisone and glucose would help him recover, but it may take more than a week.

Dr Janet asked Dr Rama about the condition of the boy.

"His blood pressure is normal except for a slower heartbeat. His pulse rate will improve in a day's time. X-rays showed the lungs and heart are normal. Blood and urine test results were normal. Liver activity is slightly elevated, though safe. The patient came in with chronic bronchitis and exacerbations with thick, viscous hyper-secretions. Skin was dry with rashes on chest and back; they will subside with cortisone over a few days. All other markers showed average readings. He is OK for the time being." Dr Rama wiped his palm on his forehead brushing his hair backwards, and he grinned.

"How is he doing now?" Dr. Janet asked.

"There is some recovery, but he's still dazed from the long dehydration. He can't even force a smile to greet people. He could be frightened or afraid of someone. There could be intimidation or a threat on his life."

"He will recover in a few days?" Dr Janet said.

Dr Rama looked at Dr Janet with shifty eyes. "He will need a crutch after discharge. I will do the follow-up. You told me he was with the eight-year-old Caucasian boy placed at the orphans' home, and they were friends."

"The police will need his testimony as well. He and Tom were around the crime scene after the skeletal remains were found. They overheard the drifters' conversations. It's important to link the killers." She read the notes written by Dr Rama and clipped to the aluminium tray in the patient's daily chart. "Tom says his name is Harun. Let me know when he is in a better condition to speak."

"Yes, Dr Janet, I will let you know." Dr Rama gave her with a comforting smile. "And before discharge I want him to be sent to the orphans' home like Tom."

"I'll let Nurse Joanne know about this," Dr Janet said as she flipped her stethoscope across her thin shoulders.

Dr Janet left the hospital at 5.00 PM. She had arranged a meeting with Det. John at his house. She signalled for a cab buggy driven by one horse. This time she was dressed like an Amish woman.

She could be the cynosure in silhouettes in any Victorian ballroom dance. She was tall and slim, and the farthingale gave her extra weight around her athletic, beautiful frame. Her cleavage was quite visible, though the Amish tradition forbid exposure of a woman's bosom in public. She wore a cloche with an inch of blue ribbon around it and spiked with a ruby stone on both sides. There was another thin yellow ribbon with short ends tied to the ruby stone. She looked magnificent.

The Amish disdained unorthodox living and lifestyles other than their founding fathers' seventeenth-century social and cultural traditions. The close-knit tradition was practiced by the Swiss-German community in Switzerland.

The buggy stopped before the cobbled pavement, and she entered. She told the cab driver to proceed to the police quarters.

She had a German look that needed no advertising. The wind blew her veil out of her face. Her looks were like a mannequin from a fashion boutique's glass-door display. She took out her lipstick and held a small mirror, a L'Oreal Ashley, and she glazed it across her thin, soft lips. She took out her Helene Rubenstein and sprayed some on her creamy bosom.

She took out a small piece of white paper with handwritten information. She read the contents and smiled judicially. She opened her small crystal ruby-coloured bead handbag, which featured a zigzag and crescent line of turquoise blue beads.

The buggy reached John's home. Sergeant Blue was at the entrance attending to a line of clay pots and holding several species of orchids. The morning glory was still visible, but it had shrank and tilted before falling off from its cradle. "Good evening Dr Janet. What brings you here?"

She alighted from the buggy, paid the fare to the driver, and said thanks. The buggy left. "Am I interrupting your evening, Sergeant Blue?" she asked politely.

"Not at all, Dr Janet. You are most welcome. John is having a shower, he'll be ready in a couple of minutes, I think. So you are indeed of German descendant, Dr Janet?" He smiled at her.

"Yes, I am, and I'm proud of my heritage. You can't take Germany out of a German woman. Our forefathers fought the bitter wars with the ancient Athenians. The Aryans always believe in reality, not illusions."

"I understand, Doctor. Please make yourself comfortable here."

Dr Janet looked at the orchids when John came out and greeted her. "Dr Janet, good evening. Do you want to see me, and do you have any news about the Malay boy in the ward? Is he recovering from dementia? I hope he will. And I would like you to recommend him for the orphans' home with Tom. After all, they are buddies. Their testimony may hold water. I was hoping to link the drifters with their conversations downhill. The boys heard them loud and clear."

John's mind drifted back to the scene when the stalker tried to put a bullet in him. He grinned at Blue, and his eyes danced to the tunes in his mind. The stalker was after his hide, or Blue's. Nothing had surfaced, and there were no evidential links to the murderers – yet.

John smiled at Dr Janet, hiding his bitterness behind a shallow smile. "I'll get you a cup of tea which I have prepared." He took out a tray with a teapot and three cups. He tilted the three cups and put them on plates. He poured the tea into the three cups and offered her a cup. "Blue, you can join us if you want."

"Not at the moment," Blue answered." "I'll have a cup later. I'll have a cigarette at the porch. Excuse me, Dr Janet, if you don't mind," Blue added sheepishly.

He left the two of them on their own. "So Doctor, do you have any news for me?" John asked.

Janet took out the piece of paper she had written at the hospital. Clipped to the small piece was another smaller piece of paper. It was handwritten.

Don't let the cat loose.

Darling J. M. 95?

"John, I found this at the doorway near Nancy's home yesterday, while I was passing by the road. I was on my way to the grocery store. It could have blown out from somewhere, or someone may have accidently dropped it. I wonder what it means."

"Are you familiar with phrases written in this form, Doctor?"

"Well, I think it is in Latin and handwritten with an artistic brush. We have someone here who is very educated in Latin. or he may have had years or decades of training with brush writing."

"It's intriguing, with the letters J. M., and the number. I am confused, Doctor."

"I'm confused too, who wrote it, and for whom?"

"I'll keep this in my file here at home, to analyse it further. Thanks for the latest information. I appreciate every step you have made. You're of great assistance. Now, how is the Malay boy doing in the ward?"

"His name is Harun, according to Tom, his best friend. They are buddies."

John said, "When he's discharged and sent to the orphans' home, just let me know."

"OK, you're the boss." She smiled with that inherent hope.

CHAPTER 6

THE NEXT MORNING, AT THE other side of the moor, young Salmi played in the wet, marshy land. It was the torrential rainy season again. In small pockets of bed of water, tadpoles survived and could be seen wading to and fro in search of freedom. These tiny black swimmers would gradually graduate into frogs.

Salmi sank her hands into the shallow, clear water and scooped with both hands. "Got you, small little fellows. You'll be lunch for my *ikan kalui*, but I'll need more of you!" The bamboo container tied round Salmi's slim waist was filled with tadpoles. She was also a hunter for the birds *merbok* and *tekukur.*

Minutes later, Salmi noticed a big shadow cast over her from behind. As she turned, she saw Ai Ling walking towards her with red sandals. She had a round basket filled with a small bird, the burung merbok. The trap they fixed had captured a new visitor.

"Hi, Salmi, look what I have here." Ai Ling winked and smiled at Salmi.

The two girls giggled and played with the mud. They painted each other's face with stripes on their cheeks and foreheads. The new mime face made them look like aborigines awaiting a dance ritual with no spectators.

"Comrade Ai Ling! Here, I have two goose feathers. Take one and slip it on with a rubber band round your head." She laughed with a long, girlish yawn.

"Kind of fun, Salmi," Ai Ling said, and they started walking and wailing in a trance.

They smudged stripes of white from the mud with layers of white and black, ink-like colours on their noses, neck, and brow. It drowned the sallow complexion with daffodils blooming in the background of lustful meadows.

Salmi's bashful smile curled bigger, and with that girlish charm and the doleful past of her sister's death, she trudged with uncertain steps towards Ai Ling. "Let's go back home, or just hang around a little bit longer," she said with a short yawn.

Suddenly, Salmi noticed a piece of red cloth partially buried in the mud. It is a fragment from someone's garment.

It was breezy, and the cold wind chilled the girls' soft skin. Salmi's mouth turned into a smile. "What is it?" Ai Ling asked.

"Oh dear! Someone left in a hurry, I guess!" Salmi said.

Ai Ling examined it. "It's a small piece of torn garment. Looks like these footprints lead up to the canyon, Salmi." Ai Ling cast her eyes far ahead at the wasteland. This young woman looked like a detective. Her intuitive manner earned her that hat, and she had psychic vision. Ai Ling was more passive and always presumed that everyone is good and kind.

Salmi examined that torn garment. "I think it's from a shirt. Could be man or woman. But I reckon it was ripped by a force so strong to have severed it. Let me keep it in my pocket."

"The canyon is so far," Ai Ling said as she raised her hands and pointed at it.

"Not far enough for someone to walk, if you have a purpose," replied Salmi.

"You mean …? Oh no, no, no, Salmi. Not that canyon! It's spooky." Ai Ling blushed. "I'd rather stay at home and knit my cardigan."

Meanwhile, in the home of Big John and Sergeant Blue, the drizzle kept these two men at bay. Minutes passed, and the drizzle turned heavy. They decided to stay indoors.

While holding his pipe, a *meerschaum* with the Irish tobacco Erinmore, Big John reviewed the evidence. "All right, where was the victim's body? The widow found on the hill," he said aloud. "Coroner's report states the victim was dead two days earlier than when the body was discovered. Is that right, Blue, or am I wrong after more than a decade in homicide?"

"The flies were at their third day cycle in the decomposed body, but some specimens were just at the egg stage. There is a mix," said Blue.

"We can't tie the suspect with the French twins, but they were seen six minutes from the scene of the crime, walking downhill towards the Song Song Inn," Big John said hesitantly.

"The hookers at Sleeping Pleasures Inn claimed otherwise. When questioned, they said that the French twins were having that 'moment' with them. They were in the same room.

John puffed at short intervals. "I think the widow was killed in the early hours when she was about to perform morning prayers. Yes, she was living alone as a widow and with no kids. Her small cottage is the only one on the hilly slope." Big John raised his head after resting his chin on his chest.

"According to Dr Janet, the X-rays showed an inclined injury on the head with a blunt object. We have haematoma to the rear of the skull. The blunt weapon may be the pistol they had with them, but it's still too early for us to identify that."

"She may have been doused with *laudanum* to put her to sleep," Blue offered.

"Flies in the third-day stage could have been implanted on her body by the murderers."

"That is quite possible."

"This could be a carcass of a cat or a small animal. We have a small, contributory, circumstantial evidence. They could have scooped it with a spoon and planted it on the widow's wound at the forehead, and at the deep stab wound in her stomach," John summarised.

"She was not raped, no sexual attempt made, and no signs of force because there were no bruises on her hands and body."

"Perhaps she heard them talking about the two murdered ladies at the lake. A mere mention of the names Lily and Iris could have raised her suspicion."

"To silence her and kill her. That's my theory. That buried their alibi, I guess."

John said, "In homicide, you have to think and walk like a murderer, if you want to think further on circumstantial evidence."

Blue countered, "That is not adequate. You need to do a prognosis like a doctor."

"Do you have anything different? Blue, please let me know."

"Well, why were the dried leaves and hedges burnt?"

John replied, "To draw attention from the village folks nearby."

"Their alibi will be intact when we find the body. Pretty smart move, huh?"

"Blue, could you have the entire area scanned one more time? Take along two Malay constables with you. I'd be quite worried if you were alone. "Meanwhile, I need to speak to Dr Janet. Once you have completed your task, meet me at the hospital. Try to find the skeletal remains of any small animal. That's the reason why we can't find it near the crime scene. We have murders still unsolved."

The crowds looked at Det. John and the police department with some kind of hope. They had faith. However, their hope was running wild and was not long for this world.

Detective John's lips twitched, pressed firmly together due to disappointment. "If we can't get the killers, the people in Lanang will give us death certificates."

"The police are not saturnine."

In the streets, the cold glances were sardonic. Their mood was nine pounds of frustration. The people wanted some form of retribution. The crowd jeered each time a policeman walked past. A newspaper read,

A blue satire on the police, a parody.
The murderers' still at large.

Back at the police precinct, Detective John browsed through the coroner's and victim's report and the monthly newspapers coverage. The spike memos were piling up, and he scrutinized them one by one. A magazine had arrived from Singapore and had been placed on his table a week earlier. It was *Punch Magazine* from London, the English language British weekly magazine of humour and satire. The front cover showed a group of prisoners walking free out of jail while the police looked on. The euphemism was great, but not the frustration. John filled his pipe with tobacco and lit up with a match. The small strike sizzled into a small fire, and he torched the cup of his pipe. Smoke filled the room, and the breath of tobacco from his mouth gave him the adrenaline to go on for the day. The smoke floated like a penguin walking subtly and disappearing after a few minutes.

"No credible eyewitnesses at the crime scenes. No good alibis to trail any suspects. And no one came forward to provide evidence for the police," John said to himself.

Nurse Joanne was dressed in beige pants and a white silky short-sleeve shirt. She held a small purse and walked towards the buggy stand. A small Malay boy carried a light brown leather bag strapped to his shoulder. He was Harun and would get a place in the orphans' home. He lifted his head and looked at Joanne with sparkling eyes.

She signalled a buggy that was a short distance away. The horse stopped and whinnied. The buggy driver pulled the front strap to restrain the single-horse cab.

"Good evening, Nurse Joanne," the driver greeted her. He grinned and was happy to have two more passengers.

Harun said, "Hi, sir, please take me to the orphans' home." They entered the buggy, and the journey for the orphan boy was a constantly moving landscape as the horse galloped.

The orphans' home was a large, long barracks setup of wooden homes sandwiched with a promenade of shrubs. At the front and along the arcade, an old Malay man sat in a rocking chair. He was playing the harmonica and slid the instrument across his lips with ease. The old Malay tune "Tudung Periuk", a sad ballad rhyme, was one of his favourite renditions.

Joanne greeted Pak Samad as soon as she came out of the cab with Harun. "Pak Samad, selamat petang, good evening," she said primly.

"Good evenin', selamat petang, Joanne. So you have brought a Malay boy to this orphans' home. What is his name?"

"You can call him Harun. He is Tom's best friend."

The boy greeted Pak Samad with pride, and he lowered his jaw to his chest. Joanne held Harun's hand and walked inside. The front entrance was a world of hope for Harun. He was very shy and was put off by his ugly ordeal. He knew he would have a better future here with proper food, shelter, and education. He blinked and held his belt, adjusting new pants and shirt (bought by John and Blue as a gift). The morning sunrays greeted the window and enveloped the doorway.

He stared at a portrait, *The Potato Eaters* by Van Gogh, hung on the wall. The work caught his eye; the Dutch post-impressionist painter was known for emotional honesty. The other two corners had *The Starry Night* and *The Yellow House*. The large, long quarter was like a mirror into hope and salvation. Harun, like Tom and the rest of the orphans, couldn't read or write. Tom and Harun learned the spoken language by heart and became good at it. Harun couldn't understand the writings on the walls, but he could only imagine what they meant.

The other end of the quarters was also a place for old folks, the unfortunate, the deformed, and the mentally handicapped. This shelter homes was a manifestation of the British for everyone. It gave hope to the orphaned children, the unfortunate, and the aging folks left by their children or kin's in the streets.

There was scripture on the wall that read, "We must not care about the length of his hair or the colour of his eyes."

The other shelter and orphan quarters was separated by a fence for girls and old women. The home for the girls was also a redemption house for "fallen" women.

This was a world of divided society. You have to be humanistic. A beauty to one society is one a utopian hallucination to the dreams of the affluent. These shelters taught orphans to read and write, and to learn skills for later stages in life when they became adults and returned to society.

Joanne looked at Harun and Tom, and then at the rest of the kids, who came to welcome their new guest. They seemed thrilled to have a new inmate.

The warden was a nun around forty-five years old. Her name was Jill Martin. She was slim and tall, and she carried the beauty and charm. The young boys walked behind her and paraded in a long line to fill the hall. The other half split and stood in front to form two lines. These boys had the magic to turn grey clouds and countenance away with just a few gestures and smiles. They looked hopefuls and spoke amongst themselves with muffled tones. They signalled a message: they were orphans, and orphans needed protection from society. It was not a self-parodying groan or sensation aimed at higher society. This was not about the rich and affluent society, but to break the chains of legitimacy because all men were born equal.

The nun stood at the other end and raised her hands. Soon the boys begin singing "Auld Lang Syne", a Scots poem by Robert Burns. The sad ballad could seep through the mind and heart of any mortal soul. It flowed like the rapids, finding its path along the plains.

The sweet melody faded slowly. Harun was still amazed at the indoor, prophetic confinement. As he walked around, someone patted his shoulder from the back. A smiling and happy Tom hugged his buddy. "Harun, my good friend, it's been a long time since I parted with you." Tom had his tears rolled down his freckled face cheeks. "Thank God you're alive. I'm glad you lived." He stammered and cried.

"I am glad you're safe too, Tom. I thought I would never have the chance to see you again. I thank God. I see you here safe and standing right before my eyes. You are in good shape, Tom." He smiled with bright eyes and pushed his shoulders backwards. It was his habit because he had stiff joints.

Tom said, "Come on, I'll show you around once we get your bag into the dorm. You will learn the other boys' names later; it will take time to memorise."

The next morning after breakfast, Tom and Harun were greeted by Sergeant Blue. He came with a buggy with two horses. The nun Jill Martin was standing at the porch entrance with a tray of muffins fresh from the stove. She then passed it to another nun for distribution to the boys and old folks.

"Good morning, Sergeant. It's surprisingly early," she said.

"I came to fetch Tom and Harun for the precinct. And could you keep this confidential?" Blue was tongue–tied, staring at her beauty.

"OK, I will fetch them." She went in and came out with the two boys.

Blue and the boys left in the buggy.

At the police precinct, Big John was reading the pages of the murder victims. He took a pencil and made sketches and mind maps on each murder. John's forefinger went into circles as he diagnosed each event deliberately, hoping to find a missing link. Somewhere was a hidden answer. His holster was on his table.

"John, I have the boys with me," Blue said as he walked in with them.

"Good morning, Detective John," the boys spoke, and they weren't sure what they had to do next.

"Sit down, boys. So you are Harun, Tom's best friend."

Harun's bony body and fingers trembled a bit.

"Calm down, Harun, there is nothing to fear. We are the good guys. We are the police," John said with a smile. "Now, tell me again, Harun. You were with Tom when you overheard the conversations of the drifters, right?"

"Yes. We heard it loud and clear, when they walked downhill. What Tom told you earlier was what I heard as well, sir." He was a bit uneasy in a police room.

John showed Harun the piece of paper but knew Harun couldn't read and write just like Tom. He read what Tom had said earlier.

"OK, Harun, do these men in the sketches look familiar to you?"

"Yes, they do. They look like ... I think so, yes, they are those men who walked downhill." Harun squinted his eyes in disbelief. "Detective John, these men ... What have they done? Are they the ones who killed the Malay girls?"

"No, they are simply suspects at the moment. So you and Tom know about the skeletal remains found at the lake."

Harun said, "The people in Lanang know about it. We hear everyone talking almost every day. Yes, Big Man, sir, I heard them with Tom, but we were frightened and quickly hid in the bushes. If they see us, they may harm us. We are frightened, sir. Will they come for us and kill us, because we let you know the truth about what we heard?"

"Do not speak to anyone regarding what you and Tom have told me. Keep silent and pretend you and Tom did not hear or see anything."

"OK. We heard them quarrelling as they walked down the slope. They said, 'What is done, is done. No one will know what happened.' The shaggy man scolded, "Shut up, idiots – don't put us in danger.

"Then later in the evening, another group of men came out of somewhere. The other group, the giant man, we heard him scold his men." The boy scratched his earlobe and cheek before sliding his hand down to his chin. "The giant said, 'You sex crazy' and 'peeping Toms'. We don't know what sex means."

"I told Tom you will learn about it when you are older. There is nothing wrong with this word. OK, I think it's time Sergeant Blue takes you and Tom back to the orphans' home. That is all, boys. You can go with Sergeant Blue to get something from the grocery store. Then go home quietly – and remember, do not talk about this. Understand?"

"OK, Detective, we'll keep this a secret." The boys giggled and smiled at the big man. "You're very tall and big," Harun said with surprising eyes.

"When you and Tom reach eighteen years of age, you will be full grown." John patted the two boy's shoulder again. "Remember, do not speak to anyone, especially any strangers who visit the orphans' home. What you have told me remains a secret? Is that OK, buddies?"

They crossed their fingers with John and laughed.

CHAPTER 7

ACROSS THE MOOR, A BEVY of beautiful young maidens with mahogany skin toiled in the hot sun, plucking tealeaves. They had beautiful eyes with thin brows and oval faces. They were dressed with white and light blue sarees that waved against the wind like flags. These young Indian girls had natural beauty, and they could walk the aisles of a beauty pageant. Their oval features look so well defined and symmetrical. A natural heritage came from the Indian continent.

They were hard at work. They walked down the hill after sundown, when all the day's work was completed. Bullock carts were waiting to transport fresh tealeaves in round baskets. The young girls walk home joyfully.

"The killers want to play a game with us. A chess game, or Russian roulette. Check the size of the shoe mark. The killer travels with gloves to protect his prints," John told Blue. "Get the prints done immediately."

John browsed the papers on his table, and he was mad. "I have to get things done in the right perspective. Time is running faster than a horse."

Doctor Janet looked at his face and could imagine a small forest fire flickering in his sallow cheeks. “John, do you know that you have a very good diplomacy look when you are annoyed? It reminds me of the gospel hymn ‘Higher hands are leading me’. You can move mountains if you want to – literally. Try meditating at night before bedtime, big man.” She smiled sheepishly.

“All men are the same when it comes to waltzing a woman into a bedroom for copulation.”

“Are you any different, Detective John?” came a sharp tone from Dr Janet. She wavered her lips and placed her fingers on her thin chin. “You don’t find a lone wolf dying in atonement, do you, Chief Inspector?”

“Aren’t women made for men to look at?” sighed Big John.

“You’re neither a saint nor a prophet, I presume.”

“All right, Dr Janet. Where have you been in the morning?”

“Taking steps of treason against the hospital, I guess,” answered Dr Janet.

“You are absolutely right. Just stay informed,” John told Dr Janet to calm her down. “Keep an eye on the surroundings and any changes around you. I’m looking into the case of Nancy’s husband and the two girls. We have premeditated murder.”

“Do you call that redemption, Detective John Hayes?” rebuked Dr Janet. “This is intimidating. They are walking like saints.”

“Cool down, Dr Janet. We are not after psychotic killers. These men raped and killed on the spur of the moment. When there is an easy getaway, they assume they’ll never get caught. In any case, in homicide we have two characters, one good and one evil. But in them, both are evil, inhumane, sadistic. When their sexual pressure builds up, and two young beautiful women appear at the lake, a quiet place ... That's an easy target, I presume. They calculated their moves, grabbed them, ripped their garments, and satisfied their lust."

Dr Janet noted, "They went further. One shot into their necks that went through their windpipes. We have evidence left by the perpetrators: a few drops of congealed blood, left on the scene of the crime. The congealed blood from the shots turned blue and black. It could be six hours after the scenario."

"Blood is thicker than water, and it will remain when it gets dried, don't you think, Dr Janet?"

The conversation took a desperate turn when Dr Janet burst into a fury of frustration. "This crime can't be forgiven!" She was in trauma from the first shockwaves. "Two young women killed, and then the discovery of skeletal remains. Damn you, Detective John. Damn, damn, and hell with the killers!"

"Don't damn me, Doctor. I'm doing my job," rebuffed Big John. "I know how you feel."

John held the end of the cravat and pushed it back round his neck and behind his big shoulders. The piece of white cloth was twice the normal length for most cravats. John loves this white and beige cloth; it gave him a sense of Edwardian attachment to the old styles of military stance during winter war between the British and the French armies.

"Four women and two men murdered. Don't get emotional, my dear doctor."

"Can I call you John? Let's be formal?" She looked at him indulgently.

"Yes, you can, Doctor. And you're the most popular woman in Lanang. You're hot-tempered when you are angry." He lifted his pipe and held it with his hand. "You're thirty-something. Thought of getting married one of these days? With such brains and beauty, the man you marry will the luckiest man on earth."

"Marriage is not in my heart yet. Do you want to be a candidate, John? You are interested in me, aren't you?" He chuckled briefly. She blushed, and squeezed John's cheek, and said, "John, you are a very good man, and you would make a good, loving husband." Her mockery was resentful. Her mood changed, and her laughs were a spasm of anxiety. She noticed something articulate on the wooden wall, and her sarcasm forced a sweet smile. "John, I didn't know you are interested in guns."

"I was since I was a kid. I was fascinated with their beauty, I guess. These are specimens I collected while in the police force. I will increase my collection. These are the 1810 English flintlock pistol, the 1830 Scottish percussion pistol, the American Derringer from 1875–1900, the American Colt .44, and the Scottish Snaphaunce pistol from 1690. All are strapped in that wooden white teakwood box."

"They're magnificent." She brushed her hair back, revealing her creamy white bosom. Her strange look came back with an earnest breath. "John, do you want my Colt .45 in your collection?"

"No, you keep it for your protection, in case of emergency."

Her comprehension grew thick, and she looked at him with devastating eyes. Her footsteps grew tense and heavy. She was not in the mood to continue the conversation.

John looked at her again and smiled. Her face still showed annoyance. "Come on, Doctor, I'll give you a ride back home with the police buggy. By the way, Dr Janet, did you wear a brassiere today?"

"No, I don't believe in brassieres. I have a thin white cotton cloth rolled round my chest six times. And you can't molest me, John." She giggled at him. "Oh dear, John, you're blushing. I'm just joking. Look at you – you are stunned, aren't you, big guy? Cheer up, Detective John. We have a long day ahead of us. I'll tell you the truth, wise guy. I enjoyed this evening with you."

They left the precinct, and the door closed as they walked out of the room.

In the early hours of the morning, John was still connected to his pipe, held between his lips. The tobacco was a new addition. This time he had the taste of his life with clove-scented aroma. He puffed his pipe and rubbed his eyelids. His large fist glided down his weary eyes.

Sergeant Blue came in with six constables. They placed their caps on the coffee table and signed in at the log book. Blue said, "John, good morning."

John turned his head and said, "Good morning, guys. Blue can you get the constables to come here? I have something to say. I want a team of men to do surveillance work at the night club." He rubbed his chest to clear the flecks from his pipe.

"You mean the Silver Dreams Nightclub, boss?"

"Yes, you're right. I want Bumbung and Dukun to accompany you in plain clothes, but make sure your Wembleys and S&Ws are fully loaded and ready for action. Try to pick up something over there." John smiled. "I want you guys to go in with stealth and subtlety. Try to look like Romeos looking at the dames. People get drunk, and they start talking what they are supposed to keep secrets."

"You're the boss. We'll get it done."

Blue left the precinct with the Malay constables. They went back to change their attire and headed straight for the nightclub with the two-horse carriage. The carriage stopped at the doorstep of the club for drunkards. The nightclub bouncers lifted three drunkards by their shoulders and left them crouching on the cobbled pavements. The drunks could hardly stand on their feet. Then one guy came out wobbling with a cigar between his lips. He was shabby looking and intoxicated. His destitute beard and moustache needed shaving in order to look sane. He murmured to himself, "Can you look at me? I'm not drunk. I want to go in again." He walked back to the entrance but was denied entry by the stout guards. "Step aside, I want to go in!."

"Get lost, will ya? If you wanna live."

"I am a kickboxing champ. I can kill all of you," he murmured again. "Now get out of my way, you soft ducks." He reeked with alcohol. He wobbled again in a circle and fell on the wooden road lamp. He was about to fall like a heavy, fragile, doll.

"I'm a shipping tycoon. I own two dockyards in Singapore. You don't believe me? This is my disguise. I wear tuxedos every day, and I can pay all your salaries if you worked for me."

This poor guy wobbled backwards a few steps, crossed his legs, and fell down again. He struggled to stand up with his elbow still propped up on the pavement.

Blue and the Malay constables held him up and dragged him to a nearby wooden bench at the sidewalk. Blue said, "Stay here until you are sober."

The guards who were guarding the entrance greeted these three dudes with broad smiles, their jaws touching their chest in the normal gesture to greet customers. "Welcome, gentlemen. Welcome to paradise in heaven." They gave the salutation in appreciation of the guests' presence.

From the club came a young singer's voice, and music was a faint whisper. It grew louder as they walked in the doorway. It was very dim with lit candles and yellow and blue light bulbs.

At the platform the beautiful singer wore a cheongsam with a vase shape collar; it was side slit and sleeveless. Her creamy white breasts were visible each time she swayed her body. Her red cheongsam was a brocade fabric showing the plum blossom pattern. She had backup dancers dancing to the traditional tune of a Cantonese folk song. It was the classic "Agony in Autumn", about a woman's agony in her solitary, sad life. Her dress was loose at the chest and fitted at the waist with a long slit from the sides, revealing her creamy thighs.

The dancers were all dressed up in cheongsams in red, blue, and white fabric, with the background having patterns of sunflowers and peacocks.

Blue signalled to the waiter, and a young Chinese man arrived. "Gentlemen, can I have your orders, please?"

"Yes, we want three glasses of cocktail with lemonades and peaches."

"What about whiskey, sir?"

"No, not at the moment."

The Chinese kid smiled. He was disappointed when they refused the whiskey. Waiters received extra commission if they could get customers with more whiskey orders. “Thank you, sir, and enjoy your evening here.” He bowed and left.

The atmosphere was dim, and it could grow dimmer with women dancing all night long. They would walk down from the stage and glide in between the tables to greet men, their hands and forearms circling customers’ necks. They would slide their breasts on men’s shoulders and kiss the sides of their temples near the earlobes. Then they would whisper, “Do you want special services in the bedroom? It’s mighty cheap for a one-night stand. You’ll get a complete physical for an hour or more, if you can last that long. No man has ever exceeded the twenty-five-minute barrier. If you can break that record, I’ll spend the rest of the electrifying week with you in bed. That’s a bonus bonanza.”

The morning rain poured down like hail. The rain was long enough to soak create a muddy surface along the roads. Small kids played in the rain. They were captivating by the cold and joy, and they disregarded lightning and thunder.

As the clamour of the rain subsided slowly, a single carriage arrived. The cab driver said in a loud voice, “At last, my friend, you can get down here.”

An old man in his late sixties alighted from the cab. The horses stopped at the Sleeping Pleasures Inn. “Is this the right place, mister? Sure ain’t looking good to me,” The old man complained like a child. He walked with a light luggage bag which is two feet by one and a half feet. The luggage strap rested on his left shoulder; he must be a southpaw. His wrinkled face and wide grin flashed his yellow teeth each time he smiled. His smile was wide and long from exhaustion.

He walked up towards the inn. Tiny raindrops hurtled down from his waxy vest. He stood at the reception in a hunched position. "Good morning, is anyone around? *Chou san*, good morning." He pressed the ring bell on the table.

A beautiful woman in her early thirties walked out to attend to the guest. "Good morning, sir."

The old man said, "I need a room. Is there one available?" He grabbed a small wallet from his pocket and took out a note.

There was a loud thud as the wind blew a blanket of rain and hit the glass on the door of the inn. The old man not bemused at all.

"You need a room, sir? For business or pleasure?"

The old man was stunned by that remark. He said coldly, "I need it for business, and may I remind you to be a realist. My name is Chan Heong. I am here for a reason. I am proud of my name, lady! Chan Heong is the name of one of the Chinese martial arts legends in China. But I live with the fact that I am just good at writing articles. I am as skinny as I was when I was young. I wasn't even good in sports and games in school – I was a disappointment, to be frank."

The lady interrupted. "No, I think you are one fine gentleman, sir. Everyone is born with some kind of talent." She smiled as her eyes scanned the old man's wisdom. "Everyone and everything is beautiful and special. I apologize. I was a little hasty."

"Pleasure intoxicates the mind, but it revives the body," he replied sternly. "I don't need pleasure because I think I just need a long rest." He laid his eyes on her vehemently. "My business of meeting with someone can wait till tomorrow."

"I'll take you to the room, and may I take your luggage as well?"

The old man did not raise any objections.

When they were in the room, she watched him unbutton the button at his neck. His fingers were trembling. "Are you a lupus patient, sir? she asked. "Do you carry your medicine with you when you travel?"

"Yes, I have my medicine with me. Thank you for your concern."

"You want tea or coffee?"

"Tea and coffee will do for this evening. Do you have sandwiches, if you don't mind?"

"Yes, we do. It goes with the complimentary menu, and it's free."

The old man was shivering from the cold. "I think you need a pair of pyjamas."

"We provide this in our inn. I will give you one extra blanket in case it gets colder at dawn."

"Thank you, madam, that's very kind of you."

The old man lifted his pants, and a plastic card fell to the floor. He tried to cover it with his pants; he dropped the pants on the floor, trying to bend down and conceal the card from her eyes. But his attempt could not prevent her from noticing the plastic card.

She bent down to pick up the card for him. "So, you are a crime reporter for the Chinese tabloid in Kuala Lumpur?" She gave half smile that moulded her sweet cheeks into a small ravine. "Well, pretty amazing, isn't it? A reporter coming to Lanang to get news on all the gruesome murders here."

"I am one of the editors and journalists. Where do I get help from? Where's the information centre in Lanang?"

"The police precinct will be able to assist you, sir. I'll get you a cup of hot coffee; it will keep you warm. Excuse me for a moment."

She went into the pantry to prepare two jugs of coffee and tea, with sandwiches laid with a light brown cream called kaya, the Asian competition for cheese and butter from the West. She came back and placed the bronze tray on a coffee table, told the old man to help himself, and wished him good night.

On the way back to the police precinct, Sgt. Blue and the two Malay constables alighted from the four-horse carriage. They stopped at the precinct to collect their police uniforms. Blue blew out the lamp and left with the constables.

"It's very late, men. We have a tough day tomorrow morning."

"We are used to that, Sergeant Blue," replied Bumbung. "The night moon is bright."

"We are still single. I think it is time you tie the knot with someone you love," Dukun said as he smiled at his boss. "You'll have someone to iron your clothes, and to cook for you."

"Not at the moment. I don't have anyone special."

They walked to the carriage. As Blue held the wooden door, a shot rang out. The next moment Blue was lying on the ground. A bullet hit his chest near his shoulder blade. It hit him from behind. Blood gushed out from his wound.

The two Malay constables looked every direction but couldn't see anyone in the dark alleys. There was no sign of any figures in the dark; it happened too fast. Dukun rushed to one corner with his gun, hoping he could get a glimpse of anyone. It was a futile search. He ran back to Blue and Bumbung. "There's no one in that direction, Bumbung." He was exasperated.

"Never mind – quick, lift him up! We will take him to the hospital now."

Bumbung and Dukun held up Blue and put him in the carriage. They drove him to the hospital. Once there, they pushed out a trolley and had him lifted slowly. Within minutes he was in the triage unit.

Dr Rama was on duty in the accident and emergency unit. The victim was pushed into the operation theatre while awaiting the arrival of Dr Janet.

As soon as Dr Janet arrived, Dr Rama gave her a medical analysis. The diagnosis was a complicated one.

"Dr Janet, this is going to be one difficult case. The patient has lost too much blood."

"Never mind, we'll get the surgery done now. Push the patient into the operation theatre. We will remove the slug in his chest. I think he will survive, Dr Rama. This is the first time a police officer has been shot in our town." Her face was stiff. "Shot from the back! They want to kill him. Someone out there wants the investigations stopped."

Blue survived the shooting, But he was in a coma. Detective John arrived at the hospital with Bumbung while Dukun stood vigilant.

"How is his condition, Constable Dukun?" John asked.

"Sir, he is still inside, fighting for his life."

"Tell me, how did it happen?"

"We were about to get in the carriage when a shot was fired."

"I have with me four more constables, and I want them to guard Blue in the ward. I hope he will pull through." Big John sighed.

After two gruelling hours, Dr Janet came out of the surgery. She took off her cap, and her flaxen hair waved and came to a slow trot. Dr Rama came out with four nurses. Blue was caped with the oxygen mask, and his breathing was heavy. John went straight to Dr Janet and looked at her with worry in his eyes.

"How is my man doing, Doctor?"

"It is still too early to tell, John."

"I have given the order: four constables will guard his safety. Whoever did this wants to shut us up. I will get this guy, I promise. Dr Janet please let me know as soon as he awakes."

"I have removed the slug. You will need this for your police work, John. Give me a copy of the photograph of this slug from your precinct. I need it for my patient file, post-operation."

"Don't worry, Dr Janet." She gave John the slug in a transparent plastic bag. "Let me see ... Oh! This is a .38 calibre, but we won't know the type of gun used."

After the shooting incident, the police were on the lookout for possible suspects. Almost everyone was screened and questioned about alibis on the night of the shooting. No positive answers surfaced.

One quiet morning, John was making the rounds with Sergeants Chang Wen and Sujak Ramli. They passed by a detour sign that read, "Detour – Wooden bridge to Takima District collapsed. Take another route."

There was a tall, dark figure with a blue raincoat and a coolie hat crouching near a wooden hut. His face was covered by the long brim of the hat, and he was smoking something.

John and his sergeants headed towards the tall figure. "Put your hands up, mister. Don't move or I'll shoot."

"Don't shoot, don't shoot! I will raise my hands," the man said. He could hardly stand straight.

"What are doing here in the early morning hours?"

"I am an addict. This is just opium rolled into marijuana leaves. Is it a crime to smoke opium, Detective?" The man was panting, and his head tilted to the left. He was intoxicated with the opium. It would take a day for him to wake up.

There was a well near the hut. John pulled up the pail of water and poured it on the man's head and body. "Take off your raincoat now. You need to get wet, mister." John repeated the dunking five times to wet his clothes. "You will have to walk in the morning sun to dry up. That is the only treatment. Were you at the town near the police precinct forty days ago at around 2.00 PM?"

"No, sir. The only thing I know is marijuana. It is my daily companion."

"What is your name?"

"Jason Low, sir. I am a born-again Christian. I don't carry a gun with me. I was an addict in the past but I just could not kick the habit." His eyes were wet with tears. "The Church tried to revive and rehabilitate me. They tried very hard to help. I failed everyone." He cried. "I am pathetic! Don't lock me up in jail. I work in the vegetable farm, and they pay me by the day."

"Come on, we'll give you a ride to town," John said.

"I am staying with my sister about a quarter of a mile from the orphan's home. Thank you, sir, for your kindness."

John and his men left him at the orphans' home. "Jason, walk home in the sun. You will feel better by the time you reach home."

The police carriage went back to town. John lashed at the four horses to kill time. When it was dark, John and his two sergeants browsed through the papers in the precinct. Chang Wen prepared hot coffee for them. "Here, boss, this is your cup."

"Help yourself with Sujak." He smiled at them. "We will make our rounds again tonight at ten. Any strange, tall figures walking in our sight, I want them questioned. And be alert." His smile came back like a block of ice on his cheeks.

"Yes, boss, you can bet on us." Sujak spoke in a deep and raucous tone. He'd had throat inflammation for the past two days.

They walked along dark alleys with their Wembleys tucked into their holsters. John held a Lee-Enfield rifle with one arm, and they had torches with them.

"Sujak, you guard the rear. Chang Wen, you take care what is left and right of us. I will concentrate what is ahead of us. Is that clear, boys?"

"Yes, sir!"

The street lamp cast a shadow of a man lurking in the dark. The shadow was still and tall, and the man's Stetson hat was very conspicuous. The shape and design was completely different that the British and French hat styles.

John and his boys moved with stealth near the figure, silent as cats on the prowl. When they were within reach, Sujak rushed forward and grabbed the man from behind.

"Good work, Sujak! Let's see who this is."

They walked him to the street lamp down the street, near a wooden stand for carriages. The guy was stunned with surprise.

"OK, wise guy, don't make the night darker. What are you doing in the dark alley near these shop-houses? What is your name?"

"Hassan is my name."

"Sujak, browse through his clothes to see if he has a gun."

Sujak checked the pocket in the man's pants and pulled out a gun. It was a .44 calibre magnum.

"You don't carry a .38 calibre with you, my friend."

"Why, Detective? Are you looking for someone with a .38?"

"Just shut up and answer the question, wise guy."

"Of course, gentlemen. I see you have a very beautiful and sexy Chinese lady officer with you. She makes a good loving wife in the bedroom."

Sergeant Chang Wen hit him on his back shoulders with her fist.

John warned, "Cool down, Sergeant."

The man said, "So you are a sergeant. Sexy lady, you are a beauty. I want a wife like you. Are you good in lovemaking?"

"You will lose your front teeth if you don't keep your mouth shut."

"And who is this Malay man? He looks like a wrestler to me." The man laughed to himself.

John said, "You are very tall, around six feet three inches. I think you match our blueprint. Sujak, take this man to the precinct; he is a suspect from now on."

"Yes boss!"

"Hey, you crazy cops, I have my rights."

"Yes, you have your rights. Chang, read him his Miranda rights."

"Right on, boss."

"Sujak, you're on tonight's watch. Guard the jailhouse. I will take Chang Wen home."

When they reached her home, Chang Wen invited John in. "Why Detective John, aren't Chinese women attractive to you? They don't turn you on, big man? Don't they have hypnotizing power? Are you afraid to be alone with me in my home?"

"No. You are one of my deputies, and you are a good cop."

"I am twenty-nine years old and am a big girl now. When I was a little girl, I watched the police parade with my mum and dad. The white uniform of the police force fascinated me. The steel shining sabre when they kissed the blades during graduation or any celebrations. That is the most mind-boggling, authentic, and creative scene I have ever seen."

She laughed, and her hair rested on her nape. Her snow white skin tone and her milky round bosom were an enigma. "When I was nineteen, I made up my mind. I told my mum and dad I wanted to wear the uniform. They had no objections. The rest is history."

She and John walked in together. She held John's hand and took out a key to open the front door. "Welcome to my home, my dear detective." She giggled and gave him an inviting look. She lit the candelabra with three long, white candles.

She went into her room and lit the small lamp. John could only see a king-size bed. A single woman who was so cool one moment and voluptuous the next.... He could see the silhouette and flickering shadows of a curvaceous body taking off her clothes. She was bare with her half-cup bra and panties. Then she walked out of her room like Cleopatra, walking slowly and without looking at her partially naked body.

She went to another big lamp and lit it. "John, I will get you French champagne while you sit at the round marble table. I have chardonnay, but I'll reserve that for another night. Chardonnay goes down your throat with a bone-dry taste. It's quite a stinging and pricking sensation."

"You are quite an expert with wines," John noted.

"I learnt it from *Life.* Magazine. There's nothing great. This marble table is from China. I bought it at the exquisite furniture shop downtown when I arrived here." She smiled at him. "I bought this small house for single woman because I thought of settling down here in Lanang." She poured out the champagne into two glasses. "Here, let's celebrate for tonight. Forget about your work in the precinct, and stop worrying about Sergeant Blue. He will live, I strongly believe. I baked my own cookies, cupcakes, and muffins. Come on, let's have supper together."

She repeatedly poured the champagne into John's glass. By the sixth glass John was drunk. She held John up and walked him to the bed. Then she unbuttoned her bra hook and held him tight. She was like a wild cat who wanted a good evening of lovemaking. She undressed him, they made love, and it took more than an hour to subside. When the sensation faded, they were soon asleep.

The next morning at seven, the alarm clock rang. John woke up and saw Chang Wen laying her head and body on John's chest. John saw they were naked. "Gosh, I was with her all night in bed."

She opened her eyes, and John could not resist the temptation when he was sober. John held her and kissed her over and over again. She wrestled back like a young cat. There was no turning back. John lifted her and put her down on the floor. They did it again, and John couldn't let her go till the last count. "You're a great lover. You're wonderful, my dear woman.

She said, "It looks like my two Siamese cats will sleep without dinner. They are in the cage, in the kitchen. I haven't fed them."

"Forget about the cats for a moment, dear. Let me look at you. You are a beauty. How could I resist you, with that body? You are like a live mannequin with a living soul."

"Oh, I love you John. Can we get married? I'll be a great wife."

"Yes, you will, dear. But we have to go to work, remember?"

"I have no regrets, John. Do you want this every night? I am always here, my dear. Last night was my first encounter, big man. You gave me a new breath of life, a new hope."

Twenty minutes later they had taken a shower and got dressed. They sat at the table, and she stood up and looked at him. She then poured hot coffee into two cups. They took their breakfast with muffins and laughed together. John knew it was not ethical, but in life the love cycle went round and round like a carousel.

John held her fingers and said, "Keep this a secret between the two of us."

"Yes, dear. You are my man, and you will always be."

At the house next door, a twin white lantern lit the entrance to a front door.

Three little girls were giggling and laughing at John and Chang. Chang went near them and kissed them on their temples. "How are you doing, girls?" They laughed and giggled with their palms on their mouth. "John, let me introduce you to these little darlings."

Chang introduced Man Ling, Chin Ling, and Wai Mun. Wai Mun was adopted by Madam Lum when she was born. "John, Madam Lum is my neighbour. These three girls are aged six, five, and four."

They were dressed in pants and the Chinese upper garment with large beads as buttons. The colour was red with machine-made cross-stitch embossing a grapevine with pink tulips.

The girls put on a show with an old Chinese Mandarin song mixed with English. They danced and sang a very humorous and catchy tune. It was hilarious. They twisted and turn with the Chinese folk dance, giggling till the end.

One of them said something to the other siblings. They held their fingers to their mouths and then said simultaneously, "Miss

Chang has a boyfriend! He's very big, and a white man too. He kisses her too!"

Chang Wen went to them and said, "OK, girls, go back to your mum. Go home now. Your mum is waiting inside."

They waved and said, "So long, Miss Chang. So long, Inspector John."

John laughed at Chang. "Chang, you know very well we will be dancing every time we see them."

"Ha! You'll shed some pounds at your waistline," she shot back.

They left her home and took the carriage to the precinct. His watch said it was 8.30 AM. They reached the precinct just before 9.00. They signed in and took to their seats like total strangers.

John whispered to Chang Wen, "Remember this, no pink dreams. Don't even dare to dream in the line of your duties Is that clear, Sergeant?"

"Yes, sir. You are the boss here." She smiled at him with a sly wink. "But somewhere else, *I'm* the boss, remember." Her eyes roamed across the room.

"Shh! Quiet, my pretty lady!" Just then Sujak entered, and John said, "Sujak, have you had your breakfast? What about the guy in jail?"

"Yes boss, he had his an hour ago. I took care of that." Sujak sighed and said, "He looks like a good guy."

"Be wary – looks can be tricky, Sujak. We are cops. Bring the tall Malay man here. Get him handcuffed behind his back."

Sujak soon came back with the man and sat him on the chair. Sujak's biceps looks like wild weeds; the veins ran like stalks and were thick and muscular.

John said, “Good morning, Hassan. You feel better now? Let’s talk. I want some answers from you. Do you own a .38 calibre handgun?”

“No.”

“My man is in the hospital bed. His life is on the line. He was shot from the back, and I want this cop shooter. The slug removed from his chest is a .38. What is your game in the dark alley?”

“Nothing, big man.”

“But you have a .44 colt. You like American firearms, I presume.”

Hassan said, “I bought it in Thailand two months ago. It’s for my own protection. I read about the gruesome murders in the newspapers. People have fears, Detective. Don’t you think so, big man?”

“Do you have anything to do with Nancy’s murder?”

“The Chinese woman? She was hung by a rope.”

“No, I have no idea on this. Where were you forty days ago on the night of the shooting? Are you the guy who shot my men?” John asked.

“Absolutely not. You people in the police, you are all crazy.”

“I have the right to retain you for seven days pending further investigations. This is the Police Act. After that, you will be set free. I have informed you your rights. After all, we are the good guys. You are one of the suspects we rounded up after the shooting. OK, you can get in back to your cell.”

“Sujak, take him away.”

“Yes, boss.”

The clock on the wall read 11.45 AM. Chang Wen went out to buy lunch. The other two was for them. She called John for lunch. "OK, I'm ready."

"Sujak, guard the precinct again with the other constables, will you?"

"Yes, sir!"

"I will have lunch with Chang Wen outside."

They walked out of the office and went to the carriage. They headed straight back to her home. The carriage stopped at the arcades filled with morning glories and blue velvets. They walked to the porch holding hands.

"Welcome to my home, dear John. You're my sweetheart." Her smile was stunningly happy. She placed the lunch with white chicken rice on the dining table. They took a fast lunch. She cleared the table and placed two glasses of champagne on it. She took a sip and went to her room. She came out with a towel and went to the bath. The shower was fast and brief.

When she came out from the bath, she took a bottle of cologne and wet her hair. Her towel barely held her breasts, which could almost glide out in search of freedom.

She walk to John and pulled him into the bedroom again.

"Not again, dear. We are cops."

"Yes, I know that. Remember one thing, big man. This is the law of nature. Adam and Eve did not resist one another. They did not freeze themselves into celibacy. The human race needs reproduction to reproduce. Where did humans evolved from, John?"

"I am a Christian, a Protestant just like you."

"You are Caucasian and I am Chinese, But we are from the same family tree: Adam and Eve. The evolution theory by Charles Darwin is farcical. He theorised that we humans came from apes at different period, starting from chimpanzees, the most intelligent primates. Humans did not evolve from the nine walking apes. There is no 'most common recent ancestor'. Humans are not the tenth progression in the evolution line. We are homo sapiens, or modern humans. We did not evolve from this progression. It is ridiculous, absolutely wrong." Her rebuke was assertive, and her face was a crimson red. "The fossils are definitely wrong. There is no 'missing links' theory to prove that. Homo sapiens, modern humans, came from the same first ancestors Adam and Eve. John, you have read Genesis. Am I different from a Caucasian woman? I am Chinese, and my ancestors are from China. What difference does it make? I can mother your children like any Caucasian woman." She started crying. "Don't do this to me, darling. "Don't do it – you're hurting me very deeply. It is not a sin to love someone who is not from your kind and race. Is it a sin to love someone, dear John?"

John held her hands and said, "No, darling, you are a woman. We can get married and can have children too."

"Talking about marriage, huh? Marriage is a ritual and cultural heritage, a covenant between man, woman, and God. Sex without wedlock is a question of selection and covenant."

John said, "What's wrong with that now, I love you and I want to do it now. What is wrong with making love in the bed before marriage?"

"It is just the time factor, John," She insisted earnestly. "I know it is a sin – we are Christians. But I love you, and I don't want to lose my man. Couples cohabitate all over the world; they live together and have kids. I don't want to lose my man. I love you, John. I want a good husband, someone I can love every night. I want a man to make love to me, my legally married husband. But cohabitation is just not right. Society will scorn us."

"Dear Chang, darling, are you listening?"

"You made me feel like a complete woman when we had sex, John. I know we are cops, but cops are humans too. We have sexual needs to fulfil. Come on, big man. You need a good woman. That's the truth, isn't it?" She laughed. "You are the man I want. Forget about what other people say. We can live together; cohabitation is not a crime." She sighed and lifted her head. "Wake up, my dear. Let's get married in the church."

"Come and live with me, darling. Please." He could see tears fall on her cheeks and down to her breasts. John was numb to his senses. He knew Chang Wen was the right woman, not Dr Janet.

"John, I know, and Sergeant Blue knows it too. Dr Janet is in love with you. But you can't love two women at the same time, darling. You like her too – her presence, her intelligence. But love is not a long-lost trail; you don't falter. It is a combination between two people, you and me. I love you very much, and if you love me as much as I love you, we can live together and be happy. I won't force you into marriage at the moment, if you need time to learn about me."

John insisted, "Come and live with me, darling."

"I want you dearly." She cried, and her face was crimson. She kissed him, and they made love again. John undressed, and she pulled down her wet towel. This time they took two hours to complete the journey. The lust and passion of these two lovebirds grew stronger.

Her yearning, her thirst was parched by the sun. This was her second long shower with rain, with John.

They became weak as two exhausted and haggard flies. They stared at the ceiling and followed the spin of the fan. The ceiling fan was slow and galloped like a tired mule.

At the hospital, ten days passed. Blue could only open his eyes; there was not even movement beyond his eyelids. The drip needle attached to his forearm was still running. There was no sign of recovery yet. This was a world of insanity, but it was a world seeking sanity. Life must go on, and Blue deserved to live.

Big John grumbled to himself, "I will get this guy. I will get him. My best friend is gunned down, and his life is hanging by a thread." He wiped tears from his eyes with a handkerchief soaked with clean water at the pantry.

He heard footsteps from behind. Dr Janet was staring at him. "Are you OK, John?"

"Are you chastising me, Doctor?"

"No, just concerned with your well-being, dear John. I know police work is dangerous every moment. The crooks are out there, and you don't know where they are. But you are out there in the open like shooting ducks for them." She paused before continuing. "John, he will take some time for recovery. His heartbeat is normal, blood pressure is normal. He will make it."

"You need God's intervention in this moment of misery, Doctor."

"God will not forsake us, John. Just say your prayers every night."

John said, "I will. I can't afford to lose a friend."

In the hospital hall, a young Chinese girl identified herself as Lin Lin, and she had come to see Sergeant Blue. She'd heard about the case from the people in Lanang.

"Nurse, I am Lin Lin. Can I see the injured sergeant in his room? Let me see him just once."

She saw Detective John and walked up to him. "Detective, please allow me to see him now. I want to look at him. He is such a good guy. Please, let me in his room, Doctor."

"Lin Lin, his eyes are open, but there is no movement. He is still in a coma status. He can't hear or sense anything, not even an injection needle. There is no reflex. Lin Lin you have to get Detective John's approval."

John said, "OK, Lin Lin, just for a few minutes. There are two constables in the room to protect him from any intruder. I have two more outside this room."

She sobbed, and tears rolled down her cheeks and fell on her wafer-thin chest. She couldn't take it long and came out crying."

John consoled her and told her, "Go home, Lin Lin, and say your prayers. Dr Janet, I will drive this girl home. It's quite late now."

She nodded and smiled at John.

"Come on, Lin Lin, I'll drive you home."

"Thanks, Detective John. That's very kind of you."

The precinct was without Blue for almost a month. John was still dealing with his paperwork. He told his constables to inform him as soon as Blue woke up.

One early, cold morning, the nurse came out running from intensive care. "He has wakened, he has wakened! He moved his eyelids and lips."

One of the nurses, Lekhsmi, an Indian, was replacing the bottle of saline drip. She was moved by the changes and watched with wide eyes. "Oh, yes! You have wakened." She whispered to her colleague Sarimah, "Your old boyfriend just woke from his long sleep.

"He is moving his eyes! He will lived, Lekhsmi. I think he will live longer."

"I will inform Dr Rama and Dr Janet at the emergency ward. I think he came out alive from a crime fiction novel, and he will be able to speak and eat after this."

Sarimah grinned, and her sleek, light brown skin captured Dr Rama's attention, who said, "You have striations of red-gold hair caught in between your blonde hair, and your eyebrows are thinner and slimmer than a toddler. You will make a good candidate for young women dreaming of the housewives' tale of having breakfast in a garden of flowers."

The two constables guarding the room were overjoyed to hear the news. The sergeant had pulled through at last! They smiled at each other, and Bumbung told the three constables to stay on guard while he went back to the precinct to inform the boss.

"I will rush back, guys. Stay on guard and protect the sergeant."

Two more days passed, and Blue was able to sit up and eat porridge fed to him by the nurses. In three more days he was able to talk slowly.

John was with Dr Janet and Dr Rama. "John, Blue is a survivor. Thank God."

John said to his partner, "Blue, I am glad you are well now. Rest in bed, and rest long."

"I am glad I made it. By the way, how long was I in bed?" Blue asked.

"More than a month, you tough guy. Rest here until you fully recover."

After another week, Blue was discharged from the ward. John told him, "I can lose you for a six-month period, Blue. I can't lose a good man on the Social Security penchant list. Rest till you are fit to work again. Understand?"

"OK, OK! You're the boss."

CHAPTER 8

JOHN HAYES LIT HIS PIPE with Navy Flake Mac Baren tobacco from Denmark. Round rings of smoke billowed into the thin, cold air. John looked upward towards the rooftops of budget hotels facing the victim's house. The muddy surface road in between would leave footprints behind.

The intermittent cobbled pathway eluded the tracks. The chances were slim to leave any footprints.

"Blue, there aren't any footprints left by the murderer. It was drizzling that night she was found hung," retorted Big John.

"The muddy road will leave some shoe prints. The only prints left were the wheels of rickshaws and the hooves of horses. Pretty intriguing," Blue interrupted.

"Or could it be someone known to Nancy Kwan? A woman jumped off from the coach and landed right at the doorstep. Nancy opened the door and let her in. The killer suffocated her with a pillow and robbed her cash, gold, and jewellery while those two men at the inn ..." Big John gave a sigh, deep in thought.

Blue said, "My instinct points me to the tall man and the small boy. The tall man could be a woman dressed like a man. She could slip out and not be seen by the two women at the inn's reception counter. She used the coach with another accomplice and jumped off at the doorstep. They killed and robbed her. They could have used the cable to cross over to the inn and then check out in the morning."

"Everyone knows that Nancy's late husband left a fortune for her in cash and valuables." Big John yawned, a sign of prolonged fatigue.

"Quite puzzling," said Blue.

"I found something else as quite a puzzle. The rope used to hang Nancy was slightly shorter than the length required to do the hanging. That means she was killed on the floor before she was hung," Big John said.

"The piece of cable fixed to the edge of each rooftop was used to hang lanterns during the Chinese festivity celebration. Someone who is small, short, and light – but strong enough to walk on that cable, like a tightrope walker – could reach the victim's roof," answered Blue while running his fingers over his temple.

"But who?" Big John held his chin and walked in a circle. "We are in the midst of a social and psychological trauma that will create fear in this town."

"Let's presume that if a small guy could have walked that cable, went in, and hung Nancy Kwan, that means he removed evidence by using the same route back," Blue argued.

"The same assumption could be the opposite. That woman jumped off from the coach and, walked over the cable, and the rest is history. I'm exhausted, Blue. We have to retire early."

"Are we closing down on this mystery? Our small man, the tall man, or the woman might have done the same crime, killing and robbing the victims," said Blue while raising his eyebrows.

"I think we are on the right track to solve this puzzle," said Big John.

"There are three small men and a woman in the revue group," Big John reminded Blue. He had to inform the district police via the High Commission about this new finding. "But remember, keep your head low at this moment. The first crime of rape and murder on the two young women isn't solved yet. I presumed they were raped and then murdered. I'm not being offensive – it's just my intuition."

"Yes, sir," Blue said. "When do we question the suspects?"

"In the morning. Don't bring them in yet, Blue!" Big John said sternly. "I want them to play a game of *solitaire*. The kind of sick crimes they have committed repulses me. We're dealing with people who are experts in the kitchen, such as chefs or assistants. Two skeletal remains without any flesh left – yet there were no knife marks left on the bones. We only have a patch of congealed blood left at the crime scene."

"Nancy's mystery guy isn't known yet, and we haven't got any lead on this fellow."

John said, "Blue, keep me informed on the five drifters, the two Italians and the three Frenchmen. I have an impression that the man with a parrot on his shoulder is linked. Maybe, the bird can be persuaded to talk and throw clues." He laughed.

Blue replied, "I've confronted the drifters with Ahmad Taming, our local constable. We have queried the Frenchman with a percussion pistol. He said it's for protection against wild animals. No bullets spent so far. Do you want me to confiscate it for a ballistic report? The paraffin test will give us something."

"The coroner's report found that Lily's and Iris's skeletal remains had a bullet wound each on their neck, inclined downwards at forty-five degrees. The shot shattered the larynx and trachea. I believe they were shot first, before they were skinned to the bones."

"This may be the red herring in our investigations," Blue said sternly. "We will track down these eggheads. Yes, they are indeed very cautious and scheming."

Big John smiled and shrugged. The smile soon retreated, and his voice grew sombre again. "The man with the parrot on his shoulder has the answer. He said the Italian C. Nicoli pistol is to protect him from wild boars and tigers? They worked in a cargo ship from Canada. They came here to experience the tropical rainforest and see the most exciting flora and fauna at the lake."

Blue took it further. "They claimed that they were not at the lake vicinity when the two ladies were killed."

"The dead woman found on the hill by kids showed the picture is bad."

"We are exhausted," Blue sighed.

"We may have icicles seen through a glass window when snow falls," remarked Big John. "Killers are outside doing multiple murders, and we have killers inside doing the same. The murder weapon could be a sharp, broken ice sheet, and when the murder weapon melts, we have no evidence left behind."

Blue remarked, "John, do you want me to talk to the residents about the forest fire? Anyone with a flint from a cigar could set ablaze the dried leaves on the surface."

"But the fire was meant to decoy everyone from the scene of the crime. The charred remains of the victims body were not supposed to be there. "John rested his big hands on his waist. "They intended to erase all evidence. The post-mortem revealed that she was raped by only one man and then brutally strangled with a rope."

"Where is the rope used by the perpetrator?" Blue asked.

"This is the same rope used by lumberjacks to fell trees. This guy wants to get wet in the playing field. It gets colder and will chill us to the bones. When we get numb, then he starts his manoeuvre. But I reckon the play he sketched is not going to last that long. We'll come close to him sooner or later," said Big John.

"Since he wants a playing field, we will give him one. And we are the players on the opposite side of the team. It makes us look numb," Blue said. He walked towards a glass of water and gave Big John a glass.

John rubbed his eyes and said, "I believed these multiple murders were done by three characters or groups. They may or may not know each other. Be prepared to encounter someone with multiple personalities."

Blue stretched both arms due to tiredness. The surveillance work all night was showing its strain. "You're right, Big John. I think we have a very hard and twisted case."

"Blue I have a serious matter to talk to you about. I have a confession to make." John rubbed his nose twice and scratched his forehead. "I am in love with Sergeant Chang Wen, and I will move into her home. We will live together in the same home and get married in a day or two. I have to protect her chastity and her good name as a woman. I know this will hurt Dr Janet. I hope she will understand that I'm not the right man for her."

John yawned and then continued. “I have summoned the two Malay constables, Bumbung and Dukun, to move into our home with you. Both men are single. It will be safer to move in a group of two or three men. I will pack my clothes and shift to her home. I hope you understand.”

“Understood, John. I wish you and Chang Wen all the best.”

“Thanks, Blue. OK, we’ll call it a day.”

John went back to pack his clothes and personal belongings. Blue helped him load the carriage and said, “I will miss you, old friend.”

“I am still around.”

The carriage reached Chang Wen’s home; she was standing at the porch. She cried when she saw John arrive. John opened the carriage door, and to her surprise, she saw the big man lift out luggage. He walked towards her and said, “Beautiful lady, I came back for my woman. I don’t want to lose her.”

“You are welcome, my future husband. Come on in, my loving man.”

“Thank you, dear.” He chuckled and held her in his arms. “Let’s go in, darling.”

The atmosphere was lively. Two people who loved each other so much would make the best of times, and the best of times would fulfil their dreams to build a happy family. They had a covenant built on love and trust till death did they part.

“I’ll cook something special to celebrate our union, John.” She hugged him lovingly. “Oh, how much I love you, darling!” Chang Wen leaned her head on his chest, her hands cradling his neck and chin like a violinist. "I think you need to shave, John – your orange beard is growing."

"I will, Chang, but I felt I should have proposed to you much earlier." He looked at her, noting her charm and beauty was like a charismatic beauty in *Vogue*.

"I was a fool back then not to notice you. You are indeed the China doll every man wants as a wife. Darling, I have thought about what you have said, and you were right. I will marry you in the church on Sunday. I will always love you, darling."

Her eyes filled with tears again, but this time she was walking in the clouds. She smiled and laughed gaily. "Come on, get dressed for the occasion, and we will go to town. At the bridal house in town, we will be the customer for Sunday's wedding."

They locked the door and rode with the four-horse carriage. They reached the town centre and walked into the bridal house. As they entered the shop, the bell rang, and a Chinese lady dressed in pink smiled and greeted them.

"Thank you for visiting our shop. I am glad to do business with you. You need a wedding gown and a suit for the occasion? We have gowns in white, beige, light cream pink, milky blue, amethyst, ruby, orange dusk, and green. Choose your favourite colours, miss. You will look splendid in any colour."

Chang Wen said, "I would like milky blue, madam. I think this design is what I like darling. Madam, can we try this on in the dressing room?"

"Yes, sure, you're my customer. When is your wedding?"

"It's on Sunday, the wedding in the church."

The lady was brimming with joy. "Congratulations!" She packed the wedding gown in a big box. She then packed a tuxedo in another box. John bought a new pair of black leather shoes, and Chang Wen chose beige, low-heel shoes.

Then they rode to the church to inform the pastor about the Sunday wedding. The pastor replied, "Today is Friday, dear, and we still have sufficient time."

"We will inform our colleagues in the precinct, including Dr Janet," John said. "I will get Blue and the constables to help us for Sunday's function. Chang Wen, we will ride to my old home with Blue. We'll inform him to let all our people in the precinct and Dr Janet know about our wedding on Sunday. By tomorrow the good news will be spread."

"You are the boss and my future husband," Chang Wen said.

"Now hold on and stop, my friends," John said as he pulled the ropes holding the horse bridles, to stop them.

Blue was standing at the porch and smoking a cigarette. He was not surprised to see John and Chang Wen. They alighted from the carriage seat and stepped down.

"Blue, good evening."

"Good evening, John and Chang Wen."

"We came to let you know that we are getting married this Sunday in the Lutheran Church."

"Please inform our buddies and let Dr Janet know I am getting married to Chang Wen. There is no time to print invitation cards to the wedding. We are in a hurry to tie the knot. Tell Janet she has been a very good friend lately. I need your help to prepare the functions for this Sunday."

Blue said, "I will, John. I have done this for my elder brother in London. You can count on me, boss."

"I have met the woman I want to marry, and love has no boundaries."

"Congratulations to both of you."

"Thank you, Blue."

They rode back to their home. The journey was a joyous one. They spent the night cooking dinner. Chang Wen was a good cook and good cop, and she would be a good wife.

It was a bright and serene Sunday, and the air was cool. The Lutheran Church had its regular congregation, but they also had one special occasion, the wedding.

John and Chang Wen got down from their carriage and walked into the church. They were ushered by Blue and Jill Martin, the nun from the orphans' home. Everyone from the police precinct attended their boss's wedding ceremony.

Dr Janet did not appear to be around. She was broken-hearted and devastated.

The music played by the pianist included a processional song for walking down the aisle. The church was filled with the magnificent ballad "Here Comes the Bride". The sacraments were read from Matthew 19:1–2. The matron and bridesmaid followed the bride; the young flower girls dropped rose petals along the aisle. The light blue wedding dress and veil that Chang Wen wore like a dove guided by angels. The best man was Blue, who stood by his boss. This was a once-in-a-lifetime wedding ceremony, a day to remember. In the future Blue would be walking the same path.

The reverend came to solemnise their wedding oath. They stood at the podium facing the people. The congregation in the church began clapping their hands. People swayed to the tune and the wedding joy that filled the atmosphere. The classic chorus rose like a wedding ball on Christmas Day.

Yes we will gather at the river,
The beautiful river, the beautiful river;
Gather with the Saints at the river,
That flows by the throne of God!

When the pledge was consecrated, John placed the ring on her finger and kissed his bride. "You are now man and wife," The reverend announced. Everyone stood up and clapped. "You can kiss the bride."

Madonna lilies and stephanotis covered the church promenade. The aisles were filled with red, pink, and blue midget morning glories in silver flower urns. The organist played wedding tunes that filled the congregation with silent whispers. The low tone voice of the church choir rhymed the soul-searching, instrumental tune from the pianist, "Ave Maria".

The newly wedded couple walked down the aisle and out of the church. They took to their four-horse carriage; the driver was a Malay constable, Banyun. A twin buggy followed, driven by Dayak, to drive home with Banyun when they reached the wedded couple's home.

John and Chang Wen waved from the carriage to everyone as the horses turn around and gallop. Suddenly the two horses whined and raised their legs in apprehension.

It looked like they refused to move at first. They lifted their front legs one more time, stood still, and then galloped as the constable pulled the bridles. The wheels started turning, and after a few minutes they were out of sight. "Have a nice day, boss," the constables said before they bowed and left in the twin buggy.

John and Chang Wen went into their home and celebrated their wedding with chardonnay.

"Darling, this is the most wonderful moment in my life. We are husband and wife!" John said.

"I am a happily married woman, dear husband." She gestured to John to carry her to the bedroom. "Don't you want to kiss your wife again and again, dear?"

"You are the greatest gift in my life, sweetheart."

The week-long honeymoon was celebrated in their own home.

"This is the greatest and most intelligent future investment, dear," John said as he kissed her neck from behind.

During John's honeymoon, the precinct's supervision was deputised to Sergeant Blue.

"Good morning, Sergeant Blue and constables. Good morning to everyone," John said when he returned.

"Good morning, sir."

"How was the precinct while I was on marriage leave? Is there any news, Sergeant Blue?

"No, boss."

"Blue, we have to pay the sisters at the inn for information. Can we go now?"

"Yes, boss, I am ready. In fact, I was waiting for your return."

They took their mackintosh and headed towards the Heong Fook Inn.

Two women were combing their long hair. They looked into the mirror and moved their lips, anticipating gestures. They hardly covered their bosoms; only a thin and semi-transparent, light blue satin covered the upper contours. They wore cotton pants that only reached the calf, and they had red sandals made of wood. They were the daughters of the inn's proprietor. They were behind the reception counter.

At the inn, John waited at the porch while Blue walked into the inn with short strides. He looked up to see the inn's signage in English and Chinese. It was a translucent glass twin door with the caricature of a young woman being lifted up in the arms of a man with a coolie hat. Blue walked in. There was a long couch at the front entrance to the reception counter. He noticed two pretty women staring at him with apprehensive cheerful eyes. He was greeted with tender loving care. Such young beauties would definitely attract a man's affectionate attention.

"Good morning, ladies! My name is Blue, and I want to talk to the inn's proprietor." He scanned the two ladies with raven eyes.

"Good morning, gentleman. Welcome to Heong Fook Inn. You want to rent a room?" Lorna said as she stood up to address him. "I'm the supervisor here. Can I help you, Mr Handsome? Is it for official business or for pleasure?"

"No, it's official."

Lorna walked near Blue and held his hands from the side. Blue could feel her nipples rubbing against his body. She laid her cheeks on his big biceps and rested her neck on his arms.

Blue could have resisted, but he couldn't resist the sexual drive incited by her marauding chest and lips. He could either hold her and give her what she wanted, or flash his police card. However, he was paralysed by her sexual advances and innuendos. He could feel her teats tantalizing his flesh, and she was bare to her legs and was bra-less. Her curvaceous and full body was covered with her one-piece satin blouse. She looked like she had just come out from some sex-driven magazine.

Lorna put her arms on Blue's shoulder again and said, "Handsome white boy, do you need a room? Poor boy, it looks like you need me as your mum to feed you. I can be a very loving mum, you know, and it's free of charge."

"Lady! I could sink my teeth on your lips and nipples If you expose your breast, I will charge you for solicitation and prostitution. Is that clear now?" Blue looked at her with crimson tide. "OK, ladies, I am here to get some answers. May I speak to the two of you?"

"Sure, handsome big boy." Lorna and Lin Lin giggled together.

Blue said to them, "I need information regarding the woman who was hung opposite this building. Do you pretty ladies have any clues, or have noticed any strange characters prior to the murder?"

Lorna lit a cigarette and smoked. She sat down this time but was more intimidating. Lorna sat with crossed legs, resting on the tea table and revealing her tempting legs and thighs. This pose was deadly.

Her younger sister, Lin Lin, sat nervous with folded arms. She sat on the couch with her legs and thighs folded and held her arms near her thin, small breasts. Lin Lin was very thin and beautiful. Her wafer chest were visible even to an old man with cataracts."

Lin Lin looked into Blue's Irish green eyes, "Hmm, he'd make a good husband," she murmured. "Blue, are you working for the district police?"

"I'm a police detective, doing my work."

Lin was attracted to Blue, and she knew she was in love with this man. "I can recall on the night of the murder. There was a very thin man around five feet ten, and a small boy around four feet six. They rented a room facing the victim's house. I could not see their faces; they had long hats that covered the entire face to the chin. When the tall man lifted his face, I could see his strange-looking nose. He had an aquiline nose." She was nervous while looking back at her ordeal. Lin Lin was going through a hard time, trying to recall her past encounter. She had stage fright at facing someone new. "They left and checked out the next morning around 6.30 AM, in a hurry. The tall man had yellowish light skin, but the small boy had light brown." Lin Lin's sudden relapse came back in full memory. "Now I remember: the small boy had a long chin like the smaller edge of a chicken's egg."

"What are the results of the previous murders?" Lorna asked.

"I'm afraid that is confidential," answered Blue in a harsh tone. "You can't question a police investigation. Please excuse me, Miss Lin Lin. I have to leave now. I will cherish the wonderful time I have had with you and your sister."

As Blue walked out looking for Big John, he could see him using a magnifying lens, looking for clues at the windows overlooking the scene of the crime.

John asked, "Have you completed your lunch today, Blue? Do I need to remind you to be aware? Your job is as an officer for the police precinct in Lanang and the Yards. You are in no position to have any affair with anyone in the execution of your duties. Your line of duties, once compromised, could cost you your life. Am I clear? Is that understood? Don't be too friendly with anyone. Marxism is a rising threat in Europe. It just found its way to the Asia continent. We have to write a report on our findings to the High Commissioner.

"Yes, sir," replied Blue hesitantly.

"Don't do that again, Blue. There are many ways to extract clues and identify evidence."

Soon the two left the inn for home. They had to start again in the morning.

The shrill cry of a rooster broke at dawn. John woke up and lit his pipe. The aroma from tobacco sent a chasm of adrenaline to his mind.

Big John was still stuck on the crime. He was hoping to find the missing link. The signature of the killers and the modus operandi were the exception. Robbing and killing victims for survival.... Was killing an option in order to live?

He was still contemplating to answer the unsolved mysteries next to a lamp lit by kerosene. His mind wandered to all the crime scenes. The killings left a trail that angered the police and their investigations. Back home in London, it was easier to narrow the suspects. There were more facilities, and travelling was made easy with better roads. However, over here people travelled on foot, bullock carts, trishaws, rickshaws, buggies, and carriages driven by horses. The railways were too far away; the nearest railway station was twenty-five miles from here. That was quite a distance to move around either north or south of Malaya.

John spoke to himself. "What would I do, if I was the criminal? I would leave no trail. I would have to mastermind and rehearse my steps. What if I could make the parrot that was with the five drifters talk? The only eyewitness is a bird who is very disciplined and quiet. I presumed it is trained by the owner to keep its mouth shut. I need assistance from a few people to do surveillance. Old Reindran and Imam Banjar from the surau will be able to help."

When there was daylight, Big John and Blue had their breakfast at a coffee shop near the inn. John informed Blue about the plans he had in mind.

Blue chuckled at John. "Where did you get that stole from, John?"

John was wearing a stole around his shoulders with the ends flagging in front. It was a gift from Dr Janet. "Stop laughing. I am your boss. What is so funny? And what is wrong with that? After all it's just a stole."

"Come on, John. A stole is only worn by women and officiating clergymen in churches."

"I can be very stolid, and you can count on me, Blue," said Big John. "Inform them to do the surveillance. We must attend to anything that appears crucial to our investigations. We are running out of time. Make sure you don't leave home without the Webley revolver, and strap an Enfield to your legs." Big John sounded furious. "Always be prepared for contingencies against anyone."

"Yes, sir," replied Blue with a stare.

The five drifters walked towards them. Then they took to the corner end and sat down. "Boys, the cargo ship will leave the bay in two months' time. We have to go back and report for duty. Port Swettenham is quite a distance from here. The train will take us to Bukit Mertajam." The macaw was not with the man for breakfast.

At the other end sat a big giant, Billy Smallboy, and his lumber tracker colleagues. They were having roasted white bread with kaya. The coffee shop attendant served them hot coffee in Chinese teacups.

Billy said, "I heard from the other scouts that they have sighted a terrain grown with cenggal, red meranti, and jati at the mountain range." Cenggal, meranti, and jati were the Malay names for black, red, and teak wood found in the Malay Archipelago. "Get your gear ready, and we will identify the location after breakfast."

"But Billy, it will take us days to search the almost one-thousand-foot mountain," protested Jacki Lanun.

"Are you chicken now? You can quit your job!" remarked Billy.

"I resent that, Billy. I didn't mean that." Jacki's face blushed with anger.

Big John looked at Billy Smallboy, who was holding a small book with one hand. It was the Holy Bible. He was reading while sipping his hot coffee. "Quite a Bible-reading man, and he could be Scottish from his intonation and manner." He stood and approached Billy.

"Good evening, Billy. I believe we have met, and my colleague Blue has made the necessary approaches. May I sit down?"

"Sure," Billy said after some hesitation.

"Can we have a cup of tea?

"Sure, suit yourself."

John said, "Do you notice other strangers in town? I'm asking you if you've seen any strange characters. What about your men? Billy, are they the loony patch?"

"Nope!" Billy insisted. "There was nothing that I knew of all these years. I was with them all this while."

"Are you sanguine?" remarked Big John with a low tone. "I'll ask you again, Mr Smallboy. "Are you and your men sanguinary?"

"Are you crazy, Big John? What kind of accusation is that? We are not sex crazy. You're going too far, mister. Don't implicate me and my men with your list of suspects." Billy stood up instantly with clenched fists, and he pushed the round table against Big John. "So now the prodigal brother has revealed his identity. You are with the Yards, aren't you?" he rebuffed. "I knew all along you were one of those bluecoats from England. People from the Yards don't travel alone."

"Shall I call you Pastor or Reverend, Billy?"

"Don't sass me, Big John. You know I can hurt you. I'm two inches bigger than you."

"All right, I'm not pushing. I just want to talk to a Bible-reading man. Tell me, Billy, were you and your men around all the crime scene?"

"Detective John, I think you know the history. I'm not looking for dream merchants. And I'm not a dreamer either."

"Are you a dreamer? You look like one, Billy." Big John raised his voice at this point.

"Yes, because I don't damage society with opium. I don't operate opium sucking and brothel centres. The Japanese forced it on the Chinese decades before the escalation of the Opium War with the Allied forces. You suck opium till you turn into a bony cadaver. Your lips will be parched, pale, and twisted until you drop dead."

"And Billy, do you frown in the presence of women?'

"You are wrong, Detective John. No, I don't need to do that. My adrenaline doesn't get aroused with women around. What kind of question is that?"

"Just simple police procedure. Give me a call if you know anything, Billy. Good evening." Big John smiled at Billy. "That's all for today."

"You can count me out," rebuffed Billy. To hell with you blue coats."

"My partner Blue has interrogated your men earlier, but the answers are too remote, thin, and hazy." John looked into his eyes.

"To hell with your suspicions, John. You are high-brow. We earn our living with our bones and soul."

"I have a son back home in Scotland. It's been six years now. He is eleven, and his mom died of pneumonia when he was two years of age. His grandma is raising him. When I finished my job here, I will return."

"You know I would never hurt anyone, and my boys are under my supervision. They are within my sight. There's no way they could've slipped away and done the killings."

Big John summoned Ahmad Naning, Malay Constables Banyun and Raini, and Blue to a brief meeting. They had to overstep protocol. Time was running out.

"The sequence that you have witnessed does not lay down the answers," Big John said as he raised his eyebrows. "I want you to look at it with strong convictions. I strongly believe the murderers are still around. Each case is different with different perpetrators. No witch-hunts. No premonitions. And don't even dream." He was bold and angry this time. "Do not dare to speculate. "We are not dream merchants – we are the police. I want my men to be tactical. Think like cops, and think like them, like the criminals."

John changed his tone a little. "When you want pure honey, you go to the beehives. You don't go to a grocery store to buy a bottle of honey."

"What will be our next move?" the men asked.

"When we plant a mouse trap, go right at the entrance. Do it at your own pace without getting noticed. Don't let it slip by your noses." John smiled lightly. "Ahmad and Blue, I want you to summon all the revue people and the five drifters to our local police department. Question them again and ask the same questions. See if they slip up. We will get the glimpse of it. Check to find any recent scars from a small blade that we found at the lake enclosures. Let them have the freedom to roam the wilderness. Let the hounds lead us to their playing fields." Big John grinned further. "Remember, and do it with tact. We're indeed after hounds who dine with us, not foxes."

"Yes, sir. We will get it done and recorded," Ahmad answered firmly.

That evening at the police department, each suspect was screened thoroughly in the hope that something significant would evolve.

"Nope, we weren't anywhere around that, period. Is everyone a suspect?"

There was one small man in the revue group. He had a round smile that disappeared in a guile of hate.

A thin, tall woman raised her eyebrows, simmering in the stream of questions bombarded at her. "You people do not have evidence to hold us or anyone. Do you have a court order to detain us? *You are denying our rights.*"

"We are narrowing down our suspects," retorted a constable next to Ahmad. "You don't question police work, lady. Is that clear?"

The morning breeze engulfed the streets in Lanang. It was cold, and a Chinese gentleman walked in long strides. He was dressed in a light blue long-sleeve shirt and black pants. The belt was tight, giving him a very slim waistline. He had a pigeon's hunchback posture and walked with his head down, heading towards the police precinct.

At the precinct's doorstep, he knocked on the glass frame with his thin knuckles. A constable opened the door and greeted him. "Come in, sir."

"Can I see the detective, young man?" the Chinese man said with a grin. His cheeks had lines.

"Sure. The boss is inside."

"Good morning, Detective. You're Detective John, aren't you? I am Chan Heong. I am with the *Hua Ren Daily News* in Kuala Lumpur. I was told I could get help from the police department." He kept it brief. "It's about the murders in Lanang, and I need an overview for my articles."

"There is not much I can give you, Chan Heong, except a brief account to the chain of events." Two cups of tea were placed on the table with the teapot. "Come have a cup of tea, Chan Heong."

An hour passed, and the old man was satisfied with the story. "Detective John, I will scour for some information from the Chinese folks here. If I get anything, I will let you know." His smile was wide and friendly.

"Thanks, my friend," John said politely. "We appreciate any kind of assistance and information from the public."

"Have a nice day," the older man said, and he walked out of the precinct.

CHAPTER 9

THE EVENING WAS BREEZY. OLD Reindran was walking with his walking stick and a crescent-shaped hunch. He was aloof with his white shawl and loincloth. The slim, round frame of his spectacles gave him an older look. His sparse and thin hair at the rear of his head looked like a dull, torn flag.

The public hall had a classical dance play, a mystical Indian dance called bharatanatyam. The young dancers were draped in red sarees, moving in sequential steps that only experts could do.

A group of five women dancers doing the karhak dance moved subtly on the dance floor. The light sky blue sarees had a beige linen weaved across the shoulders. Indian kids were excited, playing on the floor. The adults and old folks filled the seats and ate popcorn.

In the middle of the hall, there was a large Malay crowd waiting to see their favourite stage actresses in the prominent dance drama *Mak Yong*, originating from the northern belts of Peninsula Malaya in the Kelantan-Pattani region. The dance drama was only performed by beautiful women, with a supporting cast of male musicians playing the serunai, gong, and rebab behind the scenes.

Meanwhile, at the other corner a Chinese opera show was running with full concentration from the ancient Chinese folklore and legends of the *Autumn's Tale*. The opera was symbolic of ancient Chinese Broadway shows and dealt with almost every topic that besieged society.

In the crowd where people were mesmerised by the shows that filled their minds, all the kids were playing *hopscotch* on the floor, jumping onto squares. The old folks were too quiet and reticent, but one of them had a rheumy nose and eyes, probably from a cold.

While the middle-aged folks were closing in on the excitement and entertainment, a man with a twisted lip walked around looking for a place to sit. He'd had typhoid since infancy, with no hair on his head; even his eyebrows were gone. It was a poor sight for a man with good-looking features, except his twisted lips that drew the attention of everyone who passed by him.

His name was Juan Ling. He worked as a carpenter in a shop that received orders for beds, cupboards, tables, and chairs. He was an old veteran but a loner who didn't like people around him. Juan was a pipe smoker. Opium had left him with darkened and parched, twisted lips due to years of sucking and inhaling.

Timang Sani, the mayor, was enjoying neither mak yong nor the Chinese opera. Chan Chan pushed his wheelchair from one arena to the other, and his friendly gestures and greetings made him popular.

"Mr Mayor and Chan Chan, it's surprising to see you here," Dr Janet greeted them.

Timang Sani and Chan Chan smiled and gave their excuses. They were observing someone. "Please excuse us, Dr Janet, we have to move along," replied Chan Chan.

"OK! Good evening.

In the crowd, Blue and John appeared eating popcorns. When they realised Dr Janet was around, they walked towards her, and she was sandwiched between them. John said, "Dr Janet, can we stroll along? You're wearing a very stunning, crystal-studded robe. Do you remember the autopsy report done on Nancy's husband?"

"Yes, I remember, there were minute remains of an alkaloid substance in the intestines. I can't be sure if it's strychnine or cyanide potassium. It could be something else. The amount is too minute to be classified as poison. He had seizures and asphyxia. He's a heart patient, and that makes it difficult to narrow the exact cause."

"If you have anything new, let me know, Doctor."

"I am not at liberty to say anything yet; the evidence we have is far too remote."

"We need penetrating evidence to tie them. At the moment we don't seem to have any yet."

"Beg your pardon, Detective John, but what about the other cases?"

"Let's concentrate on the first case, and then on Robert and Nancy's deaths. We can't afford any waiting games. The people in Lanang are getting restless. They want answers, and I can't give them right now." John paused and rubbed his chin and cheeks.

John sent Dr Janet home and wished a good evening to her. "See you tomorrow, Doctor."

"Bye, dear John." She winked at him and walked towards her doctor's quarters. "Go on, big man, I'll be all right." She smiled widely, "Don't worry about my safety."

John lashed his two horses and journeyed back to the police precinct. He had left his ivory pipe on his table, so he had to go back. He reached the police precinct and unlocked the door. He lit the lamp, and second thoughts swam to his mind. "I'll sit down and do some soul searching." He took some papers in his drawer and put them on his table. He took a large white blank paper and made mind maps with a pencil. The research began with the two Malay girls, the skeletal finds at the lake, the widow, Robert Wong, Nancy Kwan, and the vagabond.

John looked at the wall: it was almost eight in the evening. He lit his pipe, scratched his head, and released circles of smoke from his pipe. John then squeezed his forehead with his fingers and rested his cheeks on his palm. "This is one long riddle. I have to get answers."

There was a soft knock on the door. He saw a silhouette outside the door: a dark figure stood facing him. A woman dressed in black with a veil and hat from the Victorian period. She turned the knob door and walked in. "Are you Detective John? Can I see you, then? I'm working late at night. Let me introduce myself. My name is Julia Tokugawa. My dad is half Japanese and half Chinese. My mum is from a place called Fegersheim, France. It's an industrial city and is very robust. It rose as early as the industrial revolution in England three hundred years ago.

"I was orphaned when I was fifteen. They died on their trip to Tokyo. Their ship sank in the Straits of Malacca, but I was with my aunty in Kuala Lumpur." She sobbed and looked pale. "The news hit me like a split iceberg in the ocean. My parents are Protestants. I believe everyone is innocent until proven guilty in court. The mind tries to figure out right from wrong!

"By the way, Detective, I have some clues which might interest you about Nancy's death. However, I have to go back to my cottage.

Would you be kind enough to send me home with your two-horse buggy you have parked outside?"

"OK, give me five minutes, lady, and I will be ready." John gave a half smile.

John had no idea what was on her mind. She was well dressed and pretty. She had a mole hidden in her veil on her cheeks. Her bosom was big but well kept and hidden underneath her tight gown; John couldn't see her cleavage at all. Her skin was vanilla cream and was very tempting to any men's eye.

She entered the buggy, followed by John. John gave the command, "Now get moving and drive on, guys." He lifted the lashes, and the horses started running. Her cottage was in the suburbs, about fifteen miles from the police precinct. The chimney was big and well built. The porch had two levels of split-design roof, like the Minangkabau ancient architecture.

The horses whinnied and came to a screeching stop. The pavement leading to the entrance was made of orange cobbled stone.

"Well, Detective, this is my home. Please come in."

"Dear lady, I am obliged."

They walked in as she opened the door with her keys. She lit the lamp on the table and lit the five-piece candelabra.

She went into her bedroom and lit the white glass lamp. The room was bright, and there lay a large bed with a pink bed sheet. There was a three-piece silver candelabra, and it shone and sparkled.

She came out of her room in a transparent satin gown. "John, can we have a glass of Russian wine together?"

"I have no objection, lady. You like Russian wine, do you?"

Her room was exclusive Victorian style decor featuring a very colourful and flagrant lifestyle. She was an enigma. On her wardrobe dressing mirror table stood an 8-piece gold candelabra with five lit candles; the remaining three were not lit. It was obvious that Julia was an avid collector of candelabras made of silver and gold.

John stood there, subdued by her stunning figure. Her eyes started swimming across the room. Her face was the face of a dying woman, a placid and frozen face with no signs of an experienced woman.

John asked her, "Are you a virgin, lady? "How old are you?"

"I am thirty-eight." Her face and curvaceous figure came out of a photograph. Her sweet grin curled back and she drank the glass of wine. She poured another glass, and another.

"Can you stop drinking, lady? You'll get drunk." John held her hands and grabbed the glass from her soft fingers. "That is one deadly hint," John said, "one supposition. There are many ways for any woman to kill a man in the bedroom."

She had great calves and thighs, and her bosom was big. She released her bra on her bed, and her wry stone face could pump any men's adrenalin.

"Em, er ...! I think I am stuck here now with a romantic woman who wants love. What shall I do? She'll think I am impotent and incapable of loving a woman," John murmured to himself with fear and agitation. "After all, she is one beautiful dame. The door to temptation is wide open for two souls. I just can't deny her that visitation."

She had John guessing in anxiety what was going to happen. Her eyes were slowly closing, and she wanted the heat to begin.

"Julia, I am a cop, and I can't do this."

"What's wrong with that, John? I am the one making the offer. Come on, dear. This whole episode will be over in an hour."

"You think so, Julia?" John undressed his coat and hung it on the bronze stand. He unstrapped his holster and placed it on the mirror make-up table. The holster on his calf was unstrapped and placed softly on the table. The Wembley .38 and Smith & Wesson .38 were placed with the barrels facing the wall. This was standard police protocol.

Finally, the big man undressed. John's six feet five inches and 260 pounds were bared. He had veins that stretched down to his chest, back, and thighs.

John looked at her mesmerising flesh and stepped forward. This was John's second encounter with a woman in the bedroom, but this was her first experience with a man. "It looks like we have two amateurs learning the laws of nature."

She looked into the dressing table mirror and turned towards John again. She pulled the red ribbon tying her long hair, and it fell on her neck and shoulders. John's eyes had gone with the wind, and by now he was delirious.

"John, I know you are after the mystery murderer. Now we are the mysteries within this hour of contentment. Spend the night here. I'll take care of you like a good wife. I will make you breakfast with oat cereal, bread, omelette, and fried potatoes. Come on, big man, you are a good lover in bed. I am a virgin, and this is my first experience with a good man."

"I am a cop, Julia. Let me know about the mystery guy tomorrow morning over breakfast."

"Yes, sir, Detective John! Let's do this again and sleep the night away."

"Let's celebrate this reunion, my dear."

The next morning John woke up, and Julia was in the kitchen preparing breakfast. He said, "How do you feel, dear? Oh, I feel tired. And about last night—"

"No need to apologise, John. We earned that together. A man needs a woman, and a woman needs a man."

"That's natural, I guess."

"Breakfast will be ready in half an hour," she said.

"I will take a shower, Julia." He smiled at her. Her smile in return could shake the Rock of Gibraltar.

John dressed, and they sat facing each other on the white square teak table. "Coffee or tea, John? Here, let me pour you a cup of coffee first. Your mind will get sharper in minutes. I wanted to help with the police investigation and the mystery guy. This guy is like a phantom. He's an illusion to the police." Her red-veined eyes swam across the dining table. Her face was full of hope, and her cheeks were swarthy and white, but the vanilla-coloured flesh was dominant. She took a shallow breath and offered John a cupcake. "Here, taste this. I baked it this morning."

He thought, *She is a good cook, and a baker too.*

She said, "I am sorry if I did not satisfy you last night."

"No, I had the most wonderful moments of my life. I will cherish the beautiful moments with you, Julia. You're a very good woman." John stared at her tempting eyes. "Have you thought of starting a bakery shop? If you need funds to start the business, let me know."

She began narrating what she saw on the night of the murder at Nancy's home.

"Well, John, I am nervous. That night I wanted to have a late dinner under the bright moon. I came down to the town centre to have some local delights. When I was done with dinner, I looked at my hand watch, and it was past midnight. I took a carriage at midnight and passed by Nancy's home. The cab driver rode fast, but I caught a glimpse of a man standing at the door of Nancy's home. I checked my watch again, and the time was 12.20. She was murdered on that night.

"It was a very tall man, I suppose. Someone above six feet tall and wearing a mackintosh. It looked like a raincoat to me, but it was dark, and I am not sure about the colour. That night the moon was bright. I could see his face, and he had this long, slim nose with a lump across the bridge, just like a camel's hump. He was someone from the Asian continent, obviously not a Caucasian. You are not looking for a Caucasian." Julia sipped her coffee with her fingers still cradling the cup. "In a way, John, he looked like a woman. Oh! And he wore a Stetson hat."

John said, "Yes, Stetson hats are popular with American bourgeoisie society, the rich and affluent."

"The raincoat covered his attire. He has a taste for American attire as well. Quite intriguing, I think."

"My mum and dad had been to New York, I was a kid back then, nine years old. My dad bought one of those hats, the Stetson, and a collection of American Wild West and modern-day hats. Perhaps, we are looking for someone who has travelled to the United States of America."

"I think you are looking for a woman," Julia said. "Have you come across cases like this in the past, John?"

"Like what, Julia?"

"A man caught in a woman's body. Or a woman caught in a man's body – twin personalities." She held her breath for a moment. "I am just guessing."

"No, Julia, I haven't."

"As the buggy passed by Nancy's home, a few minutes later I turned my head and saw the front door open. It looked as though they were talking. They may be friends, John."

"But a woman will not open her door after midnight when she is all alone," John pointed out. "This guy is known to her, and they knew each other."

She said, "Maybe you're right."

John smiled at her, and they finished their breakfast. "Julia, you're a wonderful woman. I think you would make a good wife."

"Is that a compliment, big man?"

"And about last night … thanks anyway."

John strapped on his holsters and kissed her one more time. "Goodbye, Julia. We will meet again under different circumstances." John could hardly release her from his hands. Julia was a good woman. She was lonely and needed a man to love her. "Julia, I will treasure the sweet moments we had together, and I promise you this will remain a secret till death do us apart."

"I will miss you too, John."

"Take care, dear."

CHAPTER 10

AT THE NURSES' QUARTERS, THE sun's rays beamed down the corridors. The nurses were tying their headbands with colour stripes of blue and green. The green colour was for student nurses, and the blue was for staff nurses. They were young and vibrant, with enthusiastic eyes that could melt a man's heart.

At the edge of the quarters, a quiet room brewed an air of anxiety. A new staff nurse occupied the room. The newly arrived nurse had short, soft auburn hair with some patches of dark wine colour at the back. She was marvellous, standing at five foot nine with long, sexy legs. Her calves were as voluptuous as her creamy chest nestled between two white breasts. Her mother was Dutch-Flemish, and her dad was Anglo-Saxon. Her smile was as shallow as a short grin.

She had a visitor in her room. It was against regulations to have a man in a nurse's room, but he was her boyfriend. He was tall and tanned, but he was adamant: if she was caught, she could lose her job in the hospital. They were both hugging in the single bed meant for her. It was unethical for her, but she was in love.

She was happy and smiled; her energy remained vibrant and virile as a fox. She looked at him with loving amazement.

"I think we should stop here. It is not so right. I can't go on making love like this. Please leave before anyone sees us in this room," she gasped. "I will get a reprisal or dismissed from this hospital. I hope this is the last time you see me, and I mean it. Please leave – I have to start the morning shift."

"Ok, Lucy, I will leave. I am sorry I have offended you."

"Oh dear," Lucy said, uneasy with her bare body. She covered her chest with the pillow and took a brush from her handbag. Then she leaned backwards and brushed her hair several times as she tried to tame her short hair with a hair band.

"What's the matter, dear? Do you have to go to work again tomorrow morning?" he asked hopefully, smiling wanly at her and kissing her hand."

"I have to get back to work because I'm on shift. "There is still time to reach the hospital's emergency department. Meanwhile, just stay in touch."

"My darling, have you made your decision?"

"Not yet," she replied, giving him cause to doubt. "You know what I want: I want to have a family."

"I know, and I have my reasons. But I do care about you," he said.

"You don't really care." She wiped her chin as tears ran down her cheeks. She controlled her emotions and stood up. Then she got dressed immediately. She asked him, "Do you want me to prepare a mushroom omelette with peaches? Do you want a glass of bourbon or hot milk?"

"No, Lucy, just get ready for your work. Bye, see you another time." He walked out of the room without any remorse.

At the emergency and casualty department, a sixty-year-old Malay man came in after he was harassed in an affray between two men. At the bed, Dr Janet listened to his heartbeat with the stethoscope.

"His pupils look pale, not enlarged yet. His heart is palpitating," she cried. "Patient is partially conscious. Nurse, put him on a drip with saline and monitor his blood pressure and pulse rate, every thirty minutes." Dr Janet stood up to face the old patient, who lay in bed with loud, heavy breathing.

"It looks like he had a fall on the pavement. I'm not worried about hematoma; there's no indication right now. But I'm worried about whether there is a brain aneurysm." She looked at Sarah. "He has angina. Could you get the student nurses to help you push his bed to the nurses' centre? I want him to be seen by the nurses. A spasm of pain could trigger fits of suffocation." She paused. "Nurse Sarah, you look very tired. Remember and learn this from a doctor. If there is a sudden decrease of blood flow to the heart, the patient may get *angina pectoris*."

Dr Janet checked her watch. "Sarah, do you want to join me for lunch?"

Detective John managed to get help from Sujak Ramli, and they decided to look for new evidence. John stood beside the terentang tree, a tall tree with large patches of grey and light-coloured bark. The tree's trunk grew at a height of thirty to forty feet above ground, and the circumference was around thirty feet. The trunk was big and sometimes gigantic, but the branches were slim. Across the hill, the wind blew and swept over the foliage of the tropical rainforest. The canopy could be a five-hundred-foot-high hill. Where they stood, the green mosaic looked so near and small.

Downstream from the forest, a large stream of waterfall flowed profusely and revealed a green-coloured nudity. The flow of water showed tiny rapids as it wove its way across with hissing, pulsating ripples. Large boulders stood as guardians to the smaller ones, with a disarray of small rocks ranging from dinner plates to coffee plates. There were boulders of white, black, grey, and dark brown. Some of the boulders and stones were prisoners to the green mosses that rested on them like a lawn. However, the most captivating was the orange-coloured mosses giving birth to a mixed-fruit-pastry-coloured lake.

A blue and green kingfisher stood gallantly, hopping from slab to slab and watched by the frightened merbah beringin, predominantly found in South-East Asia, Borneo, and Africa. They ate red berries only and were very selective birds. They were a smaller predator to insects and fireflies, also known as Lampyridae lighting bugs. Fireflies lived in abundance on the wetlands, mangrove swamps, and river tributaries.

The merbah beringin was smaller, faster in manoeuvres, and agile. The stream flowed down to lower ground and to a vast field of marshy, shallow swamps. The marsh surface unfolded into a swamp of clay-coloured water.

The monotonous waves had water running across the boulders. The sojourn was glaciered by a huge serpent with a pale maroon and crosswise bar of greenish-blue parchment with scales. It glided and surfaced on the boulder. Then it drove the surprised kingfisher into flight.

"What is that?" remarked Sujak Ramli, a Malay crime reporter.

"I think it's a boa, the distant cousin of the python and anaconda papyrus," Detective John replied. "The boa is an Indian, Vietnamese, and Burmese Asian species, whereas the anaconda is a South American cousin. The anaconda papyrus came from Amazon python species. The tropical rainforest Asian python is bigger but is slower and awkward. Yes, it is much bigger than the anaconda and boa."

John Hayes took a few steps closer but was not prepared to invite risks. He had his Smith .38 revolver and Wembley .38 mm with him. However, gunshots from any pistol could hardly damage the snake's body.

"We need a rifle to blow its head apart," said Detective John. Now a new visitor flew past the boa. "What's that thing in the pink shawl doing here?"

Sujak Ramli was numbed by the presence of the visitor. He knew what it was. "I'm afraid she's a vampire." Sujak looked at John. "The Malays named it *langsuir.*"

The drapery blouse shawl flagged subtly against the cold wind. Her eyes were crimson as red tears. Her long locks of hair were pulled back into a bun in the middle, and the hairs on both flanks were loose and messy. She had contours like a beauty queen. Her breasts were firm, slender, and close together. The waistline was very thin and revealed a curvy torso. Her look was beautiful but very pale and blue.

"Beware of her flirtatious antics," warned Sujak. "She copulates with men before destroying their souls and flesh. Be aware of that, Detective John. Centuries have passed, and men are still doomed by her transformation into human form. This vampire only visits lonely men who are home alone. Men with very strong lust will be hypnotised by her night charm." Sujak took a step backwards.

The boa slithered away. The length of the boa's trail was almost twelve forearms long. However, the apparition whiffed past the snake within seconds. The serpent trundled on dried leaves from the canopies above. Wild ferns waved back and forth from the strong wind. The ferns were rocked by the heavy thud of the serpent.

At the lagoon's vicinity, a heavy drizzle of rain fell. The colour was yellow, and the stench was like urine. "It's a common sign of the visitor," remarked Sujak. "She brings along a small shower or a drizzle of rain to announce her presence."

The vampire stood on the surface of the small lagoon at the rear end. The lagoon was a sea of mossy algae. Belladonna lilies were glowing, with red, pink, blue, yellow, and white buttercup-shaped flowers forming a cream of colours. Small toads with green, wet warts on their bodies glided very slowly on the water lilies' round leaves. One or two small toads suddenly jumped into the water and resurfaced again. The leaves acted as cruise-ship platforms. The trumpet-shaped flowers looked like colourful sail masts in the open sea and gave the leaves a strong anchor on water. The roots acted like the keel of a ship.

Repeatedly little toads swam back and forth, submerging and resurging like small submarines. They then jumped onto the lily leaves, gliding slowly to the middle and crouching like an athlete waiting to be garlanded with medals. Giant leeches were also seen on the leaves. Their grip was so strong that they remained adhered to the leaves. The thuds of bigger toads landing on it in a splash could not sever their grip when the leaves overturned.

"Well, Sujak, I think we have done enough here. We couldn't find anything. We'll do it again next time. By the way, your undercover status and Inspector Chang Wen still stand until we have apprehended all killers."

"OK, you're the boss, Detective." Sujak raised his hand in a salute.

CHAPTER 11

SERGEANT BLUE WENT OVER TO the nurses' quarters. He had to interview Joanne to see if she had seen any strange events. Any information gathered was important to corroborate the investigations.

Blue knocked on the door. Joanne greeted him, having just finished a shower. She was wearing her pyjamas and was about to sleep.

"Good evening, Miss! I'm Sergeant Blue from the police station." Blue flashed his police ID. "Can I come in?"

"Wait, should I allow you in? Is it safe for me to open the door? You're not a con man, are you?" she said.

"Do I look like one, Miss Joanne?"

"Oh, dear, how silly am I! You are the police from the precinct. Is there any woman out there who says you are charming? You are handsome, tall, and tanned like an ancient Greek aristocrat. Please, come in," she said in earnest.

"Thank you, miss. Are you living alone?"

"Yes, why?"

"I'm kind of thinking."

Joanne was also working as a volunteer at the orphans' home. The home was on a donation drive recently.

"Here's a cigarette!" Joanne said as she took out a slim, rectangular silver canister tucked beneath her bra. She flipped open the cover and gave a cigarette to Sergeant Blue. "Try a Marlboro Classic. Do you smoke?"

"No, thank you, I don't." Blue turned to see if there was anyone in the room besides her. "Very few women smoke, so you're an exception. You remind me of the first batch of women who were accepted into Oxford University in August 1909. They were pioneers in the Women's Rights liberation.

"Your donation a week ago at the bazaar means a lot to the kids and orphans in our society."

He asked, "You're a foundling too, aren't you?"

"How do you know?"

"By your generosity, I'd guess."

"So you're a mind reader," she said.

"Not exactly; it's just a wild assumption."

"Do you want a chardonnay?"

"No, I think it intoxicates the mind. I'll take a red wine."

"Are you single, Mr Blue Deighton?"

"Could be. In London you'll find many unmarried men. Where are you from, Joanne?"

"I'm from Reading, Scotland."

Blue Deighton took a small notebook from his pocket. He turned a page and jotted down some clues. He was on the trail and following police procedures, but he could not deny the fact that Joanne was very tempting indeed. "Do you believe in Nessie?" he asked in a soft tone while he earnestly scanned the conversation they'd had a while earlier.

"Oh, the big guy with a long neck."

"The big riddle that captures the mind and imagination of researchers for centuries, since the days Scotland stood."

"You're talking about the mystery man, Sergeant Blue. Have you ever been to the lake?" asked Joanne.

"Yes, I have. I believe she's a prehistoric dinosaur that lives in water."

Joanne changed the subject. "I have a twin sister. She is working as a nurse at GHKL. Earlier when she was young, she had a boyfriend. However, he is a clinger and leans on women for money. That man is quite tall, around six foot two. He stands with stooped shoulders. He's the kind of dude who would scare women into submitting to him if he can't get what he wants."

Joanne cried, tears running down her cheeks and to her chin. The tears fell onto her creamy white breasts. "One morning on a breezy Sunday, he came over to my sister's nurse quarters. He had this craving for sex and kissing. My sister was not in the mood to entertain him; she was too tired of his antics. When she refused his sexual overtures, he slapped and beat her up. It was pretty ugly. She hit his head with a bottle of Otard VSOP cognac. It barely paralysed him. Then he took out a switch-blade about four inches long and stabbed her in her breast. In the scuffle, he grabbed her by her neck and shoved her down the staircase. She fell like a pack of cards thrown into the air. It was awful. She broke her pelvis and spine from that fall.

"After two months of observation in the intensive care unit, they transferred her to ward eleven. The agony lasted nine months. Thank heavens, she pulled through this ordeal." Joanne sighed. "The police arrested him for assault and attempted murder. The court charged and sentenced him on all counts in the High Court of Malaya on 9 October 1915. He was given ten years' imprisonment along with five strokes of whipping with the rotan.

"Sergeant Blue, before you knock on the door, I thought of singing the country Gospel hymn 'Amazing Grace'. I sing without any instruments." Her eyes floated like a butterfly looking at Blue. "Can we sing together before you leave? To count the blessings?"

"Joanne, I'll be glad to sing with you."

She gave Blue the songbook. "Here, this is the page. I have memorised them by heart." She smiled.

She had a crystal-clear voice and the hymn began vibrating in the room. It was like the ruffle of soft leaves blown by the wind. The soft, rumbling rose and spread across the room, capturing the angel's presence.

The two songbirds laughed and giggled.

"Oh wow! That is inspiring, Joanne."

"I am glad you like it. It was fun wasn't it, Blue? Your soul needs inspiration every now and then."

"I guess you're right," he said, beaming with shyness.

"Come on, finish your cup of tea."

He replied, "I have to go back to the precinct. I'll see you again later."

He left the room, and Joanne's eyes followed him as she stood at the door.

It was almost dark, and the sunset was turning dark orange until the grey sky turned gloomy and dark. An old man walked past a row of liquor shops. Drunkards were deeply intoxicated with the whiskey and Chinese white wine, sitting like stooping ducks, crouching, and bending with their heads almost to glasses' brims.

At one corner, a big man stood up and threw a coin at the bartender. Its edge tipped on the table and came to a slow waltz before it kissed the wooden surface. "Give me one more white wine, mister."

The bartender said, "This coin is just one cent, bro! You're short two cents. This is not a charity home, go home and drink coffee. You'll feel better."

The man's rage began to flicker, and his eyes were impudent. He banged his clenched fist on the round table. His voice reeked of alcohol, and the air was electric.

The bartender took the coin and held the man by his shoulder. He put the coin in his pocket and told him to go home. He signalled a buggy to stop and take this man home. The one cent was enough to drive him home.

Chan Heong had intended to mingle with drunks to get some information. The truth was that drunks would speak the truth on anything because their minds were intoxicated. The intoxicated mind was free from prejudice and prefabricated thoughts.

He sat down at one table with two men. "Good evening, bro! Can I join in?"

"Sure!" The two drunks obliged his presence.

"Bartender, give me three small glass of French champagne. Yes, I want the pink fizzy wine. I love the colour pink."

"Yes, sir," said the bartender as he poured the wine into three small glasses.

It took an hour for the two men to write the old chapter on the murders. They narrated what they knew. Chan Heong wrote down every detail in his notebook with a pen. When it was over, there were nine small glasses on the table.

Chan Heong stood up and said farewell to the two men. He paid the bartender with a few bronze coins. "The wine is good and authentic, bartender. And what an evening – cool breeze in the open air on cobbled pavement. Guys, thanks for the news."

He signalled a buggy, got in, and went to his hotel. The dim street lamps reminded him of his younger days with the Malayan railway. He reminisced on the old days when he was a superintendant at the station in Kuala Lumpur. The only regret he had was that he remained a bachelor. There was no wife or children to talk to when he was lonely.

At the other end of town, Reindran was walking like a small kid locked in a room. Late that night, the air was still hot, and Old Reindran couldn't sleep well. He woke up and laced his body with his white shawls and loincloth. He wore classic Indian attire for a man of both noble and peasant birth. He took out his cheroot and lit a stick to warm his anxiety. The thick smoke from the flint-laden cheroot was strong enough to drive mosquitoes away for the night.

Puff after puff, he marooned the warm night with his pleasure. Old Reindran did not get into moonshine with the local fermented drinks; not even Japanese sake could tempt him. He was educated knew the ill effects of such concoctions: it damaged the liver. Townsfolk respected him for refraining.

Reindran was someone the younger people would hang around to strike up a conversation. Usually it concerned a true tale or two to kill time. He was outspoken and displayed a strong message of comradeship if he was given an assignment.

That evening at the precinct, John was still drowned with his police work. The shuffling of papers and mind mapping of possible suspects were scattered on the table. Pencil sketches and the missing links to juxtapose the sequences of murders presided everywhere.

Blue came in and greeted John. "We have two ladies from one of the hookers' dens." He nodded towards the two ladies waiting outside the glass door. "They want to see you, John. They told one of our Malay constables in the street that they have information on the mystery guy. One is Malay, and the other a Chinese."

"Bring them in, Sergeant Blue."

Blue opened the glass door and said, "Please come in, ladies."

"Thank you, Sergeant," they said.

"Come in, ladies, and take a seat. I'm glad you came. Do you want a cup of tea or coffee?" John asked.

"Tea will do, Detective."

"Blue, please get our guests two cups of tea, and for me too. I am Chief Inspector Detective John Hayes. I'm in charge here and report to the commissioner in Lanang."

The ladies felt comfortable with the reception they had been given. The Malay woman said that a week ago at the hookers' den, a customer came in at 9.00 PM. "He was very tall, around six foot three. He was lean, and there was something strange about his eyes. He had slanted eyes with thin eyebrows but long eyelashes. He wore an American cavalry hat that was white. It's the popular Stetson. But he had on thick make-up. His face was covered like a mime, with black patches on his forehead to cover up some scars, maybe."

"Yes," the Chinese woman continued. "He booked the two of us for the night, but he wanted the same room with us. He paid a lot for us to entertain him. In the room he just sat down on the wooden chair and was very quiet. We sat on the king-size bed. We offered him whiskey, but he refused and said he wanted some information from us. He was a kind of lunatic. We undressed and stood in front of him, but he never took off his clothes. He did not even touch us. He sat in his chair and told us to get dressed and to sit down on the bed. We did as we were told. He held a light brown pipe with a piece of a ring that looked silver at the mouthpiece. The tobacco was captivating, an Indonesian clove scented aroma. He could be a Chinese or Eurasian.

"The first question he asked was, 'Is there any news on Nancy's murder?' We told him no one had any idea except the police. He asked again with a very harsh tone, 'Has anyone seen the murderer on the night of the murder? I want to know this. Did anyone see the murderer's face at Nancy's home?' He was tense this time.

"We replied, 'No, sir. Even the police can't trace the murderer.' We were quite surprised by his interest in Nancy's murder."

"That is quite strange," John agreed.

"He did not engage in any sexual acts with us. I mean, we are supposed to strip naked and copulate with him. He wasn't at all interested in sex. He was lean but very muscular. We could see his veins on his arms. He could be a weight trainer. Then he stood up and said, 'Thank you.' He was very polite now. As he walked to the door, he had this fixed walking pattern, like someone trained in the army. We noticed he had two rings on his left fingers. One was jade and the other was turquoise blue but with a lighter tone. We are sure now he is left handed because he used his right hand to turn the knob. He was big with heavy footsteps. And he left just like that, Detective. We are afraid he may come back to harm us, so we came to see you."

"I think you have given me all you knew. We appreciate your courage, ladies," John said as he smiled at them. "Sergeant Blue, please send our two lovely ladies home with the twin carriage."

"Yes, boss." Blue picked up his hat and said, "Come on, ladies."

"Thanks." They left the precinct within minutes.

CHAPTER 12

THE DRIZZLE WAS VERY HEAVY in the morning. The wind blew the drizzle like a cold mast flagging everything ahead. The mosque nearby had recitals in Arabic of Quran verses; the sound filled the vicinity with the call for Haj recitation.

The Muslims were attending the Haj course in the mosque. The imam conducted the course, and his voice was crisp and old. Every moment he was gasping for air to breathe, and his last line diminished like a retreating sea breeze.

The recitals filled the air with a catchy tune sang in a motivational chorus like distant drums.

> Labbaikallahumma labbaik,
> Labbaikala sharikala kalabbaik;
> Innalhamda wanni' mata,
> Laka walmuk;
> La sharikalak.

The Haj lessons took two hours to end. The old folks and the younger ones remained in the mosque for the evening prayers, the Asar. Some of them sat down mouth-washing the holy books they took from the selves. The holy books were in the Quranic language, the language of the Arabs.

The “muezzin azan”, call for prayers, echoed in the air again. It serenaded into the atmosphere and folded the quiet and peaceful nature of Lanang. When the imam prepared himself for the prayers, he went to the front before the rostrum. The congregation lined up in silence behind him in separate rows. The imam began the prayers, and the Al Fatihah was recited loudly by the congregation behind him. The sharp, loud tone was a basic requirement for Muslim prayers. In Islam, this was the celestial verse in the Holy Quran; this was the alpha and the omega, the beginning and the end. It was a syariat obligation and compunction by God. He was the creator of the first humans, Adam and Eve. He was the creator of this universe and all forms of life. The Malays and Muslims lived with this premonition and tradition. “How many miles can you walk? Awaken in repentance and remorse till you come to an end.”

The Malays and Muslims constituted 60 per cent of the population in Lanang. Their agriculture heritage was rice planting, bananas, tapioca, and fruits.

The drizzle grew thinner. The cold wind remained in a civil tone. Dr Janet had an umbrella and walked next to Big John. John’s tall body glanced down at her soaking, and he gave a smile. She leaned her cheek on John’s arm.

“John, are you OK?” She winked at him longingly. “I think you look tired, dear.”

They walked up to the front door of the precinct and noticed there was a dart on the wooden lattice with a piece of note. It was handwritten but written haphazardly and with shaking hands. John was surprised and took down the dart. He looked at the paper's message. "Go to Red Lantern Nightclub tonight, if you want to know the riddle of the lake."

"John it looks like someone wants you to be there."

"Don't worry about me. I'm a police detective, Dr Janet. Can I have the honour to take you there? I mean, you can be my companion for the night."

"Not at all, dear John. I accept the invitation." She kissed John's cheeks and hugged him.

"I'll fetch you with my two-horse buggy at ten tonight."

She waved at him and walked with her umbrella, heading for the hospital. John went into the precinct and laid the note on his table. He placed a large, round astray to hold it down. He rubbed his eyes, wondering who had sent this message in such an aggressive tone. "Who is this guy, anyway?" he placed his palm on his chin.

John took his ivory pipe and filled the mouthpiece with clove-scented tobacco from a small tin box; it was Gudang Garam from Indonesia, a refined combination of clove soaked in tobacco drums and then dried. The aroma hit the mind instantly, and he usually craved for more. Heavy smokers lived with that taste until old age.

The buggy reached Dr Janet's house at 9.30 PM. The two horses whinnied, pranced once, and stopped. Dr Janet walked out slowly like an ancient Frank cat dressed in a long blue velvet gown, with a maroon half-inch leather belt tied around her waist.

"John, you are quite early." Her smile was full-blown, subduing the pink facial powder on her face. She was magnificent. Her feline gaiety and charm captured the serene awakening in the cold night. Her divine beauty, charming looks, and physique was equal to any beauty queen. Her lips were crimson, her neck was slim, and her eyes sparkled like the light blue sea.

"Come on, Doctor, get in, please."

"Thank you, dear John. Do you have your Wembley with you?"

"I am the police. The Wembley and Smith & Wesson are my good friends. Now move, my drivers." John clucked to the two horses.

It was a cold, swift journey. They reached the Red Lantern Nightclub an hour before midnight. John alighted and walked towards Dr Janet. He lifted her and helped her to the ground. "You look great, my lady." He grinned admiringly at her.

The Chinese ladies at the entrance greeted them. "Welcome, welcome to the dream house. We have dream merchants in here. Tell us your dreams, and we will fulfil your dreams."

Dr Janet held onto John, her arm locked with his. This big guy was dressed in a white tuxedo with a black bow and black shoes.

They walked in and sat at a round table. All women, except the bouncers, ran this nightclub. The dancers, waiters, wine dispensers, and singers were women. John signalled the waitress, and she came with a pen and a small notebook. She smiled earnestly at the new guest.

"Can I have your orders, sir and madam?"

"Yes, give me two glasses of Russian red wine, and one glass of lemonade for this lady."

"Is that all, sir?" she asked politely.

"Yes, miss. This is the introduction, I guess."

The singer was a twenty-something woman singing the charismatic song "Danny Boy". She wore a collared blouse, and her big bosoms stood out. Her nipples were large and bulged like ripe strawberries; they were visible in her tight-fitting garment. Her creamy white breasts were a besieging pair knocking on heaven's door. Even angels would look at her. The woman didn't seem to believe in brassieres. Her bosom was naked below the silk garment. It was a freedom most women would uphold suffrage for in search of excellence. This was the suffrage for democracy. She had curves that would turn on any man. Heart patients would have palpitations when adrenaline soared upwards like the stock market.

When the traditional song "Tennessee Waltz" started, the dance floor had many couples hugging each other lovingly. One strange character stole a stare at John's table. He wore an American hat that was very tall and slim, and he had a dark mandarin coat. He was one very strange character. There was no knowing whether he has a gun under his long coat. The truth was John did not know everyone in the bar. The stranger knew him. The dim lights shrouded his face from John. John wanted to go near him, but Dr Janet held him back. She was worried her man may end up with a bullet in his chest.

"What happens if he has a gun in his pocket? Don't take the risk, John. Let it be." She held his hand tight and pushed it hard on his thigh to stop him standing up.

John observed the other guests in the ballroom, and soon the tall man was gone. "Dr Janet he's left. He could be the guy who sent the note."

"How do you know?"

"My intuition. I have this hunch."

John stood up and walked over to the table. A small note was laid below the glass of a half-drank wine. John retrieved it and walked back to Dr Janet. “Here, Doctor, our friend left a note again.”

I was passing by with my buggy and saw five Caucasian men near the lake. I couldn’t see their faces. They were a distance from my view. From their voices, they were Caucasians. It was the day the Malay girls went missing.

Good luck old friend. We shall meet again!

The Kind Phantom

“Doctor, it looks like we ran into bad luck again. I guess we lost the blind game again to a better player. “How is the lemonade? It will neutralise the Russian red wine. You will not get drunk. I am worried about you my lady. Can we call this the end for tonight? I’ll send you home, dear.” He smiled again at her.

They left the nightclub, and the journey home was a trail of laughter and anticipation. John was hoping for a long relationship with Dr Janet, and she felt the same void in her. She needed someone she could trust and love.

Ai Ling and Nur Salmi had jogged a mile in the morning. The ladies were heaving and panting for air. Ai Ling leaned with her palms on the wooden wall while Nur Salmi sat on the grass near the pavement. They soon stood up and continued again, passing by a long stretch of paddy plantation.

Across the meadows, a group of young Malay maidens clad in sarongs with headscarf batiks were waving their hands while in a stupor. They were soaked in the muddy water of the paddy fields. It was the replanting season.

The choral voices of these women humming and singing the old folk Malay song "Geylang si paku Geylang" went into a synchronised hymn. It went higher and higher in the morning hue with staccato tempo, rising and then drawing thinner towards the end. The paddy field stretched a length of approximately six acres. The end of the line was surrounded with green hedges overgrown with bougainvilleas. Morning glories stood as a promenade of Prussian blue that gave breath to a small version of the Berlin Wall.

When the morning task was over, they started walking on bunds that separated each plot of land. They were edging along narrow pathways, walking precariously out in a beeline towards the nipah palm attap pondok.

Kids were waiting for their sisters for lunch. Rice was folded in a few layers of banana leaves into a pyramid facade. Water was stored in a yellow bamboo container that acted as a long glass. Fresh water was again poured out of the traditional Malay clay pot of labu sayong, which came in a variation of shapes and sizes. The labu sayong was a thousand–year-old Malay secret and ingenuity in the archipelago. The lower portion was made of several layers of clay soil, capturing a thin layer of sludge in the middle. The sludge acted as a cooling wall like a thermos flask. This portable pot-drum cooled water like a small refrigerator. When placed on the ground during the day, it cooled down like a pack of ice immersed in water.

The sweet smiles and sweat rolled down from the ladies' foreheads. The women wiped the streaming sweat and dried themselves with their headscarves. The day's work was soon over. The square platform with a roof was a scaffold at ankle height above the ground. They were seated on a range of colourful tikar mengkuang. They would walk before dark, as soon as the sunset turned orange and grey.

CHAPTER 13

THERE WAS A MASSIVE EXODUS of people into the compounds of Lee Ai Ling's wooden house. Lee Chan Chan and Lee Ai Ling were wearing black attire. Mayor Timang Sani was wheeled around in his wheelchair by another assistant for the first time. Her mum had just died from old age; she was eighty years old.

It was customary for the Chinese culture to wear black as a mark of respect for the deceased. They laid her in the casket. The top cover was still open for relatives and kin to look at her face for the last time. It was open up to the neck area, exposing the facial features. The band played a trombone and trumpet to the line of wailers. They were about to make the move towards the burial ground, which was a mile away to the suburb hillside.

The band playing the funeral dirge helped everyone sink into a deep, compassionate mood. It was melodramatic and temporal. It was so spiritual that it could leave men, women, and children in tears. When the hearse started the procession, Salmi was with Ai Ling, trying to pacify her sister's grief.

"Stay calm, Ai Ling. She's gone now," cried Salmi. "All that is left is just memories of her when she was still alive. I can only pay my respects here, and give you my condolences on behalf of my parents. Please understand my boundaries in Islam." Salmi sobbed further.

"I know," replied Ai Ling.

Umbrellas, white drum-shaped lanterns, wailers, and the band were a few of the religious and cultural protocols for a Chinese funeral. Three monks were chanting the holy verses from the ancient texts.

Kuanyin,
All–compassionate,
The most merciful,
Forgive us our sins.
Kuanyin Pousar,.

The red joss sticks, incense, burners with paper money, lanterns shaped like horses, and a castle-like house added the blue atmosphere with amulets hung over their necks. The dark brown beads, held in a circular form and laced by a string, and the size of large pearls filled their fingers as the counted the chant's repetitions.

The monks raised the horsehair whip towards the red shrine of Kuanyin, the goddess of mercy who was a beautiful and divine woman in white robes. The rest of the congregation stared humbly and in silence with their chins touching their chest. The sad chant acted as buffers against evil so that the deceased may enjoy peace and prosperity in the hereafter, forgiven from all sins and reincarnated to a higher degree in the heavens. The prayers and chanting, the cries and wailings from the deceased's family and kin, and the paid wailers raised the crescendo to a sad episode.

When the hearse moved towards the cemetery, wailing and crying in repetition filled the air. The prayers continued with the sacred verses.

Kuanyin, Immortal Maiden,
All Merciful,
All Powerful,
Deliver us, deliver us.

The gravediggers had the platform ready to lay down the casket with ropes. The casket was slowly sent down by family members who are men. Then it was the final moment. A shovel lifted clay soil to cover the casket. The band started playing the funeral dirge again. When the tombstone was completed, an umbrella was opened and placed on the grave. It was dusty, and the turbulent wind caused a stir in town. People veiled themselves from the agonising sand storm.

That evening at the Scotch Inn., there was a group of men, hazy and almost intoxicated by the fumes of wine, brandy, and scotch. They were so drunk they could not utter a word.

Liang Yin walked into the inn. The wooden stumped leg varied his footsteps compared to his other leg.

"Mister, do you want scotch or soda?" the bartender asked. "Are you new in town, sir?"

"I don't have to answer your questions!" Liang Yin replied in a loud tone.

A woman in a long-sleeve gown sat across from him at the other end. It was a gown with a long, square neck. Her round, creamy white breasts were nearly falling out from her half-cup bra. Her chest was muscular, and she has a mole below her lips. She was an athlete type and was quite tough as a woman. She has a cleft, a sweet and shallow dimple, and very thin pink cheeks. This young woman sat by herself, playing a pack of cards to her own amusement. On the table in five rows with three cards each, the last card was separated from the line of five rows depicting a strange reading pattern. She had with her a glass of red wine, and more than a dozen coins were arranged horizontally like a pole. She was a card reader.

Liang Yin went near her and then bowed and introduced himself. "May I sit down, madam?"

"Go take a hike, stranger."

"Don't test your authority, lady. Can you read the cards, then?"

"It depends."

"Come on, read my future, madam?"

"The salutation is miss, and you can sit down, tall man."

"I am very delighted indeed," Liang Yin said with a grin.

"Thank you, but please don't start any emotional love scenes here," the lady said. "I'm not your woman."

"Let's be practical in this case." Liang Jin said. "Do we need a dramatic evening with wine? I don't buy flowers to please women. That's not my style."

"I resent that sentiment." She blushed. She looked very grim as her brow raised in defiant retaliation.

"Are you orthodox?" asked the man with the wooden leg. "Listen, lady, I have a preposition. But I'm quite reluctant – I know the risk. My cousin was murdered. Her name was Nancy Kwan. Was she suicidal inclined, or was she indeed murdered by someone?"

The charming lady smiled and bringing her nearer to what she had in mind. She laid the cards again like a gypsy queen with a crystal ball. "Are you hooked to alcohol, mister?"

"It would take a small drum of brandy to drown me, pretty lady. Not even a beautiful woman on a remote island can seduce me." The man with the wooden leg gave a half-smile.

"She was murdered," the woman gave a quiet reply.

Liang Yin smiled and felt the emptiness in his mind being fulfilled now. The beautiful lady smiled and nodded her head. Her chin touched her creamy chest, and then she gave him a limpid, cute stare. "Do you have anything else, tall man? By the way, the crystal ball gazing is free. I know how you feel now. It's just hard to accept someone you know died." She released a wide smile with some indications that she would still be around in the cafe. Liang Yin then stood up, and his six-feet-four-inch frame jolted the round table slightly, but no coins were displaced. "Have a good evening, tall man," the lady said.

"Thank you," replied Liang Yin. It's been a pleasure, beautiful lady. Bye."

The big man left the cafe and went along on his unknown journey. As he walked, all eyes looked at his tall figure. It was odd for an Asian man to have that kind of height.

The charming lady buttoned her shirt button to close her revealing white breasts. She was done for the day. She scooped the coins into a small beige cloth bag. She slid the cards into the card cradle and held her white blazer on her back with two fingers. She walked out of the cafe. Her skirt was short up to knees. Her calves were athletically shaped and full. Men would crave for that kind of women. Her catwalk was tempting, and all the drunks were mesmerised by her beauty as she passed through the door.

CHAPTER 14

THE DRY SPELL THAT COVERED the region was a thin catastrophe. Rivers were gone, parched by the sun. The lake's water level receded. The folks conserved water in their homes in big clay drums. They knew the event happened once every few years. The grasses were dried, the hedges turned brown, and the sorghum wasn't spared either.

An old woman known to the folks as the harridan in the hilly region of Lanang raised her hands to the sky, crying for rain. "Oh please, gods in heaven, give us the rain. Our crops are dying," she wailed. She then strummed the harpsichord. She plucked the strings in a series of sad, musical tones. Her prayers followed, a mantra in an eerie, ancient tongue. She then cast incense powder (kam-i-yan) onto a small orange clay urn with flamed charcoal. Smoke with sulphur dioxide filled the air. The scent was venomous and intoxicating to the lungs.

Lanang, lanun, nang pak nang;
  Come back to us,
The God of rain, we need rain,
Bring forth the rain, nang pak nang,
  Nak nak lanun, lanun lanin,
Lanun lanin, have mercy on the living,
  Nang pak nang, lakang, lakang.

Soon the sky turned grey and violent with emotion that showed the moving clouds in turbulence. The wind grew stronger and greeted the foliage with incessant salutation. Then the raindrops start to fall. It rained and continued to wet the atmosphere. The grounds were drowned with water flowing and finding its way to every parched surface.

It rained until midnight. The next morning, the sky was bright across the horizon. And the sunrays rise above the meadows.

Along the shores of the lake, the waves yielded to the wind.

Detective John was having breakfast with bread and coffee. Dr Janet Walker was seated next to him. Sergeant Blue was also enjoying his coffee.

Detective John stood up, looking at the wild possibilities as to where the clues stood. "Take a look at the drifters' clothes; get Dusty to scan every piece of garment worn by them." John rested his chin on his palm. "The trail left behind by the drifters or the perpetrators can be detected by Dusty. She's a highly trained German Shepherd. I personally requested she help us in this investigation."

"Yes, sir," replied Blue with a smile.

"Sergeant Chang Wen, give me what you have now. Any suspects that fit the description," John told her.

"I have one good candidate: the man with the wooden leg. But he claims Nancy is his cousin. He asked how she died, suicide or murder. Sergeant, anyone who fits the hat is our suspect. You wrote in this report he is six feet four inches tall. The man is mighty tall, and he has a wooden leg."

"Is that a genuine wooden leg or a disguise? I want to know," John said intensely. "Blue, get two Malay constables to bring him in for questioning. Sergeant Chang Wen, I want your undercover status terminated."

"Yes, sir, you're the boss here."

Blue and the constables went to a grocery store. They encountered Liang Yin getting a packet of Rothman cigarettes and a box of matches. Blue confronted him brusquely, and the man was caught by surprise.

"I am the police from Lanang police precinct," Blue told the man.

Liang Yin knew what was coming with bitter anguish. He still managed to force a sweet smile, showing a strain of reluctance. In the interrogation room, Liang Yin sat with his arms on the table. John walked in with Blue. A Malay constable was standing on guard, facing the table. He had two handcuffs tucked into his belt.

"My name is Detective John, and this is my assistant, Sergeant Blue. I think we have met, and we have several questions we want you to answer honestly. Is that clear, Liang Yin? Where were you on the night Nancy's husband died?"

"I was at home after my carpentry work. You can check my alibi with the shop owner."

"And where were you two days after Robert Wong's death? This is the day Nancy was found hung from the roof trusses at her home."

"I was working to complete a wardrobe for clothes; my boss wanted to speed up delivery time, so I worked till late at night."

"What time did you finished and go home?"

"I can recall that was around ten, if I'm not mistaken. My hand watch ticked at ten sharp."

"This is the watch you wore on that night. This watch is broken, and you threw it away. Our men found it on the pavement near your home. Seiko of Japan is a very durable watch, unless you knock into something hard and broke the glass frame. Now, you have a new Seiko watch. You must be fond of Seiko, the Japanese legend. Where did you get this new Seiko, Mr Yin?

"I was in Tokyo three months back, on a visitation. I have a daughter with my Japanese wife, but I divorced two years ago. I have visitation rights from the Japanese court in Tokyo." He smiled. "I see her once a year, my only daughter. I bought another Seiko, the same make and year, in case the one I was wearing got damaged. Is that a crime?" His husky tone gave an ugly inflection. His voice was a slow wheezing because he was an asthmatic patient.

"OK, Yin, take a slow breath. You can rest if you want, and this conversation will be over in a minute. We apologize, Yin. Are you Nancy's relative or her husband's?"

"She's a distant cousin on my mother's side."

"Is your wooden leg genuine? Can you show to me that your leg has been amputated?"

"No problem, Detective John." He grudgingly obliged the command, folding his pants up to knee length. "You see, from my knee onwards, this wooden leg is made to fit so that I can walk like any normal man. It is genuine." He was not lying. John told him to stand on a chair with four legs. He stood up without any inconvenience but had trouble getting down; he almost fell.

"OK, thanks for your cooperation with us. You can go home." John said.

Liang Yin left the police precinct in bitter tone. He was a suspect. He knew the police always found a fall guy to take the blame.

"Sergeant Chang Wen, have you seen our Malay undercover, Sujak Ramli?"

She said, "He is moving around diligently, and he's a very good actor."

"Blue, get Chandran, Bumbung, and Sujak Ramli. Chang Wen, I want you to be here with me. I still need you to be the undercover agent. Blue and Chang, do we have any Malay candidates above six foot two?"

"We have someone who fits the hat."

"I don't mind exposing Sujak's position, if the people know he is police with us."

"What is his name?"

"Lolong Sudin, sir."

"I need more men around the clock. Dusty, you are a police dog. Guard this precinct from intruders."

Dusty looked up with bright eyes, like he understood. He had worked with the homicide department before. Dusty was highly trained as a tracker and sniffer, and as a special guard, well versed in tactical fights and attacking techniques.

"Come on, take your lunch. And sorry for the late lunch," John said. He patted the dog's shoulders and rubbed his head with his palm. John stood up and gave the instructions to his men. "We are still plagued by the killers. Get one more single buggy to Lolong's home. Bring him in to me."

When they reached Lolong's place, he was smoking a hand-rolled cigar made from tobacco leaves filled with something different; it smelled like marijuana. The Malays called it ganja.

"Never mind, guys, this is police work. They call it democracy."

"Good afternoon Lolong, we need you at the police precinct. You know your rights, and we'll send you back later," Blue told him blandly.

"Am I a suspect too?"

"No, this is just police work. And can you throw your cigar away. It suffocates us."

Back in the police precinct, Blue and Chandran brought in the last hope. If he was not involved at all, he could perhaps give the police what he had seen before and after the killings.

"Good evening, my name is Detective John, and these are all my men. What is your name?"

"Lolong Sudin, sir."

"How old are you, and what do you do for a living?"

"I am forty-one and work in the rice fields. I have two daughters, aged eight and ten, but they are with their mother in the state of Pahang. I'm a divorcee and live alone here; both of my parents are dead."

"OK, Lolong, you said you're a divorcee." John gave a wry smile. "Are you interested in Chinese women? Lonely and good-looking Chinese women?"

"Detective John, who wants a rice field worker like me? You think I murdered that Chinese woman? What's her name ... oh yes, Nancy Kwan. I read it in the Malay newspaper, the *Utusan Melayu*. A tragic death, to be hung, but I'm not the man you are looking for, sir."

"A day before the death of Nancy, where were you, Lolong?"

"I was in the fields working. I retired late at 6.30 PM and went home."

"But you came to town to buy groceries, didn't you? The grocery man told us you were there at 8 pm in the evening."

"Yes. After that, I took a buggy home and paid the cab driver. I cooked my dinner. I went to bed at midnight after my last cigar was exhausted. I've been living like this for five years. Wait, I remember now. Two days before her death, I was in town to replenish my cigar-making leaves at the grocery. I noticed a very tall person in a mackintosh and a cocked hat. That is the kind of hat worn by rice field workers and tin miners. But this guy looked like a man and a woman. Pretty strange looking, and very tall like me and Sergeant Blue. I'd say around six feet five. He was left-handed." Lolong wiped his forehead with a piece of cloth. "he signalled a cab and then was gone."

"Lolong, thank you for your time with us. I appreciate what you have given us. Blue and my men will take you back. If you see any strange characters, come and see us. I want you to know this is police procedure. We are the good guys. Have a good day, Lolong."

CHAPTER 15

THE DRIFTER'S HAD MADE A mockery of the Yard's undercover agents. The first encounter with revenants or the apparition of Lily and Iris should have given John and Blue some intuitive feelings. The drifters and Ahmad Naning were elusive. The revue group and the mute man with twisted lips managed to decoy the entire episode into confusion.

"I should have better hindsight, like a roach," murmured Big John while resting his head on his hand. "Do I have a clairvoyant instinct?"

Blue interrupted. "Now cool down, Big John. It ain't your fault, and besides ..." Blue touched John on his shoulders and reversed his steps to get a glass of water for John. "I believe we are not racing against foxes alone. We're running with hounds who dine with us. The intention of hunters revealed the reasons why they were here. Testimony given by Salmi and Ai Ling should have closed up the findings. There was 'strange ectoplasm' that appeared as human form during séances. There were poltergeists of a posse running across the lake till the far end that leads to the once legendary Fort Cornwallis; sometimes they drowned in the middle of the lake, but sometimes they reach the far end and gallop up the hill. Some of these revenants return with kindness to protect and inform the living. They were once humans like us, but now they are history."

"Why? Why does it take so long to visualise an answer?"

The confusion of the case grew beyond human understanding. It was riding high on the mark of the paranormal.

John and Blue reached for their guns. The drifters were one suspects, however they had to have grounds to hold them. Tracking the perpetrators was not a new experience for these two Metropolitan police detectives.

John filled his pipe with Danish tobacco and held the unlit pipe towards his lips. He inhaled as though he was smoking. Sometimes he lit the pipe, but most of the times he did not. "I'm recording every detail in my pocket diary. I need a full report after this is over," John said to himself.

John and Blue got into their buggy pulled by two horses. Along the outskirts of Lanang, there was a small tea plantation owned by Chan Chan's uncle, Kwan Lung. A bevy of beautiful young Indian maidens with mahogany skin toiled in the hot sun, plucking tealeaves. They had beautiful eyes with thin brows, and their white *saris* waved against the wind like a flag.

The men waved at the smiling workers carrying round baskets tied to their backs. The young women smiled and giggled as they walked past the road leading to a long wooden truck parked near the road.

John and Blue reached the police precinct before noon. Just outside the police precinct, two small boys were running with their small kites. They ran to keep the kites afloat, because there was hardly any strong wind blowing against their direction. The kite flown by one boy came crashing down on Dr Janet's hat, and the thread entangled around her shirt. She freed herself and gave the kite back to the boy. "Come on, kids. Take your kite and play in the open field," she laughed.

She walked into the porch and knocked on the twin glass doors. She could see Sergeant Blue and three constables talking while holding a few sheets of paper. Big John was holding his pipe and enjoying the tobacco aroma. However, it was not lit, as usual.

Dr Janet pushed the glass door open. She said, "Can I come in, and is Detective John around?"

"Yes, he is at the middle cubicle," Blue said as he raised his head.

"John, I'd like to have a word with you. Is that OK?"

John looked up at her and smiled. "Sure. Please take a seat, Dr Janet. We have one wooden rocking chair, for relaxation therapy."

"Thank you, but I prefer the normal, upright chair."

"What brings you here today?"

Janet said, "I thought I could discuss something with you. I think it's important. It's about the post-mortems I did on Nancy and her husband."

"I have done thousands of post-mortems in London, but these two are quite mysterious."

"Here, I'll show you the medical report. It's my copy. The copy you had is with the coroner's office." She pushed the papers in front of him. "The killer travels with gloves to protect his fingerprints.

But the size of the shoe marks done by your men outside Nancy's house are quite puzzling. It's pretty big, a shoe size eleven. I mean, someone who is six foot two or even taller.

John rebuked, "Now hold on, Dr Janet. I am six foot five, but my shoe size is just ten."

"Well, Detective, some people may be taller than others, but the size and length of their hands and feet are different. Not everyone has the same genetics."

"But I can't presume the killer is a man or a woman. Do you want a cup of coffee, Doctor? Sugar cubes are on the tray, and you can help yourself while I look into the victims' files.

Janet said, "I think the killer wants to play a game with us, in a chess game or Russian *roulette*."

"Nancy's death is one big mystery," John admitted.

"Who is this mystery guy? I want to know too." Dr Janet's voice was sharp and clear. "Have you a lead anywhere?"

"Not at the moment," John walked to his table and sat down on the teakwood chair. He looked at her, his eyes wide open and looking at her brunette hair sandwiched by a tinge of orange. Her long hair fell behind her earlobes and along her neck, resting on her creamy bosom. She was a beauty.

"Detective John, are you undressing me in your mind right now?" she asked.

"Could be. You have great charm, and you're beautiful. You'll make a very good wife."

"Is that remark for pleasure? All men are no exception. They will daydream and waltz a woman into a bedroom for copulation. Are you any different?"

"You're neither a saint nor a prophet, I presume."

"How is the work in the emergency department?"

"I think I have committed a crime of passion," said Dr Janet. "Steps of treason against the hospital, I guess."

"Are you OK?"

"I'm all right. What is the investigation like, Detective? Have you got all the clues right? Have you placed all the dominoes in place? Come on, big boss. You're the chief here in the police precinct, other than the commissioner."

"What kind of clues, Dr Janet?"

"Do you call that redemption, Detective John Hayes?" rebuked Dr Janet. "This is intimidating. The killers are walking like saints."

John said, "Can we have a special cup or two of raw coffee from Sumatra? It's trapped with the cengkih flower for a sweet aroma."

"Are you doing advertising for the Malay peninsula raw coffee?"

"No. Coffee is good for the mind and makes one think further. By the way, that's my own assumption, and nothing legal. My men are working diligently on the killers' identities, and also our mystery guy. I believe we will succeed." He checked his watch. "It's late, Dr Janet. Can I drive you back to the hospital."

"It's my pleasure, John. Let me get my hat. Oops – I think it's a little too big for my head."

John took his mackintosh and put it on. His .38 Wembley was tucked into his holster and strapped to his shoulder and the side of his ribs. He bent down to place another Smith .38 in the holster strapped to his calf.

"By the way, can I just call you John from now on?" Janet asked. "It is neither aristocrat nor illegal."

"Yes, you can, my dear doctor." John gave a half-smile. "Let's go then, Dr Janet. I'll walk you out."

They left the police precinct, heading for the bay where the bogeys were waiting. "That's magnificent," remarked Dr Janet. "Where did you get these two mustangs? From the Arabian desert? They are magnificent. I just love horses."

"There will be a multi-racial cultural show a week from now," John told Dr Janet. "It is to revive old traditions."

"Can you be my bodyguard? I'd appreciate your presence."

"Certainly," John replied. "Do you want me to carry a rifle or a Colt .45? And is that a poor subterfuge?"

"My late father gave me one Colt .45 before he died. It is fully loaded and encased in a teak box. I put it in my closet because I had no experience with guns. I guess I can learn how to shoot an intruder during emergencies. John, I'm just a vulnerable woman. You are supposed to protect me."

The Malay shadow puppetry, or wayang kulit, had set the foundation for Malay folklore legends interpreted in shadow plays. The script was either memorised or done impromptu. Percussion instruments added background music.

However, the most prominent dance drama was the Mak Yong, originating from the northern belts of Peninsula Malaya in the Kelantan-Pattani region. Women acted with a supporting cast of male musicians playing the serunai, gong, and rebab.

At the hospital, the flow of patients was continuous, like a line of light black ants scrounging for sugar pellets. The nurses and doctors were at the accident and emergency unit. The number of casualties from accidents had almost doubled and reached a high tide. Dr Janet was doing minor surgical procedures on one patient one after another.

Back in one of the rooms, an Indian doctor was attending to a patient. "There's elevated blood pressure. The patient is having trauma from a fall from the wooden staircase at her home."

Dr Rama Raj was having a tough time after three surgeries at the operation theatre. He was thirty-five with wavy hair curled at the temple. His hair was receding to the point of baldness. He had thin hair like a newborn baby, which gave him a boyish look.

"There is no sign of cardiac symptoms," remarked Dr Rama. "Get patient admitted to ward two and monitor the blood pressure. "Check blood pressure hourly. This patient is to RIB."

The Malay nurse replied in a light tone, "Yes, Tuan Doctor."

Prior to this, there was a slight commotion when Dr Rama examined the patient. Her parents were touchy and agitated when Dr Rama diagnosed her chest and abdomen. All the nurses were supportive of Dr Rama and tried to assure the parents that this was a normal procedure.

The nurses gave Dr Rama assurance that if he ever needed their testimony in the police station or in court, they would be there. Sometimes it happened with eighteen-year-old Malay girls.

"What is wrong with that?" a nurse asked the parents.

"A doctor who is black, and he is an Indian!"

"He is human, and he is equal to any humans in the eyes of God."

Dr Janet was swift to identify the situation. She said in a very candid tone, "This is a hospital, and doctors diagnose patients with the stethoscope. Doctors have to diagnose the patient's chest to listen. This is standard medical procedure. There is no need to get the patient's permission, just because you are an Indian. So what! What is the big problem if the colour of one's skin is black, mahogany, light brown, or dark brown? It's not a measurement of human intelligence and competency."

Dr Janet was pleased with herself and her reply. "Always remember, Dr Rama, you're a doctor. And black or white, we are humans." Dr Janet raised her head and looked at the ceiling fan. "The medical profession is no heavenly beauty in *Vogue*. Dr Rama, you're a good doctor and surgeon, but expect this aftermath. The Malay parents may come back with molestation charges."

CHAPTER 16

"SALMI, ARE YOU EXPECTING SOMEONE?"

"No, Ai Ling," Salmi replied while showing a demure smile. "I have had my loneliness. My two dead sisters, they gave me that emptiness."

"Can I dine with you for dinner at your home?" Ai Ling asked softly.

"Sure, why not? You are my dear sister, Ai Ling."

"When I look back on the night they were murdered, I have this blurred vision. They were undressed, walking with tears towards me, crying to the moving rows of white tombstones. They were wet, drenched to their feet. Their long hairs were soaked with very greenish water full of seaweed. Lily shut her left eye twice, trying to tell me something. One-eyed vision. The other eye had a dark patch. It's very strange indeed, and gloomy."

"I can't understand this, Ai Ling. I really don't know what it is."

That evening saw the two young ladies in their attire. They were dressed in kebayas" the Straits Settlement unique style that transpired in the eighteenth century in the Malay Peninsula. Salmi wore a black translucent kebaya laced with handmade kerawang, which captioned her elegant, soft complexion and contour. The sides were held by kerongsang along the embroidered edges. She was a perfect sight, the slim-fitting kebaya reinforced with a maroon batik sarong.

Ai Ling was magnificent with a beige kebaya laced with hand-sewn trimmings and tinged with gold kerawang. Her wafer-thin chest showed her stunning white breasts that stood up, held by her push-up bra. She had a pink batik sarong.

They had dinner with a three-piece candelabra on both sides of the tables. On the mounted round rotating platform made of redwood from China, there were five Baba Peranakan dishes. They dined with chopsticks made of cedar wood with three-inch ivory embedded into the cedar wood. There were two jars of red liquid filled with watermelons. It was a quiet toast for the evening, with two close friends confiding in each other's traumas.

"I'll cherish this evening with you, Salmi," Ai Ling said with a smile.

"Do you want some grapes with salad and *daun pegaga*? It's good for the body's defence system from ulcers," Nur Salmi said. "Do you think the killers who murdered my sisters can be arrested?"

"It's a matter of time, dear Salmi."

At the hospital, a new patient came in for admission to the ward. Dr Janet rushed over after receiving news from one of the nurses. There was an unending mound of work, examining patients and doing minor surgeries. Dr Rama attended the patients in the casualty room.

Dr Janet walked with big strides, and she took some running steps to assist Dr Rama. "How's the patient?" she asked.

"She was brought in by her son," replied Dr Rama.

A visibly shaken young student nurse had her first exposure in the department. Her name was Lisa Harun. She helped to retrieve the patient's pillow, which had fallen. She adjusted the patient's head to the middle of it for better comfort.

"Dr Rama, give me the diagnosis," remarked Dr Janet.

"The patient has angio aedema. Blood pressure is 160/100, and pulse rate is 110. We have sent the urine and blood samples to the lab," Dr Rama replied.

"Ok! Saline drip looks perfect. Do an IV with 0.5 mg morphine every four hours."

"The pain is continuous."

"Get blood pressure every six hours. Get her put in ward nine, the ladies ward. Put her in the middle, near the nurses' desk. That's a severe manifestation. We have swelling of the face, tongue, glottis, and larynx with dyspnea. Perform a renal function test. Exacerbation of renal impairment may occur because she's old. Reduced blood pressure can lead to cerebral infarction. Get prepared for everything."

"OK, Dr Janet," Dr Rama said with a smile.

At the police station in his quiet office, John Hayes was in moody resignation. "OK, I will summarise the possibilities of events to Nancy's case," he said to himself. "Nancy opened the door and allowed a visitor in at a time past midnight. That's pretty unusual. The visitor doused Nancy with laudanum and strangled her to death, and then he tied her neck to the nine-foot horizontal roof trusses. We found the hangman's rope was two feet shorter. It was too short to do the killing. That was a deliberate act and was unprepared. She was killed on the floor. Someone who is very tall and used a wooden chair would be able to throw the rope over the wooden trusses.

"After the murder is done, he dashes out in a hurry. An unknown vagabond was walking past the front door and knocked into the old man with sudden impulse. He was scared and stabbed him to death. The accomplice arrived with a buggy, or a single or twin carriage, or a wagon. In the confusion, the carriage wheels hit and killed a barking stray dog about ten yards from the crime scene.

"Nancy's case is still a mystery. We don't have any leads. No fingerprints. Nothing to tie it together." Big John placed his thumb on his temple. "I think the killer went in with the intent to discuss things with Nancy. He could be her lover, or partner in the murder of Nancy's husband. There could have been a deal offered, but she did not buy it. He was someone known to her; she had nothing to fear. This is my assumption, but it could be something else."

CHAPTER 17

"LET ME IN. COME ON, April Hwang, let me in. I'm not going to hurt you. I just want to talk."

"I will smack your face, Brandon Kwan. Why do you talk to the girl Lin Lin?" sobbed April. "I'll make mincemeat of you, and you're history!"

"April, it was just a soiree. Everyone was there. You came ten minutes late," replied Brandon. His fingers glided on his jawbone, and he held his temples. He had a face set with frustration and guilt.

April yawned for a moment and slid back across the dining table. She was hungry and had an anger that gave her a crimson but pale look. "You're a snob, aren't you, Brandon Kwan? Go and make a public statement. Say you're in love with her." Her anger began to subside. She opened the door and put her fingers on Brandon's lips. "Brandon, how do you make your approach with a woman?"

"I believe I'm destined to be with you, dear."

"Don't 'dear' me – you've hurt me. Are you hungry?" April look at him in earnestness.

"Yes, dear, let's sit down and clear the misty confusion."

Brandon pinched her cheek and rested his right hand on her thigh. He whispered into her ears, "Simmer down, darling." His sudden impulse flushed her modesty to icy cold scorn that made her hug her knees to her wafer chest.

Across the wall on the chest of drawers stood a big, oblong Chinese ceramic bowl that housed a beautiful mummy *bird-of-paradise*.

April took out and laid a tea set made of dried tea leaves from Yunnan Province, China. She began to humour herself and poured the aromatic herbal scent into six small teacups. She took a sip first and laughed. “Do you have diplomatic obligations, or are you a cynic living with fear? I'm sorry I couldn't control my emotions. It was my suspicions.” She paused further and came with this reply. “How I long to kiss you.” She smiled, took his hand, and placed it on her thin shoulders, which revealed her push-up bra.

“My quest is to find the murderer who killed my sister Nancy.” Brandon's face had almond blue eyes, and he retained his father's Chinese looks more than his mum's Caucasian features. Nancy was the opposite, with a stronger Caucasian heritage. Brandon placed two logs in the wood-burning stove to warm the room. There was a continuous, cold evening rain.

The police department in Lanang was a big building with three rows of single-storey quarters. The reception area was in the middle with long wooden seats on both sides facing the counter. The second row had the detention lock-up with two interrogation rooms. The lockup itself had two layers of brick walls reinforced with steel bars. It would be a mistake if there was any attempt by suspects to escape. The walls were fenced with barbed wire atop the two-layered wall.

There was a two-storey sentry at the entrance door, fixed with two rotating spotlights. There sat a guard with rifles.

Outside the police station was a meeting place for the folks here. The empty space had one row of parking spaces for the people. Adjacent to this was a big place for any small event.

There were a few Malay boys in sarongs and songkoks, and they were playing the *sepak takraw*, a game with a ball made of rattan. They stood in a circle kicking and heading the ball to one another. It was a game of accuracy and ball control, and they were good at it. This was no aristocracy game; anyone could play.

At the police department, Detective John and Sergeant Blue were in the interrogation room. This time they had the one-eyed man alone. John needed to crack the puzzle with a series of repeated questions.

"Good evening, Mr Romulus. Can you give me what you know. Can you recall anything?"

"I don't have anything. Look here, you can detain me, but you can't force me to say anything I haven't done."

"Oh! Do you want a blind game?"

"You're hitting at nothing,

"You're very sure your French twins were with you? They were not at Nancy's front door?"

"Why are you so cocksure, big man?" Romulus tried to set the tone right with tranquillity.

John said, "Let me tell you this, my old friend: we have an eyewitness. Because the subject was seen by the witness and was dressed the same way as your French twins, in a trench coat and a hat." John raised his eyebrows in a desperate attempt to crack the missing link.

"If you're the man known to Nancy, she would invite you in. There were no signs of broken latches or doorknobs. Is that right? You're the leader of your team, and you went there alone. You used carbon monoxide gas filled with a bottle of red-coloured syrup. Shake the bottle many times to mix the poisonous gas into the solution. Carbon monoxide is colourless and odourless. You wore gloves made of cloth to destroy all evidence, and we have no fingerprints. A very smart move. No trace, no fingerprints."

Mr Romulus squinted with a sullen face during the intimidation. John thought, *Yes! He is being intimidated, at least.*

John continued. "You are doing a perfect murder. You hit the victim unknowingly, because you masterminded the plot and drama, I suppose. I'm also anticipating the deadly cyanide potassium. Both poisons lead to the same symptoms: a heart attack. The haemoglobin gets intoxicated and leads to the heart. Ain't that right, Romulus?" John leaned on the wooden wall. The threshold looked like it was going to fall like the Roman empire. "You glazed it on the brim of a glass, a complete circle, to capture the victim's lips at any position she held her glass of chardonnay. Did you kill Nancy Kwan?"

Romulus looked confused for a moment. He knew he wasn't involved with this murder – because he was one of the killers of the two young women. He knew the media and the police needed a fall guy, but not him with Nancy, whoever she was. His mind drifted back and segued to the scene of the crime at the lake. The rape was worth the aftermath; it was sensuous. They were pretty, young, alluring, and kinky. They were easy prey.

"Does a woman's soft cleavage in between her breasts inspire you?" Big John advanced the assault. "I still believe you are sanguine.

Let me have the names of those involved. The sixth perpetrator – I want him exposed. Otherwise you will go in for a long period, while he walks free. I want the sixth killer, my friend. You and your men will get the death certificates when the time is right, unless you help. Your auburn hair and snaky ponytail needs a new hairdo. Do you want a free haircut? I will read you and your men the *Miranda rights*. I think you don't need an attorney in court." John walked out in a hurry.

The room next door was damp with frustration. One couldn't shake the dust. The light from the twin lamp was dim. The words on the calendar looked like Egyptian hieroglyphics.

John went into the second room. The French twins were at the table with their hands shackled behind their backs. He said, "Allow me to introduce my undercover police agent, Inspector Chang Wen. She's from the Kuala Lumpur Police Contingent." Detective John forced a confident smile. "You were noticed by a woman at the scene of the crime." Chang Wen smiled with her finger on her lower jaw. "What were you two doing at the Hooker's Inn? Your dark brown suit and moss green trench coat reek with opium. The upper region at the chest had marked residue of wine patches. We can run a lab test to identify the make. Tell me, which woman with big melons seduced you? Let us question them. If you are clean, we'll let you go."

"I think you look quite stubborn," Inspector Chang Wen retorted. "You refuse to cooperate with us. Do you think we can't trace all the links to these murders? Mind you, we have sufficient evidence to place all the missing links. Once we reach there, we will get you. Meanwhile, you'll be under police surveillance and are not allowed to leave Lanang until the case is closed. Is that understood?"

They nodded.

"Good. Do you men get touchy for a mile, and when you snap out from your passion, you just can't cool down? It grows in you and then explodes. The cauldron gets higher till your mind drops dead. You hold something in your hand while the victim is still frozen from fright. Then you strike with the hard object. You leave the victim no chance to beg for mercy. You hit her several times until her standing shadow falls. Is that what happened? If you decide to change your mind, let us know."

The atmosphere outside the police precinct was very dull. No civilians were walking near the vicinity. The strong wind blew pockets of tiny sandstorms across the streets. The cobbled driveway resisted the accelerating, raging wind.

Soon the news spread like wildfire. They knew somehow that suspects rounded up by the police were still in jail for interrogation. Just as the wild strong wind began to simmer down, more than one hundred men and women crowded the street. They carried effigies nailed to wooden crosses, only this time the effigies were the police. The hearse was lead by a mock funeral with a long parade, with cymbals clapping a funeral rhyme. The trumpet, saxophone, and violin completed the orchestra. The wailers added colour to the entire dramatic act.

The crucifixion was ugly, a reincarnation of the police's failure to catch the killers. Crucifying was a sign of frustration: they wanted justice to be done. They wanted the killers caught. There was no silence without nightingales. Soon the noise began rising. As soon as they walked by the police precinct, a group of men surged forward and headed to the precinct's front entrance. They were armed with sickles and machetes. The police were taken by surprise. The angry mob outnumbered the police.

John, who was going to light his pipe, was shocked and moved his head left and right. However, his voice was still an authority in the police precinct and in the town.

The throng of pallbearers pushed their way into the aisle of the police department. They were swift like soldiers taking over an enemy's position in the frontline. They were mean and crazy. This scene took a few minutes to play out in the precinct.

The leader of the pack rushed to John, who did not anticipate such a violent attack. His face was a mocking sneer that was defiant as he wielded the sharp sickle. "We demand justice, Detective John. You know why we're here." He placed the sickle on John's neck. "If you resist, you will die, Detective John. I'm sorry to do this, Inspector, very sorry. I don't mean to hurt anyone. All right, everyone, listen now. We have taken over this precinct. Nobody moves, you hear? Nobody moves!"

His face was violently sullen and graven. His voice was a baritone that sent a chill down the spine. This guy meant business, and he was willing to slash and kill. His eyes roamed the room, searching for more room for his men.

They grabbed all the police officers, with machetes and sickles put to their necks. Some of them were familiar faces with the police, however a vendetta knew no boundaries. The police were terrified, and they couldn't shoot these people because they were civilians.

"Now, don't put up any fights or retaliate," the mob leader said. "We won't hesitate to cut your throats. Is that understood? We want these five men. We will hang them by the trees and the thick wooden lantern posts. We will hang the five suspects." The twitch of the leader's lips was bold and cold. "Just give us the suspects, and we will hang them in the street. The pallbearers were adamant, and they couldn't care about the consequences. Now move, you mother-suckers. Say your prayers, and see ya in hell!"

"Now calm down, folks, cool down. I know how the people in Lanang feel," John said, raising his voice slowly with some authority. "Our job in the police is to serve and protect. We preserve public order. There will be no lynching in Lanang District. Everyone deserves a trial. After all, they are just suspects. Everyone is innocent until proven guilty."

The big crowd blasted their way into the prison cells. They were livid. There was no remorse, and they were adamant about what they had in mind. Within minutes all the suspects were tied up and manhandled.

"Hold on, people! I won't allow this to happen. The police commissioner, Stephen Lark, is in KL for an emergency meeting," John told them firmly. "He will not approve this. There will be no kangaroo courts either."

"Just let us have the suspects, John!" the big man in the mob answered. His face was sullen, and he was serious.

The suspects were shoved from the precinct like POWs. The mob outside had the hangman's ropes. Soon they were ready for the hanging at the end of two big trees.

When the mob was busy erecting hanging ropes. John held his rifle and told his men to put up a fight no matter what happened. Soon they overpowered the unprepared pallbearers and pointed their pistols at them. John instructed his men to line up facing the mob. They were armed with Lee-Enfield Mk 1 rifles. John raised the rifle and fired six shots in the air. He spoke over the loudspeaker. "Now people, stop this lynching. You have been warned now. The first man who starts the hanging will be shot dead. This is a public order. You are inviting the police to install public order, facing a mob. All my men are heavily armed with rifles. You know how powerful this rifle is. I don't have to draw the line." Big John's face was cold. "We have twenty-three men and two women." That was twenty-five armed police, not including John and Sergeant Blue. "We have the authority, people. Don't waste your lives. Let the court decide." He fired three more shots in the air. "Now, disperse and go back to your homes."

John fired another shot and hit the leader on his thigh. The man dropped like a piece of dead wood, screaming in pain. He fired five more shots at the mob. Each wave hit the pallbearers erecting the hanging ropes. The others were shocked and retreated with fear that they might be shot. They moved backwards, looking glumly at the police. They were numb to their knees. They knew the police would execute their authority in the line of duty.

In the confusion, a lone figure pulled something from his pocket. He had a revolver in his hand. It was a brazen silver pistol, a .38

Smith & Wesson. He raised his hand like a marksman aiming in a hunter's game. His face was cold like a debt collector doing his rounds. He grinned, and his canine teeth came out in a sullen, icy face. The muscle spasm on his face went tense, and he fired four shots wildly at the five suspects. The bullets hit two of the drifters, impacting hitting both their heads and chest. They fell forward in a pool of blood. One of them was the Italian, and the other was a French twin. It was an ugly scene.

The mob was satisfied because two suspects were dead. The crowd screamed in hysterics, and the mob was devastated. They did not expect this kind of bloody aftermath. This episode was an agony, the wailings of men and women gasps and grunts filling the air. The chain of events could seal their fates with the police department. They had broken the law.

Romulus screamed, "What have you people done? You mad killers!"

John, Blue, and the constables stormed into the lynching mob and pushed them aside with their rifles. It was do or die in this heated moment.

The lone gunman was knocked on the head with a rifle butt by Blue and handcuffed. Blue dragged him to the precinct's front porch and made him kneel down, facing the crowd.

"You will stay here. I will come back and send you to hell. You just killed two men."

His face was calm about what he had done. He looked provocative and adamant. "Justice is done, Sergeant! Justice is served on these idiots. I have done God's work. They will get the wrath of God, I promise you. The other three will die." His lips twitched, and his body and face were full of swagger.

Blue pushed his back and rapped his knuckles on his shoulder. He went back to secure his position with the other constables and inspectors.

The bloody experience and the deadliness of the Lee rifles paralysed the mob. They simmered down and tried to remain calm. No one wanted to be shot. They understood the game now: they were going against law and order.

In a few minutes, the police had the riot under control. John shouted to the mob to back off and put down their machetes and sickles. “Listen, it’s all over now. I told you not to take the law in your own hands. Let the court decide. Put down all your weapons, and put your hands on your heads. Stay where you are and don’t move. Understand?”

The police precinct locked up the remaining three suspects for their safety. The police then arrested the leader of the mob who had threatened John with a sickle. He was under police custody for inciting the mob. Thirty-eight men were also taken in for interrogation. The rest of them were told to go home in peace.

The whole episode popped out like a movie scene: the bad guys versus the police. It was tense, and the police precinct was just short of anarchy. Those men were desperate, smoking cigarettes mellowed with marijuana. John and his men noticed a big crowd of them. They were hand-rolling cigarettes with marijuana leaves. It took them a few minutes to get the spliff done. They were smoking and transferring the cigarettes from one mouth to another.

No wonder they attacked – they were high on that cocktail. Their minds and bodies were hallucinating, their anger elevated by their leader. Their minds and hatred were reinforced with the urge to incite against the police. Their invasion was swift but failed.

"Blue, make sure the violent mob remains handcuffed, and get their statements."

"But the lock up is overcrowded."

"Let it be, Blue. We have no choice. The surviving three drifters will remain in a separate jail for their safety. Sergeant, get me the undertaker. His name is Sam Sang."

"He is on leave today, Detective."

"Then get his deputy, or his handyman. Take these dead bodies to the hospital for post-mortem. I want the certificate of death papers. After that, make arrangements with the undertaker and give them a decent burial. We are humans caught between the good, the bad, and the unfortunate. The police department will pay for the funerals."

"OK, boss," Blue said, and his flickered enthusiasm and guilt was buried in his sallow cheeks. His mind drifted to the moment the lone gunmen fired those shots. *These guys didn't have to die like that.*

John, Blue, and a few constables stood outside the police precinct. They looked tired and apprehensively appalled. The incident had taken them by surprise. Something came to John's attention. There was a barren climbing rose at the end of the front entrance. The trellis was as parched as a dead fig tree; it looks like a barren Japanese bonsai without leaves.

"Constable, do me a favour, please. Water this small tree, will you? Looks like it needs to be drowned in a pail of water to grow leaves again."

"It's been like this for quite some time, sir – more than two years," the Malay constable replied.

In the evening serenade, Blue put on his blazer and went over to John. "I am sorry John. I almost forgot something." The sunset dimmed, and the orange bulb hid behind the clouds like a child playing peek-a-boo. The trees orchestrated with flocks of crows, pulsating the evening mist with their classic crow tunes. The grounds were filled with white paint from their incessant droppings.

"John, one of our men met an old man in the streets, a Chinese man who is sixty-five years old and kept mumbling your name when he was drunk. Old Leong, he is still around. Nobody buried him, and thank God he is alive."

John shook with laughter. "He's an old friend, a vagabond and recluse, I guess. Bring him in here to the police precinct."

Blue walked to the twin buggy to get Old Leong from the Chinese liquor shop at the bazaar. Thirty minutes later, he was back with the guy. John looked at him and put the old man in a chair. He could hardly walk and stand up.

"Here, Uncle Leong! Take this tea with lime to sober up. I told you to stay away from liquors."

"I can't live without Chinese white wine." The man looked at John with weary eyes, and his head hung back. "In my younger days as a carpenter, I was living on it. John, I saw something strange one night. Yeah, one lonely night. It was a cold night, and I couldn't see much. Two men were lighting up the torches in the street lamps; they too disappeared in the night. The stray dogs and cats were prancing in the streets, and the howling and mewing were deafening. They soon went to sleep in their beds.

"I saw a tall man in white tuxedo and a beige hat – the kind of hat very rich people wear. I remember now, it was the famous Panama white hat.

I saw him two nights ago. Maybe three nights ago. He is a big, tall man just like you and Sergeant Blue. He was holding a cigar, and he was left-handed."

"OK, Uncle Leong, look at me. How many fingers do you see in my hand?"

"Two. Four. I think I see six. You have six fingers, don't you, John?" His head fell, and his chin rested on his chest. "So John has six fingers. Blue might have seven fingers." The old man chuckled, and his sleek, weak body wobbled and swayed to the side. He opened his eyes again and burped. "I think this man has six long fingers, John,' he blurted. "Can I have tea? I am pretty sure he had six fingers. Might be the man you are looking for all these months. John, he had a silver gun tucked into his holster and strapped round his ribs near the arm, like the one you are wearing now."

John said, "OK, that is enough. Blue, take him to the back room to sleep."

"Yes, John. He needs a long rest to sober up."

The old man said, "Thank you. Oh Lord, thank you Lord! I have seen angels. I have seen angels on earth, and I will see heaven one of these days. Now, where is my pillow?" He sounded demanding. "Give me the pillow, Blue. Don't hide the pillow." The poor man laid down to sleep. "One more thing, young man. What time is it? Have you been baptized, Blue? Has John been baptized? I can baptize you and John. I was a reverend in the church at age thirty-six. I was young and handsome. All the woman would look and crowd around me." He was nodding off, smiling, and hallucinating. It seemed to be a very jovial daydream. "But now I am old, an old man. No beautiful woman wants an old man. Huh!" His eyes closed more. His dreams sank and faded away, and he rested his head on the pillow. The dream of an old man was beyond comprehension, suffocating in the mind of subconscious fantasy. He had a slow dream walking towards the patches of white snow that left indelible footprints along the journey.

"Is he asleep, Blue?" John asked.

"He should be by now. Poor Uncle Leong. He should refrain from alcohol."

"Blue, if he is right, never mind that he is drunk. We are indeed looking for a man with six fingers. Quite intriguing, these chases have finally returned something. At least now we have good reasons to checkmate a suspect." John smiled broadly. "Blue, do you remember this old paradigm? Any murderer will walk the whole nine yards. Either they kill again or stop killing for a period of time to confuse the police. This man is one odd red herring." He looked at Blue with some hope. "The man we are looking for regarding Nancy's murder has this strange signature stratagem. He wants images planted into the minds of the public to sandbag the police department in our efforts to trace him. Blue, I think we will be seeing red flags every now and then, when we go near it to find the loose ends of a coloured thread."

"We still need to find the link with the other missing end," Blue said in a cold tone. He turned to the table to get two cups of tea for himself and John.

CHAPTER 18

IT WAS VERY DARK, AND the drizzle grew heavier. This time the dusk was dull and orange with horizontal lines from the rain. It was magnificent on the canyon made of limestone and gave a panoramic view downwards, overlooking the vastness of Lembah Laut, or the Valley of Sea. In the canyon standing at a height more than 150 feet above the lake lies a cavern as big as a house. A pair of deer ran into the cavern to get shelter. These two guests turned around to face the rain at the entrance.

Two tall men dressed in their mackintosh raincoats lead the way towards the cavern. They were followed by Dr Janet, Salmi, Ai Ling, Old Reindran, and four police constables by the names of Banyun, Dukun, a Dayak named Bumbung, and a Bidayuh named Lemang. Soon the congregation grew bigger at the entrance. Six torches shone besides the moonlight rays and gave them a lit atmosphere.

They were here at the wasteland, where the tall canyon stood a mile ahead. Young Salmi had had a premonition after the fragments of a torn garment was found by her and Ai Ling. The canyon was a bizarre stretch of thick and wide limestone, taking the shape of seven fingers pointed upwards towards the sky. The side of the entrance had a boulder that resembled a tall, square altar; it was around four feet in height. On top were seven partially burnt joss sticks that stood firmly in bamboo sticks in seven holes that looked as though they were hand-bored.

"It looks like a ritual practice," cried Salmi.

"They believe that with this practice, they'll never get caught by the law. But now we just got closer to them," snapped Big John.

Salmi was stunned to notice the remains of her sisters' clothing: two baju kebaya worn by them on the evening when they were killed. The mystery of their missing clothes were finally unravelled. Ai Ling tried to console her sister's tears.

Salmi moistened her dried lips with her tongue. She looked very sad but was able to maintain her composure. Her eyes were strong and limpid.

Ai Ling's fingers covered her lips. "Now calm down, my sister. Let the police looked into this evidence left by the murderers. I believe this shred of evidence will put them behind bars."

There was a gale of wind blowing from the inside of the cave.

"That's strange," said Dr Janet.

"Why?"

The sudden surge of wind blew wisps of hairs from their heads. Salmi, Dr Janet, and Ai Ling shared mingled feelings with the unseen pressure.

"Are we alone here?" Ai Ling said.

"Of course not – someone else is here."

"They could be my sister's revenant," Salmi cried. "That's quite paranormal, but it's not unusual, I think."

Old Reindran was stunned and looked pale in his shawl and loin cloth. "God is great. God is great," the old man whispered through the breeze.

When the rain stopped, they came out to get fresh air. Blue Deighton sat in front, facing the lake below. The moon was at its full bloom.

As soon as they were about to go back, a sudden chill began again, and it was as cold as ice. A full-blown, cold air curtly turned warm. In the sudden confrontation, a small white tiny object floated from the cavern's interior. It glided and landed on Dr Janet's topee.

Nur Salmi walked forward and caressed the white guest. "It's a piece of bird's fur, either from the breast or the wing," remarked Salmi.

"Is it a pigeon or other bird?" Dr Janet asked.

"This is not a fantasy you play in your dreams."

"Come on, Salmi. You have psychic powers," Dr Janet said with a grin.

"It's from one of the murderers, but we can't tie this with the perpetrators, can't we?" Detective John said. He scratched his temple, and beads of sweat fell on the ground. "But we can hold them up for further interrogation, if it's the cockatoo's feather. We then have to detain the five drifters." John raised his brow. "We don't rely on crystal gazing. We need concrete evidence to indict them. In criminal investigations, there is nothing cryptic. For every why, there is a wherefore."

The folks of Lanang District were still cautious over the looming scenario. They had doubts, and their worries kept them vigilant. The unsolved murders still surrounded their small imaginations. "Are our children safe to go out?"

In the morning, the newspaper boys were seen running in every direction to get their papers sold. They were pulsating with a boyish flare on their young cheeks. "Get your *Times* and *Utusan Melayu*!"

The call echoed from every boy gesturing to the passersby. A small Indian kid with light mahogany skin and an obese body stood on a big boulder. The boulder was cream in lustre and was the shape of an egg, about two feet in height. The boy was heavy, and thick cheekbones occupied his face with a light scarlet that ran down to his jaw. It gave him the look of Orson Welles. His eyes were small and narrow. The thick cheeks drowned the eyes into a ravine like a vortex in the ocean. He was an orator, and his voice was crystal-clear and very persuasive. He was dressed in a short-sleeve shirt with two pockets on his breasts and short trousers. He wore a hat that was too small for him. A loud voice came out from the small figure. "Please buy the papers, sir! Get the latest news! Read the unsolved crimes. Murder in Lanang!"

Meanwhile, at the police station, Detective John and Sergeant Blue had just arrived with four Malay constables on their bicycles. John alighted from the buggy with Blue. The single horse carrier was parked at the horse bay.

"We haven't got a clue to find Nancy's suspect," Blue said. "This is not an enigma resting *on pins and needles*. Obviously, I don't want the police to be pilloried by the public in caricatures." John placed his big hands on the table in despair. "I don't believe in failing my duties as a policeman, but we have done so this far, Blue. Maybe we made a mistake when we detained the tall man and his accomplice. I think we detained the wrong guys. "We have to release the tall woman and the short man. It was just a coincidence when the crime occurred on the same night. They rented the hotel room as a disguise for their sexual needs." John's voice was full of disappointment. "OK, Blue and Constables Banyun, Dukun, Lemang, and Bumbung, you know your job. Read the drifters their rights."

The policed summoned the drifters for a second time to the police precinct.

"I want the foggy man to answer a long list of questions. Check his bird companion. I am still relying on the bird. We can't make a bird talk, can we?"

The drifters were held in the police department in the evening. It took the police some time to gather them, but this time the one-eyed man had his faithful companion with him. The other French twins and Italian came with him. They looked haggard, and their moustaches and beards needed a clean shave.

John was waiting with Blue Deighton and Sergeant Chang. They were holding a few pieces of papers from a file left on the table. The interrogation room was adequate to hold ten people at any one time.

John sat in front of the foggy man named Romulus. A small fly fluttered across the bird's beak. The bird raised its feet to scratch its beak. The poor guy looked a bit helpless and was trying in earnest to lift the other feet to relieve the itch. It seemed unable to refrain from scratching its beak, but it couldn't hold its droppings. The bird's dropping fell onto Romulus shoulder.

"You ought to be spanked, you disgraced bird. I'll beat you up." He slapped the poor bird with the palm of his hands. The bird jumped to the edge of the table."

"Stop it, Romulus," John interrupted.

In a sudden rage and retaliation, the bird flapped its wings. John held the bird with his forearm. The cockatoo chattered these words. "Bad old man! One-eyed! Bad! Raped! Killed! Woman! Woman! One, two. Two woman!"

Romulus and his men had sailed in between the devil and the deep blue sea. There was no turning back to deny what they had done to the two Malay girls. "Your cover is blown now, Romulus. I think you sailed your boat without oars. You are under arrest, and that goes for the rest of your men. I think that's enough to wrap up the case of the missing two Malay girls."

"You can't take a bird to court as an eyewitness. You can't use a bird's mumblings to charge me and my men," Romulus challenged. "A bird's testimony is not admissible in court." There was silence for a moment. "Isn't that right, John? What can you do to tie us with the killings? It's ridiculous. A bird can't be relied on as evidence. I think you're crazy. You're all crazy in the police department. You just need a fall guy to take the blame."

No, you're not the fall guy. You and your men committed this sordid crime! This is no smokescreen by chance." John looked more tense than ever. "I think this bird and the shreds of clothes worn by the two Malay girls is enough to indict you in court. Now tell me the truth, Romulus. Was it you, the French twins, and the man who pulled the trigger? He uses a .38 Smith & Wesson, just like my men. "I have one man in my jurisdiction. He is left-handed. Give me your signal when you're ready. Romulus, you have to give in. It's over. For once, speak the truth. Who fired the two shots, Romulus? I know there is a third party. Give me his name. Is he one of my uniformed men?"

"OK, OK! It wasn't me and my men, John. He was a uniformed man. Yes, he pulled the trigger. It was Ahmad who did the killings. He pulled the trigger to silence them! He told us he had to redeem old scores with one of the Malay girls. I'll tell you the whole story.

"We were at the crime scene. My men noticed the girls in the bushes. As they moved closer towards our direction, we grabbed the two young women from the back. They were slapped and beaten. The victims put up a struggle against the brutal strength of my men. Sadly, they failed! They were stripped and gang-raped. The lurid scene turned nasty. When two of my men forced them on their knees to pursue further sexual pleasures, both women sank their teeth on the man's ...! Well, the intense pain made him instantly punch them in their faces. They fell like butterflies with broken wings. My man yelled. Another with a red scarf tied around his forehead said, 'Let's kill them.' That's the Achilles heel known by women.

"Ahmad, shot them in the throat to settle his old score with one of the girls. He told me he had wanted Iris to be his bride. She rejected his advances. We wrapped the dead bodies and took them to our shack below Mount Cornwallis. We crossed the lake to the other side with the floating raft. In the shack, the French twins were good with kitchen knives. They cut and skinned them to the bone. The men were cooks on cargo ships one time. We felt they needed to be discovered and given a decent burial, so we left the skeletal remains at the shores of the lake. John, you know the rest of the story. You've been trying to pin us down with Nancy's murderer. We're not involved whatsoever."

"Yes, I think you are right, Romulus. I know that. Nancy's killer is still on the loose," said John. "Mr Romulus, in this world people make sudden choices on impulse. You and your men went too far. The court will take up this case. Meanwhile, you and your men will be in police custody. Bye, old friend."

CHAPTER 19

TWO OLD WOMEN WERE WALKING slowly across the cobbled street. Street lamps covered the sidewalk with lamps lit after 7.00 PM by the night shift man. It was his job to light the lamps in the busy streets and douse them after 7.00 AM. The two old women had encountered him as he passed by. They were quite surprised to see a man who was six foot four. He was very muscular, and lean.

"Excuse us, young man, we're in a bit of a hurry to reach the grocery store. We don't know what time it is. Could it be around 8.00 PM?"

He faded into the dark and lit a cigar. The only light visible was the embers from the cigar.

The next morning, the continuous wave of people flooded the streets and pathways in pandemonium. The cries of people in the coffee shops and market were like flagpoles greeting the polo players. The men on horses galloped, and their hounds ran in a hunting party. The rabbits ran hard, hoping to outrun the hounds.

The man with the wooden leg wobbled along. The breezy mist sent chills to everyone at the morning bazaar. The man trudged along the crowded pathway with emotions that seemed to falter in a Quaker voice. He was looking across the street in sly manoeuvres to get a better glimpse. His lips quivered, and they revealed tiny cracks from a long drought. He seemed adamant, refusing to smile at anyone who nodded at him with a smile. He was weird all right, and perhaps he had his history of emotional trials.

A sudden revelation of amusement tickled his mind, and he smiled for the first time, revealing his uneven, jagged yellow teeth. His clothes were tidy and clean except for the torn spots that were hand-sewn haphazardly. He was poor, and his hair was combed to the back and parted in the middle. He had a pair of small, oblong spectacles bordered with gold that looked older than he was. He had a scar on his temple that crossed to the right flank. The keloid was round on the surface and was thick from a hornet's sting. A callous resembling a raised camel's hump rested near his neck, an enlargement from his shoulder blade joint. He may have had a fall and fractured the shoulder blade during his childhood.

The dripping, tall figure was Liang Yin, and he walked past Nur Salmi and Ai Ling. He had a bottle of corn whiskey tucked into his waist and held a calumet in his left hand. The calumet was a long-stemmed ceremonial pipe, smoked by North American Indians as a token of peace. The flash of red brown skin was hypnotizing, and the skin tone was misleading. He looked like a native from North America. He may have worked in a cargo ship and was associated with one of the tribes.

That chilled morning was as dull as the unsolved murders. At the bazaar, there was a stream of people. In one corner there was a small boy selling the dailies. The other hawkers were busy with their trades. The rousing orchestra was deafening and kept chanting their wares.

"Sweet Mandarin oranges!"

"Oysters!"

"Buy now, buy now!

"Sir! Madam!"

"Mandarin oranges from Korea."

"It's fresh, just arrived!"

"Oysters from the South American sea!"

"Taste it once, you will get some more."

The voices rose loudly and intermittently, but they were drowned out by the sea of people engaged in the buying scenario.

A small boy ran to the town centre to get attention. He stood in the middle of the road with a thick batch of newspapers. He had a singlet with tattered holes. After a few minutes, the tiny small boy with an oversized cocked hat that almost covered his eyes stood on a platform and held a pack of newspapers. He tilted his head, revealing the yellowish brim on his face and calling out to get attention.

"Six murders!" He raised his mellow, low-pitched voice in the Malay language. *"Cepat, cepat, beli suratkhabar. Jangan tunggu sampai hari kiamat. Kejadian Ganjil! Dapatkan sekarang!"* ("Quick, quick, buy newspaper. Don't wait till the end of days. The unsolved mystery! Get your copy now!")

Suddenly, a pickpocket zigzagged in the crowd and slammed through the alleyway. Then he was long gone. But along the way he fell down twice and wet his hands from the first fall. He splotched his hands and shirt in the mud. He stood up and ran but fell again along a corridor. This time he left behind a dark print of his palm and fingers on a piece of white linen hung near a wooden wall.

Along the road, horses grunted and whinnied when they stopped. The single and twin coaches rolled past their destinations to pick up their passengers. The stamping of the horses ruffled spirals of dust on the road.

Salmi smiled with a grin. An old wag in the crowd yelled, "Have the police caught the killers? Why can't they come up with some suspect? Do you need such a long time to track the killers?"

Blue was having his usual cup of coffee at the Hailam Coffee Shop. The small shop was filled with a continuous flow of customers. It was the kind of coffee, served in cups from China, that stood above the rest of the others in taste. There was one special tradition from the ancient Chinese: always pour hot coffee in a narrow, U-shaped cup made of thick porcelain. The interior revealed the contents of the porcelain, which were greyish and light brown in colour. It tasted so good. One would never leave one's seat before finished at least one cup. It was like a shot of adrenaline in the taste buds. It hit the mind and left one asking for more.

The evening drizzle was brief but cold. The wind threw its annoyance at the concourse overlooking the row of shops. Mr Blue Deighton and all the people received a very soft, icy cold coronation. The sudden, chilling drizzle looked like steams of freezing clouds that exuded from a natural mountain.

At the Heong Fook Inn, a stranger took long strides to the reception counter. He signalled to the lady; she was Lin Lin, the proprietor's daughter.

There was no client at the inn; the last client had checked out in the morning. Lin Lin was alone without her sister Lorna. This was a situation where the curiosity killed the cat. He was sly in manner and very big and tall, around six feet. He looked like someone from the higher northern Malay belt. He could be from Thailand, a drifter, an unknown intruder, or a Thai kick boxer. His fist showed marked calluses with a tough physique, and he had hardened, muscular legs. He looked handsome short black hair standing like a porcupine even when it was dry. His eyes were light reddish-brown.

Lin Lin thought, *I am absolutely right! He is from Thailand, the land of kick boxing champions.*

It was getting quieter, and the sunset took a darker look on the horizon. Lin Lin was recording the day's client movements into another book. She sat at the reception desk facing the hall.

"Good evening, lady. Can I have a room, please?" the stranger said with a grin.

"Good day, sir. The price is quoted on the board. Complimentary with first check-in, you'll get a free supper and one free breakfast in the morning, at 8.00 AM."

The stranger, whose name was Sansau, smiled again. He gestured towards Lin Lin and asked for the room. "Where is the room key, miss? Can you give it to me?"

"Here, the room number is five. Let me know if you need anything else."

"Thank you, lady." He took the keys and his small luggage to the room. He didn't blink an eye and was very unnatural.

Sansau went into his room and didn't come out until the free supper, and then he returned to his room. The old grandpa's alarm clock, which stood at the end of the hall, rang at midnight. It was at this moment that the wooden door creaked opened, and the man came out in his light blue sleeping pyjamas.

He noticed the young lady was still at reception. She was sleeping on the table with her head lying on her arms. Her light pink hair covered her slender neck, and her long hair was tied with a red band in the middle.

She was alone in the inn; Lorna had not arrived due to a fever and was at home, believing her younger sister would be all right. She was used to being alone, and nothing untoward have ever occurred to her or Lin Lin.

The man with an unknown background took his chance. He went near Lin Lin, and his fingers started caressing her hair. He was going to unveil his beastlike transformation. His molestation woke Lin Lin instantly. She sprang up from her seat and stood upright, stunned by the touch of a man's hands.

"It's you? How dare you do this to me!" she snarled. "Keep your distance from me." She pushed his chest and ran round the sofa. His lust were so strong, and his eyes were focused on her creamy white breasts.

His poise was beastlike and sly:
The rising borderless passion,
The hidden sexual purge;

A serpent heaving with contusion
Through the narrowed nostrils.
A face benign, a mask unveiled,
Hitch-hiking with peril
Like a wayward loner who was surreal,
Standing dark with hidden lust.
The victim screamed; the loner chuckled.

Nay! You're mine, undressed, doomed, breathed your last.

Walk over my graves, you fool. I'll cook stew out of your flesh!
I'll spit on your graves like a hailstorm in a flash.
Your destiny is in a mess, like a blind man with a seine,
An occult from the mariner's sass, lest he gets the lash.
A blind man couldn't feel the thrust, a threshold so fine.
Dream no more! I'll kill you in a flash.

Don't feign your past, lady. I'll get you in one rush.
I'll remind my blessings, my heart impaled.

Nay! You're going to crush.
Behold! I will kill with one rush.

Surrender, lady, surrender your lovely flesh!

In a swift motion he caught her in his arms, and his lips were all over her face, neck, and breasts. She fought to release herself, but his sexual advances grew bigger, and he pinned his big, tall body on her small delicate frame. Lin Lin knew she had no chance of saving herself. The man wanted to rape her.

"Stop it! I'm not your lover. I'll scream to be heard, and soon this room will be crowded with people," she told him with anger and fear.

"Go ahead and do it. I'll beat you up," he laughed. "A lady killer like me deserves this experience." He held her closer in his arms, but this time he began to unzip her dress. Her bra was still hanging on her soft, tender waistline.

The pain and trauma went on for an hour. The inspiration was a thorn in her flesh and soul.

Finally he released his grip on her and lay down on the floor in exhaustion. Lin Lin sobbed from disgust and pain. Her subconscious mind began to inflate while she regained her composure.

In his excitement, she managed to fool him by making love again. When he was adrift in his dreams of sexual odyssey, she jumped up, released herself from this bondage, and ran towards the chest of drawers. The chest of drawers had a revolver in it, left by her late father for family protection against intruders.

She pulled the drawer open, and a silver revolver was now in her nimble hands. She was terrified, and her cold sweat ran down her face. The chilling moment came to a standstill. Her fears were revived, and she thought, *I will survive. I will.* She held the revolver pointed at him with two shaky arms. "Don't move, bastard. I'll shoot and kill you if you make one move."

"I don't believe you will pull the trigger," laughed Sansau.

"I am without remorse now, idiot," she said, shaking in between her sobs. Her face was ashen and stiff, and her eyes were cold.

"Don't try your luck with me, you fucking bastard! Crippled moron! You are sick in the head. Rapist! You sick, dirty bastard."

He tried to move and lurched forward to grab her. She fired two shots. The first one hit his chest, and the second hit his head. She fired again. The third and fourth hit his neck and chest. He fell like a piece of white linen falling slowly on the floor, consumed with blood.

She was frightened. She cried and left the revolver on the chest of drawers. The assailant was lying with his face expressionless. The scene was a body soaked with blood. This dead body with four shots lay on the floor. The frightened victim was numb, and she couldn't speak a word.

She held her thin breath and stood silent, trying to regain her courage. Her naked body was cold from fear. She took some time to gather all her clothes and get dressed again. Then she called the police.

The telephone rang, and a police constable answered. He heard her frail, shivering voice. "I think, I think I shot a man, and he's dead. Can I speak to Sergeant Blue Deighton, please? I need to talk to him."

"Yes, he is around somewhere. He will be here in a few minutes, miss."

"Please inform him that I am Lin Lin from the Heong Fook Inn. Thank you, sir." While holding the phone's receiver, she cried. Her tears fell on her thin cheeks.

The police constable could hear every moment of cries and fear.

She said "Please, please let him know I'm in deep trouble. I want him to be here. "Please, please help me. I need somebody." Her voice was deep and weak.

Slowly she slid down, and her thighs rested on the floor with her legs folded. The receiver hung from the cradle. She looked lifeless. Tears wet her face. The crimson face of her attacker was turning pale and blue.

In ten minutes the police arrived, and Sergeant Blue came running in, anticipating the crowd would be rowdy outside the inn. The four gunshots were loud enough to break the silence in the night. By this time, a few men and women were standing outside the inn. Police constables sealed the area with tape to keep the throng at bay. Raucous tones filled the air.

Blue went in the inn with his team. Lin Lin was still shivering from fright; her face was pale and bluer than a river. She was extremely thin but attractive and very pretty. Thin veins showed below her light yellow-white skin. Though she was the bony type, she held very inviting passion from men who noticed her beauty. Her trauma and ordeal was too heavy for her. She was too gentle even to hurt a fly.

Blue put his hands on her right shoulders to calm her down. "Be patient, Lin Lin. There is nothing to fear. Tell me what happened."

"He tried ... he tried to rape me." Small drops of tears rolled down her cheeks. "Then he managed to rape me. There's nothing I could do to fight his advances. I managed to get free and rushed to the drawer to get the revolver, left by my father. That's all I can recall, Blue. I remembered I fired the shots. I couldn't control my fear."

"Come on, I'll take you to the hospital. Dr Janet will be there to help you with the medical report. We will get your statement recorded," remarked Blue in a very light tone.

At the crime scene, police photographer Mark Stone took ten shots from every angle. The body of the deceased was wrapped in plastic sheets and transferred to a stretcher. The inn was sealed until further notice. Sergeant Blue and his men examined the crime scene, taking samples of semen, blood, and sweat on the floor for the lab.

At the hospital, Dr Janet noticed very visible marks on the girl's delicate skin. Regardless of the rape scene, the sexual ordeal she went through, and the implied thoughts, the doctor gave a positive medical report. She would still need a very good defence counsel to take her case. Whether she fired four shots for self-defence after being raped by the rapist would be judged by the court.

The facts of this case had strong grounds. It looks like she would survive the storm in court. Dr Janet tried very hard to subdue the trauma Lin Lin had experienced. She looked at the girl and held her hand, giving her a warm touch of confidence. "Listen, Lin Lin, the tragedy is over. Don't cry, girl, don't cry!"

"Yes, I know, I know. It's simply awful!"

"Just calm down and relax. I know it was ugly and repugnant. I want you to go home after collecting your medicine at the pharmacy. Sergeant Blue will take you home." Dr Janet smiled.

The frightened, traumatised girl's sadness and remorse were clear. She was very pale and quiet.

CHAPTER 20

A CONFUSED STAGE WAS CREATED WITH malice, flimsy trust, and judgement on the tragedy that had happened to the poor young girl. It was a dark ordeal for the victim, but the opinions of the masses varied regarding her innocence. Did she know the intruder? Was she his girlfriend? Did she consent and make love to him? In the heated moments, did she resist his lust?

She would not reveal what happened in the room. Would the court expose every minute of humiliation she went through?

The first impression the public had on her narrowed further, with the headlines that shocked the people of Lanang: "Four bullets shot by girl."

Lin Lin was under surveillance by the police department for her protection, in case there was a lunatic who wanted to be a judge out of court. There were people who had scant disregard for the innocent. The papers were sold out, and the throng grew bigger each day while she waited anxiously for the trial.

It would be a situation between the prosecutor's voice for the deceased against Lin Lin's defence counsel. The coroner's report was ready and kept in the court's vault. Soon silence echoed with intermittent opinions of jaywalkers and rumourmongers filling the streets of Lanang; they wanted their opinion heard too.

The courthouse was a clay brick building coloured red and orange. It was a single–storey mansion. The signage was a rectangular plate that read, "Courthouse of Lanang." There were reporters and a big crowd of Lanang citizens who took the case seriously. Lin Lin is Chinese, and so the racial composition was predominantly Chinese, with Malays and the shadowy and sinister Sujak Ramli, the Malay crime reporter. There were also some Indians. A large platoon of Malay constabularies, a Chinese sergeant, an inspector, and Corporal Chandran filled the police line-up to add credibility to the language gap.

In the courtroom the judge swept his eyes across the entire room, his glasses sliding down his big, sharp nose. The prosecutor's lawyer for the deceased shuffled his papers on the counsel table. He was a Caucasian with a small ponytail tied with a blue ribbon that was neatly embedded with an amethyst. The deceased's lawyer was Mr Robert Brown, and he is a middle-aged veteran lawyer with a clean-shaven face. He had a mole on his left cheek and walked with a Victorian flair. His voice is very convincing and crystal-clear.

The defendant covered her face with a white towel and sobbed intermittently as a wife bereaved over her husband's funeral.

The bespectacled judge, Justice Jordan Faith, called both counsels to the judge's bench. He solemnly asked several questions while mitigating on the murder case of Lin Lin. He asked, "Are there any mitigating circumstances for the deceased?"

"The deceased raped the victim," replied the defence.

The prosecutor argued, "The coroner's report on the rape victim clearly states that there were no visible signs of extreme retaliation. There were no contusions on the raped victim's body and sexual areas."

"Did she consent? Was she raped by the rapist? What was the rationale by firing four shots, two shots in the chest, one in the head, and one in the neck?" the judge asked. He was pleased with the answers from both counsels. It appeared that this was indeed a very complex case, and there was no precedent of cases to juxtapose the crime. A homicide was committed in self-defence.

The defendant's lawyer was an old man in his early fifties named Mr James Chamberlain. He was a legend in the legal scene, and his specialty was homicide and criminology. He was a highly refined orator and had a distinct voice. He had beady eyes with a wide forehead. His lemonade cologne had been his signature for more than three decades in courtrooms. The cologne's sweet sensation swept the courtroom like an evening serenade. "I believe she is innocent," said James Chamberlain. "Lin Lin, you're a women, and he raped you. The truth is you are a woman."

James whispered to himself, "Damn! Damn the public opinion on her sex ordeal. The truth is she was raped by the monster rapist who raised her sexual libido." He then said aloud, "We don't have a man here with months of frozen celibacy. But we have a rapist who raped his victim on the spur of arousal in a quiet place with no one around. He raped my client. This is a profane homicide rape case." He took a stack of papers from his briefcase and read the lines ardently.

Lin Lin walked near him and leaned her breasts against the bench. She looked at him, and tears rolled down her face to the cleft of her thin, flat breasts. "Mr James Chamberlain, do you think that I stand a chance to be acquitted?" she cried. "I have to let you know, Mr James, I am a lesbian. I had no love affair with the deceased rapist. Believe me, Mr James, I am telling you the truth. Neither do I have any liking or inclinations towards men."

James turned his face to look at the deceased's attorney. He was adamant, and James's hate grew thicker. But James had second thoughts if the deceased had torrid encounters. Was there any sexual contact with the deceased in the past? Did she enjoy the inspiration? He could visualize her naked body lying on the bed, quenching her breath and asking to be stroked by the rapist. This case looked very sinister because there were no injuries on her thighs and her velvet folds. But the medical report clearly states there was indeed penetration, and it was done very subtly. Her hymen was torn as a result of that provocative penetration.

The trauma and the tragedy captured nationwide attention. The flood of speculation and circumstances surrounding the case was very misleading. The verdict may stand in favour of the deceased, but the evidence was in the prosecutor's suspicions. "Did they enjoy the sexual inspiration together? But she's a lesbian." It would throw all the evidence in a disarray of doubt.

The judge reminded the jurors, six men and six women, to remain impartial in their conventional roles as crime analysts. The jury should not be deceived by prejudice in the verdict. This was a very twisted drama. It may unfold that both sides could benefit from the facts of conclusive evidence against each other. If the verdict was passed and there was any dispute to the facts of the murder case, a judiciary review would be needed to open the case as and when the prosecutor's and the defendant's counsels deemed it inconclusive.

Lin Lin was called to the witness stand. She was crying from the prosecutor's accusations that she had made love to the deceased.

The defence counsel stood up to his client's innocence. James Chamberlain repeatedly stressed that there were no *mens rea* in the mind of the rape victim. There was no motive in the shooting with four shots from her late father's revolver, which was kept in the chest of drawers from China. The jurors observed the hearing diligently as every minute passed. The trial judge scanned and skimmed every line of evidence with deliberation.

At the defendant's counsel chamber, James Chamberlain told Lin Lin that if the trial favoured the deceased, she could still go for a plea of insanity. "We have to add that you have suffered from delusions as a lesbian. You were once on medication for delirium. You were in a spasm of shock when you were sexually stimulated and then raped, notwithstanding the fact that you your soul defied the act but your flesh was subdued to his acts of deceit. We have a legal situation under the M'Naghten Rules, an authority by which a defence of insanity could be tested. Under the 'M'Naghten Rules, it prohibits a plea of insanity."

The acts done by her by firing four shots were wrong, but she did it on impulse from fear that the rapist may not die and endanger her life. She also knew her medical inclination as a lesbian, and societal norms were vindictive.

Her lust was only with her own gender and not with men. The delusive nightmare tore her mind to defensive delirium. She did cross the line of *territorial imperative*. Henceforth, she was defensive by shooting the big, muscular rapist. Jurors talked amongst themselves.

"What could she possibly have done?"

"She's a lesbian, isn't she?"

"Lesbianism is a hormonal imbalance and with sexual issues."

"She has chosen the other horizon."

"What's the big deal?"

The judge adjourned the case to tomorrow morning at 9.00 AM.

"That is good news," laughed James Chamberlain. "We have more time to discuss the probabilities to this case. Sober up, and by God's grace, Lin Lin, you will see better days. This is just the beginning." James smiled at her. "This is one of the most complex crimes that ever happened, but I have a premonition that you will go free or be given a lighter sentence.

"The truth is, what kind of men doesn't like a woman's pussy and body? He's a man from Thailand. He has a track record with molestation charges on seven Thai women, and that speaks clearly. You're a lesbian, and he raped you. But he doesn't have any right to rape you or any women."

Lin Lin sobbed and placed her fingers on her strands of straight hair.

"You may, escape the death penalty. I'm pretty confident," James said to Lin Lin in strained tones.

She was sad, twitching her fingers in her hair and sliding them down on her temple. She was gorgeous and very captivating to the eyes of men. Lin Lin's face turned to stone. She looked at the prosecutor's counsel crushing arguments on the severity of the crime she had committed. Her light brown eyes were drawn further into despair, but James understood it better.

"You have homicide, a girl raped after her sexual drive was inflated by the rapist," he said. James tried to read her heart and mind in the court hearing, but he could not bring out the truth from a girl who was raped for an hour. She could not present the sequence in detail, and failing that she would stand a slim chance of acquittal. Lin Lin's fingerprints from the revolver proved conclusive. Her chances were even slimmer now.

Sergeant Blue could not take his eyes off Lin Lin. She's a lesbian, but so what! She is a human being, and she's a woman. That rapist's conviction history with seven molestation charges in Bangkok proved as "collateral evidence". This testimony was important in court. When Lin Lin was at the stand, Judge Jordan Faith gave her a swaggering stare but with a very concerned, humble look.

The prosecutor's counsel presented several inhumane questions. These were deliberate and meant to break her down. Mr Robert Brown posed these questions.

"Miss Lin Lin, are you aware that you're a lesbian?"

"Yes, sir, I am."

"Are you partially inclined towards men as well as for sexual pleasure in return? A one-night stand, for example?"

"No, sir. I have very little taste for men, and most of the time I don't have feelings or love for them."

"Were you highly sexed on the night you claimed you were raped for an hour?"

"No, sir, I wasn't. I'm not interested in men whatsoever."

At his juncture, James Chamberlain stood up and interjected. "Objection, Your Honour."

"Sustained. Counsel for the deceased, you may proceed," replied the judge.

"Objection again, Your Honour." James stood up. "The deceased's motive was clearly known. He raped his victim. But Your Honour, the question of my client being a lesbian is not a material fact to this case. She's a women and has every right to retaliate and protect her life."

Robert Brown continued negatively. "Miss Lin Lin, did you enjoy the sexual therapy?"

"Objection, Your Honour."

"Objection overruled," said Judge Jordan Faith. "The counsel for the deceased, please be more relevant. Mr Robert Brown, please come forward to my bench. I appreciate if you respect the court proceedings. Otherwise I will have you charged with contempt. The fact still remains she was a rape victim and she is a woman, a traumatised frightened young girl who was raped brutally. Her premedical condition, which is deemed abnormal to society and religious practices, is not applicable within the context of this rape and murder case. However, please remember the law protects the victim, and it does not censure her rights as a human being and a woman. Do I make myself clear on this, Mr Robert Brown? Please take to your seat."

"Your Honour, may I request adjournment till tomorrow morning? I need to present a material witness," James remarked.

"All right! The case is adjourned till tomorrow morning at 9.00 AM." Judge Jordan Faith banged his gavel.

CHAPTER 21

THE MORNING CROWD GREW BIGGER by 8.00. It was cold and breezy, and the courthouse would need a big drum of hot coffee to please everyone. Some folks were walking around with jackets, holding their arms to their chest. Some were not aware of yesterday's proceedings.

The judge was the first man to move into the court house. He had a bag and a file of papers held in his hands. His glasses were hanging on the bridge of his nose, and he looked prepared for the trial. He raised his hand with the stack of papers and lifted the frame of his glasses.

The counsel for the deceased, Mr Robert Brown, and the defence counsel, Mr James Chamberlain, exchanged a few comments regarding the case. It looks like Lin Lin's counsel would have a tough time defending his client. The pressure was on him this time. It would take a miracle to save Lin Lin.

The courtroom was full of people, and a young Chinese clerk in court read out, "Lin Lin versus the deceased Sansau." Everyone rose up to greet the judge, who acknowledged the second proceedings with respect.

There was a strong wave of public outcry in the Malay Peninsula, urging the press to remain impartial in their statements. A slight spark could light up a skirmish between the Siamese and the Chinese.

Mr James Chamberlain rose to call Lorna Lin, Lin Lin's elder sister, to the stand. She walked to the box stand and was dressed in a deep blue and velvet dress. She had a scarf around her head to cover her sweet-looking face. She was jittery when the prosecuting counsel for the deceased stared at her. The opening scene was poignant for her to convince the jury on her *locus standi*. Lin Lin was her sister.

The DC raised this question. "Ms. Lorna, were you with your sister the previous nights at the inn?"

"Yes, sir, indeed I was with her every night. But on the night the tragedy happened, I was at home due to a fever. I had to rest at home."

"Ms. Lorna, as far as you are aware, did you know your sister was a lesbian?" The DC raised an eyebrow and smiled.

"Yes, sir, I know my sister is a lesbian, but I had no idea whatsoever who was her pleasure partner. Which women in Lanang … I have no knowledge of it," replied Lorna with tears.

"Ms. Lorna, have you seen her making love to another woman?"

"No, sir."

"Has she made love to you, by rubbing her body on your shoulders, or other sexually stimulated parts? Has she gone to that level by rubbing her breasts and nipples against your chest or back to get satisfaction?" The DC was very practical to raise any element beyond reasonable doubt to prove Lin Lin's lesbianism. Proving she was a lesbian could save her from the gallows. It was tactical to downplay the jury's minds on her innocence. "No further questions." The DC went back to his seat.

The judge asked the prosecuting counsel, Mr Robert Brown, if he wished to cross-examine Lorna's testimony.

"Yes, I do, my lord," replied the PC. He proceeded. "Ms. Lorna, how do you describe your sister's attitude towards men? Is she sanguine and sexually inclined towards men or women?"

"I have no idea."

"I have, on one occasion, seen her kissing another school girl her age when she was fifteen. They hugged and made love, caressing each other's necks, chests, and breasts. Yes, she seemed to be inclined towards her own kind only."

"Can you tell the court what happened after that?"

"They undressed and were stark naked. They made love as a man does to a woman. It happened at the inn at 10.00 PM. During that time, there was no one who checked into the inn. There were only the three of us. They invited me to do a threesome, and I obliged. "And we exchanged panties, wearing each other's panties. It was some kind of belief to protect us."

The crowd in the courtroom couldn't believe what they heard. It was convincing and very satisfying. It was sexual therapy for the men, but it was a scorn met with icy-cold complexion from the women in court.

"Yes, sir, it was fun. I am not ashamed, at least up to this moment."

The crowd in the room were stunned. They couldn't believe what they just heard. It was shocking. It boggled the mind of an ordinary person."

"Thank you, Ms. Lorna. No more questions, Your Honour.

The Judge took off his glasses to wipe his face with a small towel. He was tired. In his mind he knew that Lin Lin has no intent to kill. It was done in retaliation, in case the rapist wanted to subdue her or possibly keep her for another rape.

The prosecutor called another witness to the stand. This time it was Dr Janet Walker to testify. She was the pathologist who did the autopsy on the deceased, and she was the doctor who'd examined Lin Lin after she was raped.

The coroner's secretary presented the inquest written statement to the judge for his examination. Lin Lin had a right to make her plea of innocence. She was told by her DC that the court would hear her plea.

One could hear a pin drop when Dr Janet walked to her stand. Her beauty was alarming. She was dressed in a white gown with long beige gloves, and she had a pink headscarf that covered part of her face. She was cool and smiled at the prosecutor.

"Please raise your right hand. Do you swear to speak the truth, the whole truth, and nothing but the truth, so help you God?"

"I do."

"Dr Janet, could you please explain the diagnosis that you did on the raped victim, Ms Lin Lin?" Mr Robert Brown raised his first pool of questions to downplay the victim's chances. "Dr Janet, was there forced entry prior to the rape?"

"No, there was excessive secretion of semen on both sides. Sexual orgasm was raised to the peak level. The only bruised part were her nipples; they were quite badly mauled by the man. They were swollen and severely splotched, like red hot chillies. For the entire duration, there was no sign of retaliation by the victim."

"On your diagnosis, was the hymen torn due to the rape?"

"No, there were no new signs of torn hymen. The old scar could have happened if she was active in sports and marathon races with hurdles, or even high or long jumps. Or she could have had prior sexual encounters with a man. But she's a lesbian," replied Dr Janet.

"Just answer the questions presented to you, Dr Janet. There is no need for secondary answers. Was there any form of retaliation by the victim?"

"No, I do not think so. But Your Honour, a women's sexual orgasm under threat to her life could be instigated by any man when certain areas are touched, kissed, and licked, especially her private parts, neck, and nipples." Dr Janet looked sad because she was not able to help Lin Lin with her statements.

"Was there any strangulation marks on her body, or were there any bruises on her thighs?"

"No, there was no marked provocation on her flesh. except her nipples."

"Was the crime scene contrived? Were all the elements intact? Were there any changes to any evidence after the death of the deceased?"

The judge interrupted. "He wants to know if there was an exhibit of her torn clothes. Where are the torn clothes?"

Janet said, "They were not ripped by her. She doesn't have that strength. And from my diagnosis, there were no bruises on her thighs, not from any marked provocations."

"Perhaps it was consensual sex at first, or she changed her mind after the sexual intercourse ended."

"Objection, Your Honour," James Chamberlain rebuked.

"Sustained."

The prosecutor said, "Your Honour, this is not just a lesbian stuff. She is charged with murder, whether or not she had intention. Mens rea and actus reus remains."

"How do you prove it will create a new picture?"

"Your Honour, we deal with the severity of the case," rebuffed the prosecutor. He continued his questions. "Was there a consensual sexual act between Lin Lin and the deceased?"

"Objection, Your Honour. The prosecuting counsel is promoting collateral damage based on single evidence – that is, four shots. My client is a rape victim. Lesbian or not, she was brutally raped. She's a minor and sixteen years of age," remarked the defendant's council.

"Overruled. Members of the jury, please consider the testimony presented in these proceedings."

"She was sexually assaulted and then raped, though there were no marks on her thighs, private areas, and body. There were not many visible signs of violence. But her hymen had been broken, and traces of semen and a little blood were around the thighs."

James frowned, and looked at the jury. "Please look beyond your judgement. Give the defendant a fair verdict. That is all, Your Honour."

Sitting quietly like a demure victim, Lin Lin's face shot a look of apoplexy. She felt there was no hope left.

"Prosecutor, do you wish to cross-examine the witness?" the judge addressed the court while looking at the jury.

"Yes, one last question. Do you think she was raped, or she consented to the sex odyssey?"

"I found no signs of extreme violence, though there was subtle retaliation by the defendant." Dr Janet frowned and looked up in despair. "I have no idea. That is not in my position as a doctor, specialist surgeon, and pathologist. I can't give you or the court any medical report that is not based on medical guidelines." Dr Janet raised her voice to get the message to the courtroom and jury.

"I think that is all for now, Your Honour. No further questions."

"Counsel for the deceased, you may take your seat." The judge tilted his spectacles with his index finger. "Dr Janet, you may leave the stand. Meanwhile, the jurors will decide the credibility of all testimony." Judge Jordan Faith reminded them that they were indeed under an oath of allegiance to the court of law. Justice must always prevail over evil.

The next morning saw the case continued. A sad event was about to consume the environment. The judge walked into the courthouse, protected by the police and his guards. This was a new case that touched one's raw nerves. It wasn't going to be a smooth case, and she wouldn't be able to face down the storm in court. When the threads were revealed, she would be hit. In justice, one couldn't free a rapist and persecute the victim.

Lin Lin was seen sobbing at the entrance. She was sandwiched between her sister Lorna and Chan Chan. This was a victim in shock from her ordeal. She was lucky she was not under amnesia or any form of relapse.

The judge sat and raised his gavel once for the session to begin. "Everyone, can you please be seated?" He remarked. He pushed his spectacles up, and then he read out his judgement for the jury to pass the verdict.

"I have this to say. This is not just lesbian stuff. This case is classified under murder. Whether or not she had intention for the crime, the mens rea and actus reus triggered is up to the evidence presented in these previous days. We are not talking about gender issues here. However, we deal with the severity of the case. Regarding cause of death, the prosecuting counsel is promoting collateral damage based on single evidence at the scene of the crime: four gunshots. But remember please, she is a rape victim. Lesbian or not, she was brutally raped. She's a minor and sixteen years of age. Because her future is ruined, that doesn't mean that she will be charged as guilty by the court. I want the jury to decide wisely on the pertinent points before you deliver the verdict.

When the jury had concluded, the spokesperson for the jury stood up and read out loud. "The jury deliberated the case to seven to five in favour of the defendant. We find the defendant not guilty in the first degree. We find the defendant guilty as charged in culpable homicide not amounting to murder in the second degree."

The judge passed the sentence to culpable homicide not amounting to murder. He pushed his glass frames up his nose and adjusted the glasses with his fingers. He then wiped his forehead and cheeks with a handkerchief. It was his most difficult case as a judge. Lin Lin was sentenced to fifteen years' imprisonment. "She will be given medical attention by the prison authorities, and she is entitled to treatment after this ugly ordeal. With good behaviour she can get a prison's pardon reduced to six years. This is the law."

The judge wiped his sweat from his forehead and pushed his wiped glasses with a 'Scotch' tissue paper.

"Ladies and gentlemen, I want you to know that this is the most bizarre case I have ever presided over as a judge. For more than five hundred years, the law books in England have had no precedent for a case like this one. A young girl, a lesbian, raped by a man. She retaliated after the rape ordeal by killing the perpetrator. This court case will go down in history. This will be published in criminal law books as a new case in England. As much as I uphold the human rights and civil liberties of every human being, the law protects both sides, the defendant and plaintiff. All men are born free and equal."

He took a breath before continuing. "This is the first verse of a republican's catechism from the United States of America. This are the words of Thomas Jefferson, one of the most refined and learned leaders in history. I am indeed very sad. This poor girl, this very unfortunate girl, must be given protection regardless of her sexual abnormalities. Society must understand that our norms dictate the demarcation lines. Innuendos are just a mirror to interpretations. How you perceive a subject is different from another person. Everyone is entitled to his own opinion. I hope the human race learn from this experience. Thank you, folks, for your time. That is all."

The judge released the wooden gavel with a slow, disheartened thud.

The heat was brewing around the courthouse, and the air was dark and damp. It looked like tombstones could fall like dominoes. Chinese guilds and associations from the business circles gathered near the courthouse. They wanted to know the fate of the poor Chinese girl, and the tension grew bigger. A large group of approximately fifty men from the Chinese Martial Arts Associations in the Malay Peninsula, known as the Chinese Boxers, made tents and rented available rooms in the inns. Business was brisk in Lanang, but the preliminary signs of their presence received different views. The number of Chinese folks grew by the day. If there was a riot, they could bring down the police station. The police line-up was just one platoon with nineteen men and one woman.

The Chinese Boxers had an orchestra. They played the "Alamo" tune, the Mexican death song that rang out moments before they plundered the Alamo. The tune was continuous and mellow.

"We will have a stampede when hell breaks loose," Big John said. "However, I have asked to the Tapah Police Contingent in Perak, and the Kuala Lumpur Police Headquarters, to send reinforcements." Big John gave Sergeant Blue and his inspectors an official police announcement with the loudspeaker. "The directive is loud and clear. Anyone who crosses the line of justice and disrupt public order will be severely dealt with."

A spokesman for the Chinese Boxers surged forward in front of Sergeant Blue and his men. They were tall and big, mostly middleweights with quite a number who stood at six feet. There were about ten heavyweights who were even taller. "We know our rights to any peaceful assembly. We have the freedom to voice our opinions and our rights." The tall boxer raised his voice. "She is Chinese and a rape victim. Why doesn't the court just hang the dead rapist? We are Chinese. It's our duty to protect our women and children. She is barely sixteen years old. Her future is damaged by the dead rapist." He raised a clenched fist in the air. "We will leave this place in peace after she is freed from the murder charge. And we don't want to hear 'culpable homicide not amounting to murder' either. When the verdict acquits the deceased rapist due to lack of conclusive evidence, we will protect our Chinese legacy. Is that clear to the police?"

Blue interrupted. "Yes, we hear you loud and clear. Please be reminded that it is our duty in the police force to protect, preserve, and maintain public order. But don't take the law into your own hands. Let the court decide. Is that clear?"

As soon as the verdict was passed, Lin Lin collapsed. The episode took a bitter turn when a Chinese youth ran out of the courtroom, ignoring the two policemen on duty at the door entrance. "Stop, young man! You are not supposed to get out yet."

A constable told him to remain calm, but the boy ignored the instructions. He was recalcitrant and flush with anger; his face turned crimson. He punched and kicked the wooden door before running further out the door. His eyes flashed when he turned his head to look at the courtroom. The commotion was already brewing in the room. Chinese folks were stunned by the decision of the jury. It wasn't right; something was amiss. The kin of the deceased from Thailand were happy. They jumped with great joy, disregarding the torn feelings of the rape victim's family.

As the youth jumped from the courtroom veranda and onto the ground, he yelled across the concourse area. The agonising moment began to take its toll. The Chinese Boxers and all the folks who had gathered to lend their support to the rape victim started chatting in their native dialects. There were enormous cries of confusion and incitement.

The police stood to their ground with the powerful and devastating *Lee* rifles. John said, "This doesn't has to be written in stone like this. There will be a stampede."

In the heated atmosphere, a large crowd of men and women were dressed in some kind of Halloween caricatures, and they covered their faces with mask. Most of them wore hoods, and one could hardly see their faces. Was there going to be a riot? No one knew which side they were on.

The two young ladies, Salmi and Ai Ling, had been following the court proceedings since the morning. Court hearings weren't their cup of tea. The last event that took place captured Salmi's attention. It was the death of Nancy Kwan and the mystery murderer. Psychic reflections in Salmi's mind kept going back over the details. The mystery man had a mask on, a long navy blue mackintosh covering his tall frame. The only people Salmi talked to regarding the mystery murderer was Detective John and Dr Janet.

There were cries of frustration over the verdict returned by the jury. The dead rapist was acquitted. This was not a feminist rhetoric – this was justice, and justice must return to the victim. A small flint that ignited the sentiments would throw the big crowd into anarchy.

Ai Ling looked around her with steely eyes. She could sense the mire evolving into a thin cauldron growing by the minute. Salmi noticed something burning behind the hostile crowd. A few Chinese Boxers raised their fists. They shouted, "The Thai people are dead!" They lit joss sticks and pierced the copper urns filled with sand, leaving the joss sticks standing. A few men rushed forward, shouting and chanting songs, clearly on a war path. "The court and the devil!" they screamed. "Because the king of Thailand had close ties with the king and queen of England, the bloody verdict was given in favour of the dead rapist. They acquitted this bastard! The poor Chinese girl is incarcerated. You and your Satan court! You British go to hell!"

The chanting went higher and higher. "The Chinese people built the courthouse and other buildings. We came down here from China and the crown colony Hong Kong, with our ancestral skills in engineering, architecture, and building skills. We helped change the landscape in this country. Why are we treated like nobodies by everyone else? Is this what we get? The court judge and the jury acquitted the bloody rapist! The court is supposed to sentence the dead rapist for life imprisonment. You can mummify his dead body and put him in a coffin, and put him in jail. The court should do that in the name of justice!"

The chanting grew higher from the Chinese Boxers. "Maybe he can play Monopoly with the ancient mummies." A voice in the crowd laughed. "Are we termed the unwanted immigrants? Idiot British courts! Is this the legal system you imposed on Chinese immigrants? You used our women and men in tin mining, plantation and vegetable farms, and poultry farming."

The big crowd chanted in English and Chinese dialects, and the cry went even higher. "Death to the courts! Heng Tai! Kor kor yan lang ching. Chap chung." The Chinese boxers' platoon leaders gathered their men into position like an army. "Listen, my brothers. The court have done an evil thing. We'll show our Chinese muscles from now on. There will be a showdown, and our enemies, the Thai kick boxers, are crowding over the other side. Let this be the day. Let them remember this day. "Oh Yeah! Cham chow chui kan."

The Chinese and Thai boxers were armed to their teeth with machetes, thick wooden sticks, and short knives. It was ugly. The riot would turn the roads very bloody.

In the blazing confusion and hate, the police was out numbered ten to one. It would take the huge crowd minutes to start to plunder and stampede. People were dancing like children to the invisible tune created by a pied piper. There would be a lynching party between the Thais and Chinese. Detective John gathered his men. "You will not see kangaroo courts here. We will do what we can to minimise casualties." He gave a stiff warning. "May God forgive us today. The dark moments have yet to happen. Blue, I'm going to get help from the Malay people here in Lanang. I think we need help from Malay Silat fighters. I'll try to get help from Guru Silat Sayong. We have to intercept the impending riot. At least we'll have extra muscle until reinforcements arrive from Tapah."

The heat was beginning to exude. Blue gave John a weary look. "There is always hope, John, by God's grace. How many men do we need to neutralise the Chinese and the Thai kick boxers?"

"It depends on how many Malay men Guru Sayong will allow us to recruit and deputise as police constables. This is total madness against a riot of three hundred men, Blue. The Malay Silat fighters are our last hope. I need three hundred men! Malays are very brave and good fighters. Malay Silat fighters, engage deadlocks with your hands and legs. The fighting styles is engaging the enemy and intercepting locks. The rest is attack and blows with hands and legs."

John sent a Malay constable to invite Guru Sayong to meet him. In about thirty minutes, he arrived and walked towards John. "Good morning John." He greeted him with a warm smile. "I know the reasons why you called. I have five hundred students. I will get three hundred Malay men to help you. You can deputise them under oath."

"Thanks, Guru Sayong."

"Don't mention it, John. It is our duty to help one another in crises like this." Guru Sayong left immediately to gather his students.

John looked into the sky. There was a thin line of confidence on his face. "Blue, first we have the mob and empty hearse. Now we have this swelling tide running wild. We can call this the constitutional riot in disguise. I can call this a constitutional walk, Blue."

"I suppose so, John." Blue held his breath. "This will give us hope and room until the backup arrive from Tapah."

Soon Guru Sayong arrived with his promised three hundred Malay men. "John, my students are here now. You can start deputising them."

John said, "I want to thank you all for this strong support. Your presence here truly saves us. You are such valiant men. Now, raise your right hands. I consecrate you as constables and deputies in the police force in Lanang. You are to uphold your duties without fail and favour. Amen."

"Amen!" came the loud reply across the lines.

Three hundred trained fighting men were under the guidance of Guru Silat Sayong Rahmat Kapilo, who was a renowned Malay expert. These men were dressed in black casual clothes. More than half were bare-footed, and the rest wore sandals called capal. Capal was a hard-based leather shoe worn by the Indians and Malays. During engagement in the frontline battles, most Malay exponents preferred being barefoot. It gave them strength with their soles anchored to the ground.

The Malay reinforcements stood side by side with the uniformed police. They were only armed with the three-foot-long bamboo fighting staff; they did not need machetes. They had come this far for the benefit of the Lanang people.

The chorus of revulsion was deafening and drowned the announcements made by the police. There was an unbridled riot in the making. The cauldron was building up slowly, leaving no traces of detection and plenty signs of a bloodbath. It was so sick it would need a heavy rainstorm to cool down the red waters. Some men were armed with pikes and shovels, waiting to hack at the nearest victim.

Salmi grinned at Ai Ling. "Ai Ling, be careful and try to get us out of this mess." Her voice grew weaker.

The taunts and rumblings went out of control. Fury ran wild. The Chinese Boxers raised their red flags, laughing and taunting the police guarding the courthouse. Within minutes the inferno rose. The courthouse started burning from the rear; someone must have torched the back of the courthouse. Fire raged savagely And looked like it would consume the entire building within an hour. Detective Lieutenant John reminded all his men to stand guard, with their rifles and handcuffs tucked into their belts.

"Do what you have to do to control the riot! I'm afraid this is not going to be a racial plunder between the Chinese and Thai folks," cried Detective John. "This is not civil unrest. I'm afraid we will have total anarchy. Anyone around is going be a victim. I'm still pinning my hopes for the reinforcements to arrive from Tapah."

Cops were everywhere. There was only one police barricade outside the burning courthouse. "The reinforcements should be here by now. They have special units of 150 men to quell riots. God, send them here as quick as you can," John murmured as he looked at his men with apprehensive eyes.

John had his men roll out the Gatling gun, a machine gun with large shells and a thousand rounds. It had a hand-crank operation with six barrels revolving around a central shaft. The stick magazine was on top of the shaft. The Gatling gun was pushed out and mounted at the barricades, facing the mob. John told his men, "In case they decide to attack the police, we have to perform our duty to protect the lives of our men." He raised his voice one last time. "I want all my men to know this is a sad moment for everyone in Lanang. In the Ten Commandments, we are to obey God's law. We are Christians. I believe this applies to every creed and religion – Christians, Muslims, Buddhist, Taoist, Hindus, or even atheists, we share the same conscience and remorse. Thou shall not kill. Please remember, we are the police. We carry guns and get paid for this. Sometimes you are forced to use it." His eyes scanned the gloomy scene just ahead of them. "Pull the trigger. You kill the attacker. You are the lawman with a gun. Even you have no call to do this. I am sorry. May God forgive us."

At the border of Lanang District, a train arrived at the old railway station. It was one long carriage train, and it took a few screeching moments before it slowed. The steam from the wheels shot out like fumes from a steam bathroom. Eventually the train came to a slow walk, and the train warden leap forward and signalled the driver, waving his hand with a small flag.

Passengers alighted with their bags, and children ran wildly and headed towards the grocery store for candies, leaving their parents to be on their own. The warden lifted a loudspeaker and told the passengers the train would park for one hour to let the engines cool.

The last four carriages opened like the gates of hell. Horses galloped down from the carriage with men dressed in police uniforms. There were fifty horses led by Superintendants Richard Wilson and Suhaimi Ahmad from the Tapah police. The other two carriages opened, and cops paraded down with their bicycles. They were the riot control police, a special unit armed to the teeth with the Lee Enfield Mk II. Each man had two handcuffs in their belts. A thick, round, rattan-made shield was strapped to their back along with their rifles. They had .38 Wembleys tugged into their waists.

Superintendant Suhaimi gave the last instructions. "OK, men, you know your duties. We will ride as fast as we can to Lanang. It is twenty-five miles ahead to the city. It will take us an hour to reach the police precinct. Meanwhile, put your guns in high gear. When you hear the howler, start riding fast." The superintendant's loud baritone voice sank their expectations.

The fifty horses galloped in two long lines, pursued by one hundred cops. Most of them were Punjabis, Ghurkhas, Malays, Indians, Chinese, and Portuguese descendants from Malacca. They formed the last line of defence to diffuse riots and restore public order. They were taught one fine judgement by the British army: "Shoot the bandit before the bandit shoots you."

The outnumbered cops at Lanang were too few to stop the stampede and massacre. Blue told everyone to hold on until help arrived from Tapah. Inspector Chang Wen, undercover officer Sujak Ramli from Singapore police HQ, Lance Corporal Chandran, and the rest of the Malay constables wiped away their sweat.

Out of the dark moments it was bluer than blue, and a loud, thundering howler cut across the streets like a voice in the wilderness: "We are here now. All you men put your weapons down. We are the police." The loud voice was Superintendant Richard Wilson. "You people know how deadly the Lee-Enfield rifle is. One bullet and you are gone. I have with us the .303 calibre tripod mounted Maxim machine gun. You people haven't seen the awesome power of this killing machine."

The Maxim machine gun was a self-powered gun invented by the American-born British inventor Sir Hiram Stevens Maxim in 1884. It had a .303 British cartridge action, and the recoil operated with five hundred rounds per minute. A four-man crew operated it.

It was hopeless because no one listened. They would rather bite the bullet than restrain themselves. The inferno razed the courthouse and the other buildings. The two feuding groups continued amassing.

The mystery man had one long history crimeography. The two girls Salmi and Ai Ling knew too much, or they may have had a glimpse of his identity.

In the ensuing riot and fistfights, men fought as gladiators with honour, burning carriages and torching wooden buildings. The platoon of cops wasn't enough to quell the unrest. All hell broke loose as shots were fired into the air, but they felled on deaf ears. John and all his men were armed with the Lee-Enfield Mk I, the magnificent and deadly magazine-fed repeating rifle, and they were the new line of defence against its predecessor, the Bakers rifle.

The two superintendants grinned. They looked at John and said, "John, we can't use the machine guns. They are not attacking us at the moment. The big guns will be our last resort. "This is one hell of a showdown, John. We have never seen something this big."

The 150 reinforcements had to rush in with batons. John stood next to the two superintendants. "Sir, we have to join the plunder to diffuse them. That's the only choice."

"You're right, Big John. We'll charge to paralyse them."

Within the rising clouds of acrid smoke and burning from buildings and the courthouse, no one could hold the carnage. Everyone went into rhapsodies of confusion over the ugly riot. People looked at each other with deep revulsion. Out of the shadows, a very strange, tall man emerged from the dusty turbulence. He was holding a pipe in his hand, a blowpipe used by the aborigines in South-east Asia to kill wild animals for food. Even rhinos, tigers, and elephants could drop within minutes. The pipe was around three feet long. The dart was poisonous, soaked and dried in the dead bodies of tiny frogs whose skin and flesh was as lethal as cyanide potassium. It caused seizures and cardiac arrest within a few minutes. It was as good as a sudden death.

"Ai Ling, we have to stay together to get through this pandemonium," Salmi said as she made progress through the aisles of confusion, holding Ai Ling's hand.

"Salmi, I think we are like a log fire smouldering in a valley of a stone hearth. We have to get out of here if we are to stay alive," cried Ai Ling.

Even stray dogs looked confused and ran in circles, afraid of the heat from the burning atmosphere. A strange character stood at the other corner, looking at them with cool grey eyes. His face was hooded with the Halloween costume that resembled the uniform worn by the Ku Klux Klan. However, this time there weren't horsemen armed with ploughshares and rifles. This stranger looked mean and stood like a stone-cold phantom.

It was like reading the Book of Revelation: the horseman of the apocalypse riding its path as an angel of death.

Salmi and Ai Ling stared at him, sensing pain and fear trickling down their spines. The girls said to themselves, "Who is this man, and what does he wants from us? This is not a game. Who is this guy? A sadist, or one lousy, very sick serial killer? No, not this guy! He doesn't want the whole world to know him."

Smoke-filled chaos was all over the place. Bottles were smashed in the confusion, and the riot was beyond reasoning. Men beat up men, using racial slurs. Salmi was shocked and Ai Ling looked frightened. The strange man was not in sight anymore.

"Ai Ling," cried Salmi, "we have to make a move to a safer place."

Black, dense smoke was all over and billowed from the burning courthouse and other buildings. Every alley was engulfed in flames and smoke. Smoke blinded the pathways and moved with the strong wind. Fire surged in the alleys and blinded the atmosphere. It was like an enormous gale taking a ship by its mast in the turbulent seas.

There were bodies lying on the streets, killed in the riot. The police couldn't shoot. There were many women and children in the alleys who needed to be protected. It was hard to separate them from the mob that was out there with one thing in mind – vengeance.

The chaos created by the mob on both sides between the Thai kick boxers and the Chinese boxers sent everyone screaming. Within a brief period, the feuding sides took everyone in the alleys by surprise. It turned the whole scenario into a war zone, and only the toughest survived. Even the voice of Detective John over the loudspeaker, calling for public order, went unnoticed.

Salmi and Ai Ling reached a narrow alley, panting from the smoke. They regained their consciousness and survival, however it was short-lived. Ai Ling tripped and fell over a rock on the cobbled pathway. She was bleeding from a cut on her forehead, had a twisted ankle, and could hardly walk. Salmi helped her walk, passing by one more dead body with a broken face bludgeoned by a hard weapon. Salmi could not identify the dead body. Blood stained his clothes, and he had a few stab wounds in his chest. A dagger almost ten inches long protruded from his chest.

Salmi pulled Ai Ling to one quiet corner. "Ai Ling, we'll be safe here for the moment." Her short-sleeve shirt was torn and revealed the cleavage of her breasts, the size of a cup of tea trying to get free from the tight corset. Even saints would stare at a woman's revealing bosom. In addition, charlatans would touch them in their daydreams.

Ai Ling told Salmi to unbutton her shirt, and she used it to tie the twisted ankle. There was no need for temptation, revealing her white clean waist and bosom. She was clad in a semi-corset like Salmi. "Salmi," cried Ai Ling desperately, "you don't think we look like two aristocratic woman right now, don't you? Do you think we are sexy women?"

"Cut that out, Ai Ling. There's no time for jokes," Salmi shot back. "And you are injured, my dear friend."

"Don't you wish we had husbands with us now?" Ai Ling giggled. "You have psychic powers, Salmi. Please get us out of here safe."

"I can't see things so often, Ai Ling. During emergencies like this, it can get very blurred. Right now, I can't see anything. The mind doesn't work that way. We don't see colours or clairvoyance every now and then." Salmi almost cried. "But I sense danger is around the corner, Ai Ling." She lifted up Ai Ling and helped her to move again. However, this time she didn't know the direction back home.

Within seconds, a dart whipped past Salmi by an inch and hit a cow tied to a wooden stand. It landed on the cow's neck. One minute passed, and then the poor cow fell to the ground, paralysed instantly. When Salmi and Ai Ling turned their heads towards the direction of the incoming dart, they saw nothing except a man moving to hide from the scene. It was the stranger in Halloween attire; he was hooded, and so they could see only his eyes. The hooded man was a nightmare, a phantom. Who was this guy? What did he want? He held a blow pipe and wore black, long, sharp-edged shoes with grey gloves. This person could send shivers down their spines.

"Ai Ling, are you thinking what I'm thinking? This man wants us dead!" Salmi said in a quiet but firm tone.

"Quiet, Salmi. We don't know if he's still around."

"This is a real tragedy – a riot, with people killing one another."

"Ai Ling," said Salmi, "when I watched *All the King's Men* the first time when I was eleven, I dreamed that one day I'd be part of this play. Robert Penn Warren, the American novelist, wrote this novel. It's about a mob against the union leader turned mayor."

"And the mob was very ugly," murmured Ai Ling.

"That's disgusting, Ai Ling. Don't even think about it at this moment."

"The hooded guy wants to cut six pounds of soul from us."

"Are our souls worth six pounds, lady?"

"I think so, psychic girl. Do something, please!" cried Ai Ling. "You can see events and tragedies. Get us out of here."

After the riot stopped, the police counted the deaths, a total of eighty-seven. Nine civilians, three police constables, a woman in her fifties, and more than twenty people were severely injured. Corpses were everywhere, and it looked like the Alamo's last stand. With so many dead bodies, this tragedy reminded them of the darker side of human nature. The bodies were collected onto bullock carts for the hospital's mortuary. The coroner's report would be a long list of names for Dr Janet and Dr Rama.

Among those dead was Luang Jin, the leader of the Chinese Boxers. His body was lying next to a Thai Kick Boxer who was as tall as he was.

It was a nightmare for Lanang. As soon as the court case was over, had it not been for the fast evacuation of the court officials, the judge, the prosecutor, the defence counsel, and the jury could have been in the official count of deaths. The hate for the prosecutor and the judge by the Chinese Boxers may turn wild on them, and they were given police protection from the courthouse. Later the carriages took them away safely.

Black smoke still rose from the burnt debris when the press officials came. They took pictures and interviewed the police and the surviving civilians, as well as the injured. It was awful. Sergeant Blue Deighton suffered injuries on his forehead. He had a cut while diffusing the fight between a Chinese Boxer and a Thai kick boxer; he needs six stitches to cover the split flesh.

It took Lanang a month to recover from the tumultuous events. They needed a conscription of fresh people to fill the vacancies left behind by the people. The people felt betrayed after the riot. People wanted migration to other places to seek peace and retribution.

The courthouse was rubble and debris, and the reconstruction was a long process. Logs of wood and planks started rolling in over the next several days. A wooden sign was erected near the courthouse and had a detailed plan of the new project for Lanang's courthouse and other buildings within the district. A new facade for the courthouse would create hope for the people. Buggies with no top and a single seat were everywhere and brought new construction workers into Lanang.

The police precinct was partially razed at the front entrance. The porch and front entrance were torched and reduced to debris; they would need some repair and renovation. Detective John was sitting in a mahogany teak rocking chair with his ivory pipe between his lips, unlit. The morning breeze was cold. John released a watery smile each time someone passed by him. He had a cynical detachment but had not fallen from grace after the tragedy.

Dr Janet walked with two young, beautiful women. They had lips and charm that could melt the North Pole. They had smiles that flowed down like water lilies coming down the steps of a waterfall.

"Can we join Detective John in his inspiration? He looks forlorn and lost," Ai Ling said. She had more enthusiasm than a lonely kitten.

"Shut up, Ai Ling," Salmi said. She shrugged her shoulders and leaned against her friend.

"Quiet, girls. Let the big man rest and have his moment," Dr Janet said as she smiled dreamily.

The morning sun climbed in the brazen sky. This was a new morning, a new dawn of hope. Let there be peace, and let peace rings across the mountainside.

Two newspaper boys were running across the streets. They had the *Times* and *Utusan Melayu* in their grasps. One was a Chinese boy with a flat face and thin shoulders; he was pink faced and handsome, but he had a brutal look like a debt collector. He had well-shaped lips and deeply slanted eyes. He raised his voice like an instrument in an orchestra. "Come on! Tragedy in Lanang. Murderers caught! Mystery killer gone! So get your papers, folks!"

The Malay boy did the same act and looked haggard from running around. His fingers twisted each time a buyer went near him to get the daily news. He had a rendition that sounded like a slogan. He raised his voice amidst the movements of traffics across the busy streets. "Buy papers, sir! Madam, buy now and get your news. Mystery killer escapes. Buy the papers! Mystery man runs free."

Big John couldn't live with the rum-running story. He was smiling softly and trying very hard to hide the true colour on his face. "These boys ought to be spanked," He whimpered to himself. He looked straight into the eyes of the boys and said, "Come here, boys. Give me the papers. Give me two each for the day. And boys, please cut out the 'mystery man' talk. He will walk free for a while, but not for long."

"Sorry, Detective John. We don't mean to offend you and the police precinct. Honest, sir, we're are just selling papers," the boys murmured, and they left.

Dr Janet stood before Big John, grinned, and chuckled. The Chinese wooden and wax umbrella cast a shadow on John's face. John stood up from his rocking chair and greeted the three women.

"Do you want to step inside the precinct? The sunshine is getting warmer," he offered.

"Thanks John, very kind of you." They walked into the police precinct followed by two nervous, astonishing women.

Dr Janet wiped her face with a beige handkerchief. So did the two girls. "How is the investigation? I mean our mystery man."

"He is still a riddle, I guess," John said.

"Don't blame yourself for every escaped criminal. Time will bring the law near to them."

"I know, but that's what the people in Lanang think. Ladies, help yourselves to tea; it's on the dining table."

"Thanks, Detective," the two girls replied.

CHAPTER 22

IT WAS COLD AND QUIET, and the precinct had a new image. The entrance had a promenade with wooden trusses as canopy, garlanded with morning glory. A new long wooden sign stood next to the window: "Lanang Police Precinct".

A loud commotion outside the precinct interrupted the evening calm. A large crowd gathered, and the transparent glass door at the entrance cast a large glimpse of men moving around.

"Blue and Sujak, go out and see the commotion."

"Yes, boss, we will take a look."

The crowd of men were numb. They walked to Blue and Sujak to tell their story. "Sergeant Blue and Sergeant Sujak, you guys have to see the dead body in the cafe. I mean the Chinese restaurant selling white chicken rice and roasted duck. The guy drop dead an hour after his meal. It is shocking, Sergeant. I mean, how can a man die after a meal in a restaurant? All the customers are still alive, except this one."

Sujak rushed in the precinct to inform John and the others. "Another murder."

John sighed. "I thought the dust had settled down. OK, men! Blue and Sujak, come with me. Dukun and Bumbung, tag along. The rest of you remain in the precinct."

"Yes, boss."

"So it's the Twin Rice Shop? Mr Huang is the proprietor."

At the crime scene, the police sealed the premises. The yellow tape surrounded the entrance. On the floor lay the dead man. The victim was a Chinese man forty years of age.

"Mr Huang, did you notice anything strange prior to when he died?"

"No, sir. My daily customers are as usual. He died after a sumptuous lunch. He was dining alone." Mr Huang tried very hard to convince John.

"Mr Huang, I want a full report on his menu that was served."

"Right, Chief Inspector John. He ordered Chinese white chicken rice with French dressing and salad."

"Let me see the menu, Mr Huang." John turned towards the owner. "Mighty amazing name, 'Chinese de French Rice flavour'. Two glasses of syrup with lemon slice and ice cubes. Mr Huang, can you remember your regular customers who had left the scene? I need a list of their names for further investigation." John raised his hands and tugged at his waistline. "Meanwhile, your restaurant is closed for crime scene investigation. Once my men are finished with the findings, I will let you know when you can commence business."

Dr Janet arrived at the crime scene, panting for air. She normally had composure, with her hair flowing backwards and a stethoscope in her blazer pocket. "Where is the corpse? Oh dear, another murder." She gasped. "Well, he could have died of a heart attack. I have to check with the hospital to see if he had been treated in the past for heart problems."

"Was this natural, Dr Janet? Do you believe this cause of death?"

"No asphyxia, no strangulation marks, no hidden small lacerations, no sutured wounds or abrasions. I need to do the post-mortem if there was poisoning. Chloral hydrate or strychnine could slow down the heart. It's strange: this victim's eyes are dilated and stiff." Dr Janet looked into the pupils and touched the neck. "I will need time to find residual remains in the liver and stomach. You have to wait for the post-mortem in the hospital John." She looked at John in desperation.

"Yes, Dr Janet. The coroner's report and the toxicology results will determine the cause of death."

"A fly paper or a tissue paper dusted with cyanide patted on the victim's neck could give him time to walk out of the restaurant. It will take some time for cyanide poison to work its way into the blood stream. If he is a heart patient on medication, it will be difficult to prove COD, if the residual substance is too small to show the effect."

"Blue and Sujak, listen now: I don't want any guessing games. This is the real world, my friends. We will look into toxicology and forensic pathology."

John lifted his chin and looked at the victim on the floor and the chalk drawing. Constable Bumbung took photographs of the corpse. The dead body was strapped with mackintosh covers. "This is murder, believe me. Do any of you have a different script for this case?" John smiled and held his ivory pipe. The pipe was like a souvenir, and he held with his hand as a signature. "Any of you have a prophecy? "I don't believe in prophecies yet. I deal with crimes and real people doing the acts."

John, Blue, and Sujak left the crime scene for the police precinct.

The next day, a local daily in English and Malay printing only two folded pages on events in Lanang created a new horror for the people of Lanang. The headlines read, "One More Murder. Is this the end?"

Someone had started a small bonfire, and this was not arsenical or antimony poisoning, but the storm that may have ended just came back again.

"Is this a God-sent revival, or something else?" John asked as he rubbed his temple repeatedly with his fingers. There was no doubt that substantial evidence would be coming through the doors of the precinct. "Death will be knocking on heaven's door for this killer. That is the sad truth. This guy knows what he is doing. Fiction writers always write the happy denouement, but we don't."

He lifted his head and said, "Boys, I think the blue moon is dancing. We are the police. Always remember: think like a killer, walk like a killer, and kill like one. In this way you will be able to trace this guy no matter how far he runs. This is just the beginning of a new episode, and the end is yet to come. Those on night duty, guard the police precinct. I don't want any intrusions. OK! This wraps it up for today." John and his men left the precinct in a hurry.

John rode home with his wife, Chang Wen. Along the way, John's mind drifted back to the past months. It came back like a dream in a carousel, turning and reeling in a string of chapters. Chang Wen knew what was bugging her husband's thoughts. The new murder had ignited a small flame in his troubled heart. There was too much to lose and too little to win. They reached home and walked in the promenade. The dusk, illuminated by the glowing street lamp lit at 6.45 PM, cast an orange, gloomy atmosphere.

The next morning celebrated with a slight drizzle. Everyone was busy with hot coffee and tea. The morning papers lay on the reading table; no one seemed captivated by the headlines. It stayed intact like a wallpaper gathering dust. They needed someone to rewrite history.

Dr Janet sent a runner to pass the coroner's report to John. It was sealed and signed against the folded cover. The young man came into the precinct and wanted to pass it personally to Detective John. He was a slim young man, and his hair was glued to his wet head. The beads of rain slid down his temple and thin cheeks like tiny drops of dew in the morning breeze. "Good morning, sir. I have a document from Dr Janet for Inspector John."

The constable replied with a smile. "He is over there, in a beige blazer."

The young man stood nervously, shaking off the raindrops from his face and hair. He was quite wet and shuddered from cold. "Thank you." He greeted John. "Sir, Dr Janet sent me."

"OK. Say thanks to Dr Janet. Tell her I will see her in the evening to discuss certain matters."

"I will, sir." The runner smiled and turned towards the door.

John opened the sealed envelope. It was the coroner's report, and the toxicology for COD was poisoning. Residual remains in liver and stomach walls had conium maculatum, known as hemlock. He had cardio myopathy, or swelling of the heart.

John whimpered to himself. "So the hemlock liquid must have worked its way up from the feet. Hemlock is found predominantly in Belgium and Italy. This guy is a traveller, or he could have purchased the yellow liquid from a seller. He could have walked past the kitchen and put the liquid into the two glassed of syrup, and no one noticed him. The red syrup dominates the colour, and with a lemon slice, there was no way the victim could have noticed something was wrong. A very smart move, I guess."

John's mind hovered between reality and dreams. "Is this the same mystery killer, or someone else? If he is a new guy, I have one new case." John's eyes looked down on the floor. "If this new case goes unsolved, it will be another cold case."

The next day the newspapers' report was a trail of prohibition and vagueness. One more man was dead in the Chinese restaurant – another mystery weaved with intrigue. This was a crime scene with unknown reasons.

John lit his pipe with Danish tobacco. A constable drove him in the twin buggy to the hospital. John needed a detailed explanation from Dr Janet's post-mortem. He inhaled and blew several round rings of smoke before he walked into the hospital alone.

Dr Janet had done a simple surgery on a woman and was walking to the washroom. John greeted her and signalled with his hand. "Dr Janet, I want to have a word with you." John had a sweet impression on his face.

She waved at him and said, "Give me five minutes."

They soon walked to a quiet corner and sat down on a row of wooden chairs. "Have you had your lunch yet, Doctor?"

"Well, never mind, John. I know you want a detailed explanation."

John stared at her eyes and emptied his pipe tobacco into the urn next to him. He wrapped his pipe with a large handkerchief and shoved it into his large pocket. "What can you give me, Doctor?"

"I found residual remains of hemlock poison in his liver and intestines. It struck me as quite strange that the killer used hemlock. Perhaps he wanted to see immediate death, leaving no footprints behind. But the victim had no covenant with death. I think either the killer knows this victim, or he wants to juxtapose his past attempts."

"I could be wrong, Doctor," John smiled again and said, "I am not the excellent sleuth. Or was this man murdered for some inherent reason? Well, I could be wrong again, Doctor. With murderous intent or otherwise – that is, to decoy us into believing this last victim was done by someone else. This new murder will sandbag the police department again. I have had enough headaches, Janet."

"Yes, John, it's the same poison used to kill Socrates by the Athenian courts." Her face was crimson. "This is my first case encounter with conium maculatum, or hemlock poisoning. It work its way upwards from the feet, to the heart and then the brain. The victim will experience seizures and suffocation. No wonder I saw dilated pupils. It will take about eight minutes to end the process. Meanwhile, the killer has enough time to walk out and slip away. I think I am right this time, John. I don't drift into caricature and dreams." Her face turned serious and flat. "You're facing a phantom, one or two serial killers with Halloween masks." Her breathing was quick, and her chest was heaving. It regained its composure after a few minutes. Her blonde and brunette hair flipped to the front like a flag as she shook her head. "I am a realist like you, John." She smiled again. "I am no champagne socialist either."

"So we have someone with a new signature stratagem." John grinned. "Police work will never end. The list of names from the restaurant owner doesn't give me any clues. This man is a new stranger, I guess."

"John you have a very shallow understanding on a woman's psychology. How a woman looks at a subject is different from a man's view. I think you are getting sharper with your police work." She smiled widely. "But you can't read my manuscript."

"Doctor Janet, thanks for the review. I'll see you again. Bye."

John walked out in serious deliberation; he wasn't in seventh heaven. His mind was bloated with images of the new killer. "Who could it be …?"

Back at the police precinct, the morning mood on this new murder came out like a photograph hung on the wall.

"We have no precedence for this new case. It is mind boggling for the time being. "Blue, do you have the lab results for fingerprints?"

"No, boss. This guy wears turquoise gloves according to the workers in the kitchen. They saw a tall man walk out about ten minutes before the victim collapsed. They noticed a tall man with a beige hat and white tuxedo with a red bowtie. He is clean-shaven with no distinct marks except a scar on the left cheek. There is no other clear identification."

"Good work, Blue." John gave a half smile. "If there is no lead, I am worried this will be the second unsolved murder."

"One of the pedestrians noticed him signalling to a two-horse carriage. He told the cab driver, 'I am moving south. Perhaps to Selangor or Johor,'" Blue replied.

"So he left Lanang District in a hurry?" John groaned in deliberation. "It looks like this man is heading to hell. There is no purgatory for him. There is no redemption or surrender. His soul needs salvation. He knows his footsteps well. Before he reaches south, he could change his attire. There is no way our men in the southern states can identify him. Anyway, Blue, can you get to the post office and telex to KL Police Contingent? Let them know we have a new killer who uses hemlock poison."

Blue gave the breakdown. "Suspect around six feet three inches tall, wearing an authentic beige cocked hat. He has light brown eyes, small and slanting like a Japanese women. He has thin, light eyebrows. Last seen at crime scene with a white tuxedo, a red bowtie, and turquoise gloves. Suspect heading south of Peninsula."

Blue rushed out to get his single buggy. He rode to the post office about a hundred yards away from the precinct. A light gull swooped across the streets. It was windy, but Blue was not perturbed. His almond blue eyes were set on the road leading to the old post office. Blue jumped down from the buggy and went straight to the postmaster.

"Good afternoon, sir. I need to send an urgent telex to KL Police HQ." His voice was muffled from exhaustion.

"Yes, Sergeant Blue. Take a seat while I send the message." The old man looked at Blue and was not puzzled at all. Blue was a regular from the police precinct. "Pardon me, Blue. The last line and authorised sender is Chief Inspector Detective John Hayes, Lanang District Police Precinct?" The old man husky voice came back and held his glasses with his fingers. He pushed the rim upwards and ran his fingers to push his logged hair backwards to his earlobes. "I just hope they will catch this Hemlock poison killer. He may kill again and again," the old man chided. "Have a nice day, Blue, and good luck."

"Thank you, sir," Blue said, and he left. There were no wild suppositions on this killer – yet. His killing style was frightening. Blue raised and snapped the bridle, and the horse galloped back to the precinct. "Who is this man? Is he the mystery man?" Blue had no idea.

The twisted thread was recoiling in silent nightmares. This new script carried with it a cold air blowing in the night wind. Everyone in the precinct was under scrutiny. There was no lead, no clues, and no links. In the frost left by the hemlock, the police precinct had a group of people doing their visitations.

Sergeant Blue went to the glass door to greet four men standing outside. "Yes, sirs, we are expecting your arrival." There were District Commissioner Stephen Lark, Mayor Timang Sani, and his personal assistant and bodyguard Lee Chan Chan. The man behind was the British high commissioner from Kuala Lumpur, David March.

"Good evening, gentlemen," John said as he stood up to greet them. "Have a seat, sirs. We will make this evening warm."

David March held his pipe and released it from his parched, pale lips. "John, I have this to say. I called for this little reunion with Stephen and the mayor. It is about this hemlock man." His eyes look pallid and sad. "He is making waves across the peninsula like a legend. At this point, it is imperative that we know his territorial terrain – how he operates and when he surfaces. I have instructed the entire police force in the peninsula to put this man in the top list. He is the most deadly killer. He's earned this reputation. Do you have any positive leads? We are not dealing with bizarre or esoteric poisons. This man is a serial killer with the most inhumane hands of death. His symbol is an execution style."

David paused. "John, I will shorten this visit. We have discussed the whole episode. I, Stephen, and the mayor have unanimously agreed that you are commissioned by us to trace this killer no matter where it takes you all over the peninsula of Malaya. This is a letter of authority from my ministry. You are given the authority to serve your duties with Sergeant Blue Deighton. Every police precinct will give you cooperation in your search for this man. I wish you good luck in your execution of the public will. It must be done to serve and protect public order. In God we trust."

Mayor Timang Sani greeted John, and the commissioner and David March bid farewell. "We know this will be a long trail of investigations, John, hunting an unknown and elusive serial killer." The men left the precinct and retired to their premises.

John held his head with both hands, his chin touching the tabletop. His long and lean fingers ran through his long blond hair. He pushed his hair back to his nape. It has been three weeks since his last haircut.

He was contemplating the two cases. The evidence holding both cases had opposing styles. Nancy's killer had strangled her first before the hanging, but the hemlock man did it subtly with stealth moves.

By evening, the flecks in the ashtray reached the brim from his pipe smoking. John had also spent six sticks of cigarettes from his Marlboro pack. John had never smoked this much to pacify his thoughts. He did not believe in prophecy and was a realist.

Blue came in and parked his hat on the hat stand. "John, I have good news for you." He was smiling and jovial. "I want to show you something. Lance Corporal Chandran and two of the constables were scavenging the ground outside the restaurant perimeters. They found this bracelet on the ground – a bracelet with an oblong piece of jade embedded with gold. Next to this bracelet is a gold chain with a round coin pendant. He must have left in a hurry. He slipped his hand into his pocket to retrieve a handkerchief, perhaps, not realizing he was pulling out his prized possession. He dropped these two items while signalling for a cab, I think. This bracelet is meant for feminine wear, but is has no inscription. The round gold coin is good evidence, though there is no significant design or alphabet inscribed. But that does not matter. At least we have a piece of evidence, if this piece belongs to the hemlock man. I have checked with Mr Huang at the restaurant. He passed the word around to his regular customers, but none of them admit owning them."

"The owner is either Chinese, Vietnamese, Burmese or Siamese. But he can be anyone, Blue. The bracelet is for a woman or a heart-throb," John replied.

"I have done the finger printing," Blue said. "John, the good news is there is a thumbprint on the gold coin. I have filed it in the hemlock file. When we have a suspect, we can hold water."

"Good work. Sergeant Blue! At least for now we have a trail left by him."

The next morning, the streets in Lanang had young boys running around selling the newspapers. "There's a new sensation, new murder. Buy the papers, sir and madam," the boys yelled. "The hemlock murderer. Buy now!"

The days that followed after such a grotesquely calculated murder always created horror in civilised society. Fingerprints only identified criminals; they couldn't direct the police to locate the killer. This last murder had created a frost that would take time to subside. The porch leading to the precinct entrance was once a symbol of hope and justice. Now it looked dull, like a row of white tombstones.

An old Malay man walked with a crutch in his left hand. His clothes were tattered and worn out. His moustache and thin beard were unshaven for days. His cheeks and jaw looked like a thin spread of green algae. He was around seventy years old. The old man kept grumbling, wobbling as he walked and weaving with bronco spasms. He was heaving, and his breath was heavy and weak. His face was frail looking, with heavy sagging at his cheeks and chin. The short, thin, receding hair was white. His eyes were big and grey from cataracts.

As he moved with his crutch, he told everyone coming his way to move aside. "Now move away from me – I need space to walk. Move to the side, will ya! Let an old man pass through." He munched on a small piece of bread. "Constable, I want to see the police chief here in this precinct. Who is in charge here?" His stern eyes followed the policeman.

"Just walk in, sir," the young cop said.

The old man slammed the glass wooden door in haste. His hands were big and strong for his age. His veins looked like weeds. "Who is in charge here?"

"I am, sir. My name is Chief Inspector Detective John Hayes." John stood up to welcome him. "Take a seat, sir. What is your name?" John asked politely.

"I am Sulaiman." He grinned with his cataract eyes, displaying uneven and thin, yellow teeth. There were only seven teeth left, blunt and standing like dilapidated wooden poles. "Hey! I have news for this hemlock man that you are after, Detective John. He passed by me and stood next to me for a while before he signalled for a cab. He was dressed in a white tuxedo with a supreme colonial hat, and he wore gloves too. He had dancing eyes, but he stopped instantly when he stared at a subject. His eyes looked like ripe peaches. I remember now that he had a perfume, intimate and intimidating. It has a lemon flavour. Wait, Detective, I think it smells like apricot. Oh, I can't remember. Wait, let me think again.... Yes, it is apricot, not lemon." The old man placed a finger on his lips.

"Sir, what else can you remember? This will help in our investigation."

"Yes, I want this hemlock killer caught. I am a good citizen, don't you think so? Oh yes, Detective. I have to take my psychosomatic pills."

That news stunned John. "How long have you been on this pill, sir?"

"They say I am treated for a psychiatry-related disease, but I don't believe them. More than three years, I think. They treated me for delirium too. They say I have dementia. I was given dementia pills. But lately I have stopped taking these pills. I am well now. I don't see the doctor anymore, and I am healthier than a doctor, mind you." He gave a raspy laugh, and his lips were wet with saliva.

John said, "Sir, here is a cup of tea. Drink it while it is still warm."

"Ah, thank you. I am very obliged, Detective." The old man grinned at John, and his eyes were dancing in circles. His smile made more wrinkles on his face.

"You are aware with what you see and hear? You can remember an event, sir?" John asked.

"Of course I can," the old man said. "Pardon me, Detective. I can remember now and recall the past. This hemlock man ... His smile was authentic, and he had cold eyes. His look was sardonic and dry, like a painting of a man with a Machiavellian look. In fact, he looked like Niccolo Machiavelli. No, wait a minute – I think he look a bit like an ancient Samurai warrior. Yes, he had broad-boned face sunk in a cobweb of profanity. His eyes looked like a ruthless killer's." The old man scratched his cheeks. "Except he is very tall and lean, and big like you, Detective John." The old man smiled sheepishly. "Hey Detective, you have a painting done by Rembrandt on the wall? I like him too."

"That is a Rembrandt self-portrait, in 1658, the masterpiece of the final style. This is the grandest of all his portraits."

"I remember again, Detective. Rembrandt Harmenszoon van Rijn, the Dutch painter and etcher. All his themes and styles are unchallenged. You have very refined classical taste, young man. You make one fine detective."

"I think that is all for today," John said. "I've gotta make a move now."

The old man walked out quietly with a cold, rambling smile. The crutch he held dragged along with his footsteps.

"Sergeant Blue, can you put this information into a piece of paper? Apricot or lemon perfume. Machiavellian features. Lean and tall, with cold eyes that looked like ripe peaches. A colonial hat for the very rich. Blue, I was thinking that whether or not the old man remembers well, the descriptions he gave us could be reliable. We will keep that for future encounters with this killer."

"Yes, boss, though it's a long trail in the future." Blue grinned attentively.

CHAPTER 23

DETECTIVE JOHN LOOKED AT THE moor with weary eyes. He could see grey clouds moving over the rainbow. It was time for his breakfast, and he took a very small bite of the spongy, orange-flavoured pancake. He could see grey clouds turning darker and billowing like thick smoke; they kept rousing strong waves, engulfing the rainbow.

There wasn't any sign of satisfaction. There wasn't any indication of a twinge of pride. The police had arrested all the killers except one: the murderer who'd killed Nancy Kwan. Nancy murdered her husband with *strychnine* pastels, and she was found murdered two days later.

The last count was the hemlock killer. Who was this guy?

"We have two puzzles to solve." John's voice was frozen in deliberation. It was not dramatic but was a customary truth. "The puzzle is who killed Nancy Kwan, and who killed with hemlock? We can't have something like this recorded in our police books. In a child's game like cat's cradle, you can do it now and then with the string looped over your fingers, and transfer it back and forth to form designs. I am sad. I think I failed to find Nancy's killer. I can't go back in time and start all over again, Dr Janet. It will elevate the minds of the folks here. We have failed the people."

Detective John held his unlit pipe again. It rested on his chin for a while and then went between his lips. The trauma from the clouds above resounded like two cymbals clapping continuously. "Looks like it will rain before noon," he noted as he rubbed his aching temple.

Chang Wen stood next to John. "I always rely on my instincts." She pursed her lips and then moved into John's arms, hugging him very lovingly. "Life is like a carousel, and it goes round and round in a circle till we die," she said in a very soft tone. "The moment you stop cycling uphill, you will slide down. That's redemption, I think."

John said, "Dr Janet, the people in Lanang need you. You're the only lady doctor here. You're a debonair, blonde-haired woman. You have a very resolute, no-surrogate stand on crimes of passion. You are a very thoughtful and considerate. The people in Lanang like you so much, and they need you. We are lucky to have you here."

John hugged his wife. "You are my woman for the rest of my life. Thank you, dear, good wife. I am delighted by your concern and tenderness towards me." His Irish green eyes focused on her, and he noticed very thin amusement and a colour of hope in her beautiful yellow eyes.

Old Reindran raced past the post office after he received a telegram from Kuala Lumpur. The telegram was addressed to Detective John Hayes and the commissioner of police in Lanang. The bullock cart was held by his two new oxen with shiny curved horns, which had bells tied to their right horns. The small tornado of dust began rising helter-skelter until it settled down when the wooden wheels stop rotating. Reindran stopped where Detective John Hayes was standing beside Dr Janet. An old tom-tom hung from his neck and swayed left and right. It was his musical drum when he got bored.

"Hail now, my companion, stop! We have arrived." Reindran said to his two majestic horses. "Simmer down, my friends. Cool down. "Detective John! Detective John! Bad News!" His old, shrill voice was soft and dry. He went on calling with a very stunned look on his face, a redeeming hope from an old man. "There's a telegram for you and the commissioner. Two rich widows – murdered in Kuala Lumpur! Right in the middle of Chinatown! Eyewitnesses saw a glimpse of his hooded trench coat. He was very tall and big, above six feet. He could be the mystery guy. The police report says he used the same signature. Both widows were hung from the ceiling, and the rope for hanging was three feet shorter than normal. It's his signature – ain't that right, Detective?" Reindran was breathing heavily. "Am I right? I mean, it could be our guy."

"Yes, Reindran, you could be right. But it could also be done by someone else. This guy could have done it, or another guy is trying to copy his riddle-like signature. He has a code and riddle." John was determined. "We'll crack his riddle. I bet we will. Maybe we have one copycat killer."

John invited Reindran to step down and take a long rest. The man's asthma looked bad.

John held Reindran with his big hands and put him down slowly. "Come on, old friend, you need help. Get down, Rein, and sit on this stool until your dyspnoea subsides. Stop talking for a while." He told the girls to get a glass of water from the precinct. "OK, big guy, did you bring along your asthma pills?"

"I have. They are in my pouch." Rein gulped the glass of water with one asthma pill. He was still heaving profusely from an attack of asthma.

The news was not new. Big John had a premonition that the mystery person would migrate for the time being. He was smart – very smart. He was a Casanova looking for rich, lonely women. Dr Janet and two girls were surprised to hear that.

"Dr Janet, we need incriminating evidence to nail the suspect, and it's not easy. You know it has never been." John nodded at her, and she gazed at him with bewildered eyes. She had no idea what was cooking in John's mind.

"We can't touch them. You know the law."

"When you kill a man who is armed, you have reasonable doubt. When you kill a man who is unarmed, they call it murder. Call it the battered wife-syndrome, I suppose." John grinned at them. "The mystery man lures women into his marooned isle. Then he traps them with his love. He sets the mouse trap and plays with his tune like the pied piper. Then it snaps open, revealing the past of someone disguised as a saint. He is a very seductive serial killer and is in possession of a mysterious character. Doctor, do you remember the piece of paper written in Latin with a brush? It had the signature 'Darling M. 95'. I had a premonition this guy is the mystery guy, and the 95 is to decoy us into believing it stands for something." John grinned. "Our guy likes to play riddles with the police. This guy could be fifty-nine years old. We are hunting for an old man or woman." John forced a conclusive smile again. "I still have this hunch, Doctor, that this enigma is a man caught in a woman's body, or a woman caught in a man's body. So we have someone with very painful past memories.

"From eyewitness reports they saw someone very tall and around sixty years of age near the crime scene at Kuala Lumpur. Our suspect is an old man, aged sixty. The telegram Rein gave me has another copy. Here's a brief police report. He is always looking for wealthy widows, and he has his peculiar hangman's rope. The rope is three feet short – his enigma, I suppose."

John lifted his pipe with his right hand, trying to light the Irish tobacco. He inhaled and said, "Reindran, could you please cool down? Let me see this telegram." He was stunned. "It looks like he is ahead of us. Dr Janet, don't get mired by my thoughts."

She said, "I am just appalled with these murders. They are a sick man's trophy."

"Just as the dust settles, we have one more killer, the hemlock man." John's breath was heavy and baritone in two different inflexions. "I have two unsolved crimes. How long does it take to trace them? There are two different styles, the mystery man and the hemlock man." The inferno had just begun, and they had awakened a sleeping giant. "We will trace them. I believe we will, Doctor."

As much as Dr Janet had loved John in the past, she knew he was Chang Wen's husband. Both were women, and they should understand.

Chang Wen looked at John and held his hands. "Looks like your first case is closed. Now you have a new case to attend to. Take your fine steps one at a time, but don't forget you're human.

Always remember men go to war and leave widows behind. They leave children as orphans. Please don't leave me here waiting for too long. I will wait for your return, John."

Chang Wen hoped for a new chapter in her life. She was pregnant and wanted to raise the baby with John, her husband.

The passion has just begun.

SYNOPSIS

THE PEOPLE IN LANANG ARE getting restless. The series of murders is like putting a square peg in a round hole. It could not fit in their minds.

The six dominoes, falling one by one, sandbagged the police. Was this the last count, the seventh murder? Did the mystery person do it? Was it an amateur or a copycat killer?

The seventh victim is a man with no strangulation marks. There are no small laceration marks, sutured wounds, or abrasions on his neck or body.

The victim drops dead after a sumptuous meal.

Dr Janet is hysterical. "You have too many murders and too little clues to tie up the killings," she tells Detective John.

They have to work fast to stop the meltdown.

ABOUT THE AUTHOR

FRANCES ZANE IS AN AUTHOR living in Selangor, Malaysia. Frances's main interests are crime fiction and poetry, and reading interests include arts and humanities, history, social sciences, and politics.

Printed in the United States
By Bookmasters